THE WITCH'S TALE

The BEWITCHED Trilogy
Book 2

KELLY ALLEYN

blackbird

First Published in 2024 by Blackbird Digital Books
Blackbird Digital Books
Copyright Kelly Alleyn 2024
Cover design: Getcovers
ISBN: 9781068650512

http://blackbird-books.com/

Contents

1

Moving on

Alice

When I'm old and look back at the night of Decima's party, I'll recognize it was when I finally grew up and learned to be myself. Admittedly it was rather late in the day, after all I was almost 26, but still. Up to then I'd more or less cruised through life, keeping a low profile. I've thought a lot about why, and realize that it came down to my upbringing. This is absolutely NO criticism of my parents. I love them both dearly. My mother spent so much time with her Mottled Screecher breeding program as well as making and marketing the *Salvheal* oil, while my father Patrick has never quite understood how to deal with me and the magic powers I inherited from my mother. He was always worried I'd do something to attract unwanted attention to the family. He was never unkind, but he tended not to pay me much attention. I sort of had to bring myself up and try not to be noticed, so I've always lacked self-confidence.

That all changed that night at Decima's, and a different me stares back from the mirror now. The 'guerilla' look that didn't suit me has gone. My curves are back. I hold my chin higher, and my gaze is direct, no longer bashful.

I am never again going to be pushed into doing something that doesn't feel right. Nobody should do that. I'm not embarrassed by my magical powers anymore but appreciate what a blessing they are. I'm going to start using them more. I haven't quite decided how, but I'll find a way.

I think that standing up to Decima made her respect me. It definitely gave her something to think about. She keeps calling me 'the amazing disappearing woman' and she's been grilling the guys about the 'secret'. It's no good asking them because they're as mystified as she is.

'Come on,' she said to me the other day, 'tell me how you did it.'

I smiled enigmatically and wiggled my eyebrows.

Ramon told me they've all agreed I must have put a drug in their drinks because there's no other explanation. I just winked.

Now I'm back up in my old office across the passage from Decima, no longer stuck in the tiny basement cubicle like a broken piece of furniture. I don't see so much of the boys except when Decima summons them. She's not meant to 'entertain' them up here anymore, the feng shui woman has banned it, but I still see them going by every day, often several times.

The studio is having a makeover, Decima has a completely new image and there's a deluge of sponsorship offers. She's buzzing with excitement about the new show. My phone pings all day long with messages from her.

She's upbeat, cheerful and fun to be around and she's promised that I'm going to have a bigger role in future.

It's funny how you can do something if you really have to. Because I panic being in confined spaces I've always avoided the elevator. Before, I could use **Broomstick** without anybody noticing, but now I have to go up and down to the top floor everyday, I've had to deal with it. People would start asking questions if I was never seen in it. The thought kept me awake all night before my first day up at the top. Then I reminded myself of that mad morning with Scorpio, and how I didn't give a second thought when I got in the elevator with him, so I knew I could do it. And it's glass, and rides up the outside of the Tower, so I can see out. If it should ever break down people will be able to see I'm trapped in it and they'll send help. The first day I gave myself a calming spell, but now I'm used to it. I enjoy looking over the town below as I glide up and down.

I've moved out of my old apartment. I wanted somewhere away from town, where I can enjoy fresh air to give Zylch space to play outside. I mentioned to Sean that I was looking for a change of scene. One of his musician friend's folks own a smallholding where they grow fruit, with a little converted barn which they are renting to me. It's fenced off for privacy, perfect really. Zylch can enjoy himself without any risk of being seen. I talked to him about the possibility of people turning up unexpectedly and said he'll need to transform into a cat while they're here. He stared back at me for a moment, then winked, so I'm hoping he'll behave.

My parents brought over a load of furniture from their house and helped me arrange it. Sean insisted on helping too, and we made it all feel very homely and comfortable. It's quite a way out of town, and twice as far to the Tower, but closer to the Brent Flats and very secluded. If I need it there's a bus service that passes by a short distance away, but I've started to enjoy jogging, and I can always use **Broomstick** if I feel like it.

Life's pretty good. I'm in a happy place.

Leaving the apartment for the last time I did feel a pang of sadness, remembering Jai standing there waiting for me that first time we met. I keep thinking the hole in my heart is mending, but every so often I'm hit with a stab of loss and longing. I push it away because it's in the past, and I must keep moving forwards.

Sean has been great. Every couple of days he comes to see if I need any help. He's fixed some shelving and a window that was sticking. He brought a couple of pizzas with him so we could share a meal when he'd finished. He says if I ever get lonely give him a call and he'll come over. I'm beginning to think of him as the brother I never had. I will never forget how he was ready to defend me that night at Decima's party.

2

The pond

Alice

In one of my mother's gardening magazines there's an article about ponds that really took my fancy. I asked my landlord if I could put one in, and he said to go ahead.

When I mention it to Sean, the next thing I know he's organized for the boys to come next Saturday to create it. I admit I hadn't thought through how I was going to excavate a big enough hole to start with.

'It'll take you forever,' Sean says, 'if you try to do it yourself. The guys would all be happy to help.'

We arrange that I'll order the materials and they'll all come over at the weekend to do the work, and we'll have a BBQ in the evening.

I invite my parents, my friend Shelley with her two little girls, and Decima, who looks so tired these days, with all the preparations for the new channel. I thought it would be nice for her to have some time to relax and chill.

At first she declines, saying she has another engagement, but when I tell her that all the boys will be there too her eyes nearly pop out of her head, and she says she'll stop by for a while if she can.

I'm anxious as I've never entertained a crowd before.

In fact, the nearest I've ever got to 'entertaining' was inviting Shelley for pizza, but Sean says he'll take care of the BBQ, my mother is bringing potato salad and apple pie, as well as some plants for the new pond. Shelley's going to hang lights in the trees and I don't have to do anything except make sure there's plenty of food and drink. Sean has talked Cory into being 'barman', using his butlering skills. Actually I'm not sure what a butler does, but Sean says Cory will nail it.

Sean's friend James, who lives half a mile away, surprises me, arriving with a mechanical digger that will make the job much easier. They start work in the early morning before it's too hot, and working together and with the help of the digger, it's amazing how fast the pond takes shape. I keep everybody refreshed with cold drinks. As it gets warmer the boys strip off down to their shorts. Physically they are so different. Josh's tanned chest is wide and muscled, covered with curly white hair. Cory ties his long black hair into a man bun. He and Sean are both pale-skinned and with almost hairless chests, and I can see their ribs. I make Sean put his T-shirt back on because redheads burn up so badly. I can hardly take my eyes off Ramon's body. His glossy caramel-colored skin is so smooth and unblemished as if it's been polished, and the muscles glide beneath it with a life of their own. I don't fancy him in that way, but he's an absolute work of art to look at.

They're all horsing around as they work, quite different from their behavior at the studio. You can tell they genuinely like each other.

By early afternoon the liner is in the pond and it's ready to be filled. I run the hose into it while they use the digger to spread the surplus soil around and flatten it out.

While the pool fills they go home to shower and change, except for Sean who says he needs to stay to set up the BBQ, so he showers in my bathroom and then gets busy in the kitchen, singing and whistling. That's what I like about having him around, he's always happy.

For the rest of my life I'll remember this perfect night. My mother and Sean bond over the cooking. Shelley's kids splash in the pond, and as the evening goes on and the guys have a few beers they join in. My father, who doesn't usually drink more than a beer a night, has quite a few and ends up chasing around with the hose and spraying us all. Cory and Ramon flirt with Shelley and play with the little girls. I notice James, Sean's friend who dug out the pond, watching us from the back of the garden. He's achingly shy and tongue-tied, but I persuade him to join us. Josh is sitting with him. When darkness comes Sean and Cory take up their guitars. My normally shy father, who is by now tipsier than I'd ever seen him, has them playing his favorite country and westerns, and surprises us all with his beautiful voice, even if he misses a few of the words. We join in, singing lazily, softly.

As the evening wears on we fall quieter and sit around beneath the stars, listening to the sounds of the night. I have never known such a feeling of being surrounded by friends and family. My parents lean against each other, and I go and sit close to them. From the corner of my eye I spot Zylch mischievously threading his way around us, but nobody seems to notice. Except for my mother – who winks at me. Yes, I'll never forget this night, when I'm surrounded by all those people who care for me.

Decima turns up, quite late, and brings me a beautifully wrapped plant as a housewarming gift. Wearing pencil-heeled sandals, and a skimpy, floral print dress that is almost transparent, with a matching chiffon scarf around her neck, she realizes immediately that she is out of place, and she stands around looking aloof and awkward until my mother goes into the house and brings a couple of chairs from the kitchen. She plants them next to my father, leads Decima to one, and sits down next to her chatting. Apart from waving and shouting out a greeting, none of the boys pay Decima much attention. Still, she seems to be enjoying the company of my parents, occasionally smiling and nodding her head. My father brings her a beer and they clink bottles. She doesn't stay long. Before she goes she gives my mother and father a quick hug and says she has somewhere else to be. When she leaves, I'm almost certain she has tears in her eyes; probably from the smoke from the barbecue.

It's after midnight by the time everybody starts to leave. Sean says he's happy to stay and clear up, but Shelley is staying over with her two little girls so there's nowhere for him to sleep. He's going to come back tomorrow. My mother says she'll be here in the morning to take Shelley and the girls home.

When we're alone, Shelley says: 'I see you've made a conquest.'

'What?'

'Sean. He's crazy about you.'

'Sean? He's a good friend, that's all. So helpful, and great company. We laugh a lot.'

'Alice, are you blind? He's infatuated. You must be able to see that. He never takes his eyes off you.'

She's absentmindedly stroking Zylch, who's curled up on her lap.

I stare at her. 'Are you sure? I've never thought of him in that way – more like a brother.'

Shelley shakes her head. 'Then there's something wrong with you. Anybody can see it. And you know, he's a really nice guy, he'd be good for you.'

'I don't want anybody. I'm happy on my own.'

'That's so dumb. You don't want to spend the rest of your life alone. And there's a genuinely decent man who could make you happy if you give him a chance. Think about it, Alice. You obviously like him, and given time you may grow to love him as much as he loves you.'

After I've gone to bed, I lie awake thinking about what she said. If I'm really honest, I do realize that Sean wants to be more than just a friend, but I try to ignore it. I like his company, I value his friendship, but I'm sure I'll never love him the way he wants to be loved.

And then there's the thing with Decima. But that could be good; that part of his life would be separate, so it could work. Although I really like him as a person, in fact love him as a friend, I am not ready for a physical relationship.

He'd never be able to hurt me, and I know he never would, but there's always the risk that I could hurt him. But why would I? I will never find anybody who could replace Jai, so I'd never leave Sean for someone else and I'd never be unfaithful to him.

Maybe Shelley is right. I can't lock myself away from life, and I'm lucky that somebody as sweet as Sean cares about me.

Thoughts swirl around in my head, keeping me awake until dawn, until at last I fall asleep.

3

Something to think about

Alice

I wake to the smell of coffee. In the kitchen, Shelley and my mother are sitting around the table and laughing while Sean is pouring coffee and flipping eggs in a pan. The girls are outside playing with Zylch, who has decided today to change his silver coat into black and white stripes, like a zebra.

For a moment I feel a flash of irritation that Sean is here, again, so early, and seemingly feeling so at home. But when he turns to me with his loving smile, I push those thoughts away.

'Mom – the cat's changed color!' Little Jessie runs up to her mother, giggling.

'Odd cat,' says Shelley. 'Why would it do that?'

'He's molting,' I fib. Sometimes I'm surprised at how Shelley accepts Zylch. I don't know whether she realizes I'm 'different'. She's always so calm and takes everything in her stride and has never questioned anything about me, and she's seen me do some pretty strange stuff.

When Sean has cleared away the breakfast stuff and gone to tidy up the yard with Shelley, my mother says 'That is a very fine young man.'

'I know what you're going to say.'

'Give him a chance, Alice. Give him a chance. I know he'd make you happy, and that's all I want for you.'

'I do know. It's just that I don't feel the same way about him. I don't think it would be fair to him. And there are other factors as well.'

'It's your choice, but think about it, seriously. Lower your barriers a little and let him take your hand. Your feelings could change if you try.'

'I'll think about it. Promise. By the way, thank you for looking after Decima last night.'

'She's not quite what I was expecting, actually. Nothing at all like that confident, abrasive on-screen persona. She seems very lonely to me.'

My eyebrows shoot up in surprise. 'Really? I've never seen her like that.'

'She puts on a strong face in public, but I can tell you that girl has a sad, almost empty aura. I felt something very dark there, and I found her interesting.'

Intriguing. I realize that I've never given Decima much thought outside of work and I really don't know anything about her. In fact that's not quite true, because I remember that awful night of her 'party', looking at the portrait of her mother, the prima ballerina Graciela Mazzelini, who was married to a racing driver. I vaguely recalled some kind of family tragedy long ago. I meant to look it up and find out the whole story, but the way that evening turned out, I completely forgot. I'll definitely do something about it and see what comes to light. I know

12

Gauld is her adoptive father, but from the little I've heard about him, he's not a very nice person. For somebody with such a high public image, it's surprising that you never see her mentioned outside of work. You never see or hear of her with friends. It seems that the boys are her only social life, but well, I mean, it's what they're paid for, isn't it?

I'm quite a solitary person, not a social butterfly at all, but Shelley and I have been friends for at least ten years, and I look on Lorelei Thornheart, Decima's predecessor and a genuine witch, as a friend too, although she's far away and I haven't seen her for so long. There's Sean as well. He's a different kind of friend, not somebody I can really confide in, but he's always there to help when I need it. I can't imagine what it would be like to have nobody to share with, or to care about.

Decima carries that old teddy bear wherever she goes, and sometimes I've overheard her talking to it. At least my sweet Zylch is actually a living creature, not a bundle of fabric. I see what my mother means about her being lonely. Maybe she needs to be nicer and then people will start to like her.

My mother drives Shelley and the girls back home. When they go I feel tense wondering if Sean is going to come on to me, but to my relief he says he has to leave, as he goes to church on Sundays.

Once I'm alone, I go and sit with my feet in the pond. Zylch bounces up to me, squeals 'Wheeeeeeee', and jumps into the water, diving under the surface, blowing bubbles, and turning over to float on his back, tapping his belly with his fingers.

'I'm glad I have you, Zylch. You make me laugh, and that's something I really need at the moment. My life is becoming complicated.'

He climbs onto my lap and lies on his back waving his legs in the air and chewing his tail.

'What would you do, Zylch, if you were me? What should I do about Sean?'

He looks up at me, rolls his eyes and pokes out his tongue.

'Thank you, that is not a great deal of help,' I say.

I sit there, staring into the water, as if it may hold an answer, but all I see is my own reflection.

To take my mind off it, I go inside and spend the evening sorting out my clothes. Decima said, a few weeks ago: 'Sweetie, we need to choose a look for you for when I let you onto the show. I think simple, two-piece outfits will suit you when you're on camera. Nothing flashy, and keep your tits and knees covered.' I've bought a few mix-and-match outfits. Shelley helped me, she's much better at choosing clothes than I am. Decima hasn't said yet when I'll make my first appearance, but I want to be ready for when that day comes. I'm both excited and terrified! Decima reminded me that it was her show, and all the attention will be on her unless she introduces me into the discussion. Once I have more experience, she said, I'll be able to take a more active part. She's very condescending, but I don't let it bother me.

When Lorelei left the show, I told her how I felt disloyal staying on with Decima, but I couldn't move away because I wanted to be close to my parents in case they needed me. Lorelei hugged me and said she was going to miss me but that it was important for me to stay because this is where I'd find my future happiness. When I asked what she meant, she smiled and told me to be patient and trust her.

'Things will turn out the way they are meant to be, Alice. You will know what you need to do, and which path to follow. Have faith in yourself. I know you will always do what is right, and you will have everything you deserve. It won't come straight away, but trust me, it will come. Take care of yourself. There will be dark times, but you are stronger than you believe. And I will always be caring for you, no matter how far from each other we may be.'

I've often thought of her words, and what they mean. I expect one day I'll understand.

Before she left she gave me a small book of pressed flowers, and on each parchment page is a handwritten spell. Inside the cover it reads: 'Dear Alice, you may find this useful one day. Use it wisely. Lorelei.'

I've had it for two years now, and the flowers are still as fresh as the day they were picked, and their perfume is as strong as ever. I keep it beside my bed and recently used one of the spells when I forgot to water Decima's precious Chinese Money Plant. It was flopping and dried out, but fortunately she's been so tied up with the new show that she hadn't noticed, and I revived it. A couple of honeysuckle flowers in a bowl of water left out in the moonlight, a simple incantation, and the plant soon sprang back to life.

It has been awkward with Decima publicly announcing that Lorelei isn't a real witch when I know she is, and all the stuff going on now, but what can I do? It's not my job to interfere and Decima wouldn't listen to me anyway. I wouldn't want to rock the boat now that we're getting on so much better.

Enough. I'm tired, so I'm turning off the light. Zylch has curled up at my feet and is quietly reciting 'Baa baa black sheep' to himself. He stumbles over 'three', and says 'shree' instead. But for an animal, he's talking pretty well.

My last thought, before I fade away into sleep, is whether Sean is the happiness I'm meant to find.

4

Cancel the witch

Decima

Everyone knows there's no such thing as ghosts and witches, right? But bitches are real, man, and when we start airing, the supreme Goddess of Bitches crown will be mine.

The sniping is growing by the minute. Turn it up, I'm in. Oh yes. 'Up the BITCH and cancel the WITCH. Take *this* Lorelei Thornheart,' I chuckle and click through to Twitter.

Trevor joins in my glee. 'Upthebitch, upthebitch, upbitchbitch,' he screams, flying around the kitchen.

'Good boy, Trevor, you're learning fast. Treats time for you.'

He lands on my hand and takes a tortilla chip oh so gently with his claw. I'm fresh out of a new manicure and it's debatable who's got the longest talons here.

'Good boy, Trevor.' I scratch his head and hit SEND on my tweet, tagging Lorelei in for good measure. I wouldn't want her to miss *The News* would I?

My coffee has gone cold but I sip it anyway and read the release again. For the hundredth time to be honest. It's real, it's happening. It's truly happening.

HAWK BAY CITY NEWSWIRE

One of the largest merchandise/TV sponsorship deals in history has been confirmed. **CGO TV, Hawk Bay City** *and* **Terikhan Dubai Beauty, UAE** *have announced a partnership to bring CGO's TV chat show* **The Witch's Hour** *rebranded* **The Bitch's Hour** *to an international audience. In a multi-million dollar deal, the show's presenter* **Decima Gauld**, *is confirmed as the US face of Terikhan Dubai Beauty's* **flagship perfume brand, #TO-ME** , *in a state-wide and global simul-launch.*

'Our long hunt for the face of #To-Me is over,' said **Fabienne Fax**, *Communications Executive, Terikhan Dubai Beauty. 'We are excited to bring Decima's powerful presence to a global audience. As we move into the Era of the Bitch, here is a woman who says it like it is. No matter the consequences. She asks the difficult questions of her guests that we all want answering. Like all successful business people, Decima* **embraces** *risk. Her recent shock announcement live on air that she is not a witch has never been a witch, and never will be a witch traveled like lightning through the web, sparking debates about witchcraft, fact or fake, worldwide. Decima will be so much more than a perfume ambassador. She brings the holy trinity of beauty, ugliness and terror to our brand, knitted together with down-to-earth, no-nonsense, truth.*

On Gauld's gutsy charisma, Fax revealed the strapline for the perfume and the TV show will be **Say It Like It Is.** *'Decima encapsulates the strong women of the world, in tune with her own needs as a 21st century woman,' says Fax. 'Her guests will all be powerful women from the international community we are becoming.'*

The show, set to screen on cable and worldwide digital, will interview leading businesswomen, environmentalists, politicians, world leaders, entrepreneurs, and wellness and beauty advocates. 'Decima will be at the helm of the global digital discussion, reaching many millions of viewers daily.'

'This is an important step in our global expansion program. Perfume sales have exceeded all expectations in Europe and Asia and, with Decima at the helm, we fully expect the US to follow. We are planning a wellness brand with Decima at the helm.'

Fax declined to comment on Decima's predecessor, **The Witch's Hour** *presenter Lorelie Thornheart. 'We refuse to give any more oxygen to Lorelei's fakery.' Thornheart left CGO TV under mysterious circumstances. Now based in LA, Thornheart's witch-focussed YouTube channel currently has 6.5 million subscribers, with 2.5 million TikTok followers. The rivalry between Gauld and Thornheart has the nation gripped.*

The Bitch's Hour *will run weekdays at 3pm EC Time.*

The witch is dead. Long live the bitch. That's because the witch never existed in the first place. Right? Josh is still insisting that they're real but it's a load of lies. Witches don't exist. As everybody in the world with an ounce of sense knows, they're a made-up concept. Mature, honest and gutsy will replace Lorelei's witchy nonsense. No deceptions. No lies. The truth hurts, bitch.

That's my personal message right there, guys. *Be you.*

And after what I've been through recently, I know one or two things about that. OK confession: I'm not strictly being ME out there. I toned myself right down towards the end of the last series. It was a tactic. A shock move.

Nobody knew quite what to make of it. It did the trick. Got the witchy ID off my back and a new sponsor too. Am I too beige now? *Too* Gwynneth Paltrow on screen with my cashmere, linen and Peter Pan necklines? I *love* to dress like the tramp I can be but, hey, who's paying the bills around here? Dressing sexy is as *natural* as it comes for a woman, Gwynnie fans, but I reserve that now for my off-screen time with my boys. They appreciate it more, I reckon. And, you know what? So do I.

For those one or two of you who perhaps have never heard of me: it all started last year when Dad set me up as a chat show presenter on his TV channel. *The Witch's Hour* was presented by self-proclaimed witch Lorelei Thornheart. They'd fallen out and he needed a quick replacement.

Now I wasn't up for it. I'm not a witch. Fake or otherwise. I only agreed to pretend to be a witch on the condition that he'd find a way of keeping my appetite satisfied.

So what better way to persuade me to rescue his show than to provide me with some hot techies? All four work on the show. Runner Ramon, floor manager and music guy Sean, and trainee exteriors cameraman, Cory. All auditioned and recruited by me. Man, that interview process was fun. No Zooms there I can assure you. But then *The Witch's Hour* director, Josh, Dad's right hand man who's been at CGO TV forever, asked if he could join in on our cozy sessions. If you saw Josh you'd know why I liked that idea, I liked that idea very very much.

So, faking it as a witch on a show that belonged to somebody else was a small price to pay for living the life. *Be you*, but don't worry about faking it a little if it gets you where you want to go. Right? We all have to push through a few barriers and half-truths to get to where we belong.

It's not all smooth sailing. Take my assistant, inherited from Lorelei. She's a pain, a niggling, prickly, pretty little irritating thorn in my side. I wanted her gone but she was part of the original handover deal and now she's included in the new contract too. Alice is good at her job, I'll give her that. She loves it and does all she can to please me. She gets my coffee just right and is always there to hand it to me when I arrive. She's so happy to work in TV she'll do literally anything to keep herself there. The problem is, my boys.

They adore her. They worship her. They're infatuated. Even Josh who's twice her age. It's like some kind of a Midsummer Night's Dream madness has been cast over all of them. If I believed in witchcraft I could even go so far as to call it a spell.

It all started when YouTuber dream boy Scorpio, who I was lining up for some dressing room fun, seduced her in the shabby little basement kitchen. She was a big fan and I let her hang around on set. Mistake. He had an 'accident' let's say, with his $900 T-shirt. Some kind of marks had got on it and Alice was sent to sort it out. She got him into the kitchen for emergency stain removal, the minx.. And there they stayed. And stayed. The crew got curious, put the security camera on and were treated to their own private show. Now they've all been put into some kind of an Alice worship trance.

I've been trying to fix it. A few weeks ago, when the news of the Dubai deal was confirmed, I held a party to tell everybody the good news. It's not only my income that's shooting up. They're all getting raises of their dreams.

To knock the infatuation on the head, I invited Alice too. Let them experience her, one by one, and end the mystery. Knock their stupid lusts right on the head. I got her real dressed up and ready for her surprise treat. It was going to be the party to end all parties. I knew she'd enjoy it.

But it didn't work out that way. Can you believe she wasn't up for it? I still can't get my head around it. Who could resist an offer like that with my beautiful boys? I thought I was being generous.

It got weird actually. Alice was really upset. And then she vanished! She simply disappeared.

It must have been a set-up with one of the boys. But who was her accomplice? Which of them is helping her out behind my back? Supporting Alice rather than me? Ha, it's not even a question. Sean is the most besotted one. But he's not exactly bright. He has other, different, kinds of talents. Talents I wouldn't want to lose and certainly wouldn't want Alice to steal.

Where did she go? How did she do that? I've never gotten to the bottom of it. But I plan to.

My phone goes crazy. It doesn't stop pinging. Great,

my tweet must have hit viral. It'll be all the usual witchy nonsense from Lorelei's stupid supporters. Well, bring it on!

At the studio these days all references to witches, fake witches, stupid witches, fake ghosts, stupid ghosts, *and* any mention of Lorelei's name is strictly forbidden. Ghosts and witches are laughable nonsense, for deluded idiots only. Any reference thereto is banned on set with the absolute, legally binding, promise of instant dismissal. And anybody who gives me grief online gets it thrown right back at them.

I scroll through. There are lots of laughing emojis and GO GET DECIMA from Lorelei's crowd. The usual names. But what is this?

She's only threatening another of her lawsuits. Quoting me as saying: 'Lorelei's fakery'. They were Fabienne's words, not mine I think she'll find. I'm in the clear there, and Fabienne has Dubai millions to squash her flat. She knows that. So she's taken it a step further. She's going to prove, online, that she's not a fake. Well, good luck with that Lorelei.

5

This bitch is on fire

Decima

I'm winding down on the couch with my book listening to the sound of Lorelei Thornheart's reputation, what's left of it, going up in smoke. If witches did exist and I was that way inclined, I'd be cackling right now.

Instead, I allow myself a quiet smile of victory, stretch out my legs and wiggle my freshly-pedicured toes contentedly in the heat. The flames dance around her hoax magic door, throwing giant shadows around the room.

You see, when they were striking Lorelei's old *Witch's Hour* set, I got my condo handyman Grant down to the studio to salvage the door and chop it up for firewood.

You've probably heard the story. When Lorelei presented *The Witch's Hour*, a fake ghost walked on set through that door. A fake so real, it rocketed *The Witch's Hour* ratings. Now Lorelei's door crumbles, right here at my feet.

Her stupid lawsuit is backfiring magnificently. She still won't accept I'm in line to become the most famous bitch in the world. I don't think that's what she had in mind somehow when she issued that writ. She has no idea how powerful I am now. *The Bitch's Hour* sponsors' limitless cash is paying for the best lawyers going whilst, over on Twitter, the world's #1 PR guru Fabienne Fax and her crack team of blue-ticks are ripping her *Witch Queen of LA* reputation to shreds.

As if it heard me, the flames shoot up the chimney in a roar that freaks me out to be honest. Trevor screams and starts flying around the room in a whirl of white feathers.

'Shush,' I growl and look over to Digby for reassurance. He sits quietly on his throne on the topmost bookshelf, glaring down at me with his black button eyes. He's annoyed. Digby puts up with the parrot but he hates fire. Teddy bears can easily go up in smoke too you know, he seems to be saying. Especially priceless antique teddy bears.

'All right, you win.' I jump up from the sofa, take my precious Digby into my arms and, with one eye on the flames, dance defiantly around the room, cupping his prickly bald left ear in my hand.

'There's nothing to worry about, Digsy. You'll see. I'm being primed for superstardom, babe, and Lorelei is playing right into our net. It's all very exciting.'

I put my book back on the shelf, settle Digby on my lap and go into my phone.

I check the enemy's hashtags first:

@VermontRose Wake up and smell the coffee, bitch, your the faker around here. #bringbacktheghost #justiceforghosts #ghostpower #thedoorisreal #witchesnotbitches

@HollywoodSam424 It's you're.

I smile. Hollywood Sam aka Fabienne Fax is so good at the one line put-downs.

I type: *.@VermontRose Listen lady, why don't you get back in your cauldron and boil yourself down to your crony old bones. #BuryTheWitch #FakeWitch #fakeghost*

Silence is dignified, Fabienne says. Let them dig themselves in deeper. It's a tough one to learn but I do get it, so I hit DELETE, sit on my fingers and watch it all unfold.

@WiccaDi98 That ghost was real, I know it. Go get the bitch, Lorelei we're with you all the way hun #bringbackthedoor #justiceforghosts

Wow, the war is hotting up. Look at this one:

@Nancy83 Get this dangerous fake off the streets NOW. Sign the Lock Up Lorelei petition here: www.lock-up-thornheart.com. #LoreleiThornheartIsAPsychopath #lockherup

Beef it up, Fabienne! Fabienne's crack team is piling onto every 'witch' who dares to speak out against me. And guess what? The more Lorelei's cronies protest, the more I trend, the more I win. That's a $10K a day PR genius at work right there. But, come on. It's only the truth! Fabienne's Law in action:

If you have a problem, what do you do? You twist it round to your advantage.

Hang on, what's this?

@HawkBayCityTimes Sexy new revelation in the Decima/Lorelei conflict, www.hawkbaycitytimes.com

Clickbait, but I follow the link. Of course I do.

'Decima Gauld was brought in to present The Witch's Hour after the sudden departure of the original show witch, Lorelei Thornheart. The Witch Queen of LA, as Lorelai is affectionately known by her millions of followers, is now the High Priestess of Malibu's Crystal Waters Coven and YouTube channel of the same name. Gauld, it has been revealed, was a struggling actor before being rescued by her father and handed the presenting job without an audition.'

I go hot and cold at the same time. What's this lack of audition rubbish? Who knows what went on there? It had to be the meddling little runt, happy family, butter-wouldn't-melt, PA Alice Archer trying to get one over on me. The more loyal she appears, the more I think she's a fake. There's something weird going on with her. My boys' ridiculous lusts continue, even after she's refused them all. Maybe it's because she's refused them all? What you can't have and all that. When I confide in Josh, he says that word again. Friendship. It's *only friendship* he repeats whenever I bring it up. Friends my foot.

My boys do still get off on our sessions as much as I love creating different scenarios for our fun, but we can all sense when something's not right.

I confided my little Alice problem to Fabienne at one of our prelim strategy meetings the other day. I only hinted at it, but she was right in there question after question like a dog with a bone. Man, could she get the proverbial water out of a stone, she could get anything out of anybody.

Repeat after me:

If you have a problem, what do you do? You twist it to your advantage.

Genius that she is, she's come up with the perfect solution to put Alice in her place.

It's nasty and I love it. The truth is, the bitch in me is already taking on a life of her own that frightens even me sometimes.

6

The price of fame

Decima

I'm already too famous to be going to a scrappy little backyard cookout on the wrong side of town, but Alice has managed to get all of my boys over and I need to keep tabs on the devious little creature.

'Ouch, oof, driver, slow down!'

'Nearly there M'am.'

'I can tell!' These streets are like cattle grids, there are so many potholes.

Cabs huh. But only an idiot would let her Porsche loose on the locals.

I lie down on the back seat as soon as we're past Main Street.

Fabienne's orders.

It's painful but I can't be seen on the wrong side of town, she says, and I can't disagree. OUCH, even if there's a seatbelt clip burrowing into my butt. The price of fame.

The engine finally stops.

I don't move. 'Tell me when the coast is clear.'

'Nobody here, M'am.'

'You sure?'

'Take a look yourself,' he sighs.

'All right, all right.' I grab my stuff and clamber out. 'Wait here.'

With a red geranium plant in one hand and my nose in the other, I follow a trail of balloons down a rutted path through a field. I come out at a building site. Beyond a bright yellow digger, I can see wisps of smoke and heads bobbing to tinny, over-amplified Abba.

Aim low and shabby, you get low and shabby. I reluctantly let go of my nose and push my way through the lowlife towards the food and drink. Who are all these people anyway?

Sean is at the barbeque, tongs in hand wearing a stupid joke naked gorilla apron.

'Hmm, quite the improvement, Sean,' I look him up and down and help myself to a sausage.

'Decima! We didn't expect to see you here.'

'Why's that? Was I not invited?' I run my tongue up and down my sausage.

His ears turn pink and he opens his mouth to protest, but I hold up my hand. 'It's a joke, Sean. Where's Alice? I expect you know exactly where she is?'

He misses the jibe but proves my point. 'She's in the bathroom there, she'll be out again in no time at all.'

I take a step back and look him up and down.

He tips his head to one side with a half-smile. He's seen this look often enough. 'Don't get any ideas here now, Decima. This isn't that kind of a party.'

'Who says?' I fix my eyes on his cartoon hairy balls and

bite into my sausage. 'WHAT the?' I spit a gob of sawdust on the ground.

Sean dashes out from behind the barbeque, frantically flapping a clown napkin at me. 'Those are the vegetarian ones, Decima. The meat's over on the table there.'

I push his head down whilst he's clearing up my spit at my feet, 'Give me meat, give me meat, Sean.'

'Decima, stop that now,' he wriggles out and stands up. 'This is a civilized event. A special event.'

'So, this is the famous Decima Gauld is it,' a woman at the next table glances up from slicing cucumbers and smiles at me in the same stern tone as her words. She comes around the table and tries to shake my hand, but she's still holding her knife.

'Oh, silly me!' she fumbles about like the idiot she clearly isn't. I get the gesture immediately and we lock eyes. Who is this? I like her. She's got guts this one.

Then I see Sean's eyes light up and, sure enough, here comes the party girl. 'Oh Decima! I'm so pleased you've come! I see you've met Astrid!'

'Astrid?'

'My mother!'

'Oh!' Oh. OK. We have a nice frosty exchange, sizing each other up, before Alice takes me to see 'the pond'. I am introduced to a man in a fit of giggles spraying a couple of squealing kids with a hosepipe.

Her father. Fun Dad, clearly.

As pleasantries are exchanged, I can see Cory, Josh and Ramon half naked and covered in mud behind him, standing beside a puddle lined with bright blue plastic. They are laughing and getting lots of attention from a shabby young girl in a tight yellow trackie squealing with laughter and twiddling with her toilet-brush hair. I know she's deluded that their attentions are going her way but my heart drops all the same. What are my boys doing enjoying themselves so much here? These are not our people.

I'm glad I asked the driver to wait outside.

I stare out of the cab window into the black feeling sorry for myself. The tears were backing up there, ready to fall. I needed to get out of there fast before anybody noticed.

I stayed long enough for one drink and a few real sausages. Those short juicy ones that squirt animal fat when you bite into them. They were good. I salivate at the memory. I wouldn't mind some late night action right now, but they're all busy, aren't they. Otherwise occupied.

My boys.

With that little bitch.

Alice has it all, doesn't she. Not only the respect of my boys, but a whole party-full of friends outside of work, a gutsy mother, a fun dad. A cat! No long-dead dear mama and papa, no gross sister (blood, unfortunately), no even more gross crook of an adopted father. Nothing but an ancient teddy and a snarky parrot waiting for me at home. I haven't even got a *dog*.

'Enough of that right now, Decima,' I hear Fabienne's voice in my ear. 'Ditch the negatives right out of that head of yours this second. Think of the positives.'

She's right. My future couldn't be brighter. I'm going to be very rich indeed. I'll never run out of my best friends – my books – as long as I live, and there's a new Mila Young waiting to be cracked open by the fire. I think about my priceless signed first editions lined up on my shelves. Voices from the past mingling with the authors of today. Now that's real magic. I smile. The past is the past. Over. Dead. Bring on the future.

By the time I'm home, I'm in a better mood. I take a cold shower. For medical reasons you understand. A drive as powerful as mine needs managing. Some would call it a full-blown *condition*, an illness, but I enjoy it too much to call it that. I throw a few planks of fake magic door on the dying embers in the grate, and cheer myself up thinking about Fabienne's plan for Alice.

In order for me to be THE Bitch, it helps to have a stooge, she says. Something to aim at, to take the blows.

There's only so far I can go with my new type of sophisticated guests in terms of my Bitch Queen profile. That's where Alice will come in. She knows she's going to be in front of the camera, but has no idea when, or what that will involve. She's under the delusion that she's going to be a co-presenter! I will spring Fabienne's clever plan on her at the last moment. When it's too late for her to back down. She's a loyal little thing and would never want to jeopardize the show. But then again she could find a way to wiggle out once she knows what's in store for her. I know! Fame should be enough of a draw, no matter how she gets there, right? She should be happy about it! She'll get a raise! And everybody has their price, right? But even I am feeling a little queasy about it.

7

Worries and relaxation

Josh

Maybe I've been working at The Tower for too long. I'd almost forgotten what it feels like to truly chill, to be myself, not to have to fake, not to be under pressure to perform in every way. To feel normal.

When Sean suggested the four of us spend a Saturday helping to create a pond for Alice in her new garden, I scoffed. Why would I want to spend one of my free days with the guys I work with all week?

'Oh come on, man, Ramon and Cory are up for it. Do you good to get out of town and breathe some country air. But, I guess at your age you need to take things easy and recharge your batteries over the weekend,' he says cheekily.

You can't get mad at Sean. He's simply the nicest guy you could find. Do anything for anyone, and always with a smile.

'OK, you win. Count me in,' I laughed.

I biked out there, and you know what? It turned out to be one of the happiest times I can remember for a long, long while. Sean was right, it was a tonic for me to mix with the guys and Alice away from the Tower and away from Decima's demands.

It took my mind off a problem, too. I love my kids. All I've ever wanted for them is their happiness. Since my beloved Diane died, I've tried to be a mother and father to them and give them everything they wanted, but now they've come up with some crazy idea about buying up and developing a derelict property in town and they want to borrow the money from me. Even if I had that kind of cash I wouldn't let them have it, because their plan is harebrained and doomed to fail. They're angry, which stresses me.

So yeah, being out here fooling around has brought my stress level right down.

I'd say Sean is getting his feet under the table with Alice quite nicely. He's masterminded the pond project and he's doing a pretty good job, managing to be everywhere at once without taking his eyes off Alice for a second. When we all go home to wash up and change for the evening, I notice he stays there, and he's acting like a host, very much at home. He's definitely got Alice's mother and friend charmed.

I don't think any of us expected Decima to turn up, but we all saw her slink in and you could feel the tension in the air.

As it turned out she behaved like a real lady. Who'd have thought! She waved at us and walked over to Alice, holding out a wrapped plant, then let Alice introduce her to her parents. She sat with them, chatting, accepted a glass of wine, and then left suddenly, saying she had another invitation and wishing us all a great night. Whatever she may have been thinking inside, she hid it well.

Watching Alice during the evening, she looked so carefree, sitting with her parents, listening to the music. She's lost the haunted look, and put on a little weight, which suits her. Not the puppy fat she once had, but some nice gentle curves. The lovely golden waves are growing back. She's found a new confidence, changed from a girl to a woman, with that irresistible combination of sexy lady and pure innocence. The eyes of every male here are watching her all the time.

Now and again I catch an expression on her face, when the happiness fades for a few seconds, and she's staring blankly, her smile replaced by the kind of look a lost puppy wears when it's waiting anxiously to be found. I wonder if she's still thinking of that Indian guy who dumped her?

8

Little acts of kindness

Alice

I thought a lot about putting my idea into practice, using my magic more, and I came up with an idea. It's simple – just little acts of kindness I can easily do.

It starts when I'm following this young girl who works at the Tower, on one of the lower floors. Insurance company or something. She's tottering into the lobby, giggling with a friend, when the heel of one of her crazy high-heeled shoes snaps. She hobbles over to a bench and sits holding the shoe and the heel and wailing.

As I walk past her I rub my thumb and forefinger together to summon the **'Fix'** spell. By the time I've reached the elevators she's yelling 'Oh my, oh my, how did that even happen!' I look back and see her and her friend staring at the mended shoe, and telling the small crowd of people who have stopped and stood around that the heel had broken off, but now it's stuck itself back on. People are laughing and shaking their heads in disbelief. I smile to myself.

So that's it. Wherever I am, I'm going to keep my eyes open for anybody who needs a little help that is within my ability. I'm going to talk with my mother, and Lorelei, about setting up a network of witches across the country. Maybe one day all over the world. We have the power to do so much good. Yep, I am really liking this idea. We could get an App made for it!

9

Gwynnie with guts

Decima

The studio at the top of the Tower has had a major refit on the Dubai dollar. Even the air up here has had a spring clean. Some kind of witchy sage air purifying treatment. When I pointed out that we have moved away from all the woo woo, Fabienne said it was nothing of the kind, but Feng Shui, a spiritual smoke detector. I'm supposed to believe that the atmosphere is now hyper-sensitive to any 'disturbances' of the peace. For which, read my Passion Pit encounters.

RIP Passion Pit. They took it down. Can you believe it? The soft pink decor survived the dressing room refit at least but my circular bed has gone. After I shouted about my medical condition to HR and complained about the lack of space, a doorway was knocked through from my dressing room to the Green Room. When I summon my boys there, together or alone as the mood takes me, they know it's game on time.

I like to alternate it between here in the Green Room high up in the Tower, and the basement control room. This morning it's only me and Josh up on the 17th floor.

He hurries towards me with that look in his eye, wraps

his big bear arms around me and snuffles into my neck.

I twist out of his hold.

He jumps right back. 'What?'

Tempted? Yes. But I have other things on my mind.

'I'm an international brand in development, Josh,' I say gently, 'and I need to talk.'

'What's that got to do with a quick one?'

'I need your advice.'

'First?'

'We'll see. Let's sit down.'

With a shrug he pulls up a couple of chairs. He sits on his backwards so he's leaning on the support facing me, legs apart either side. I rest my hands on his thighs. Dangerous, but if you could see Josh's thighs and the way his jeans stretch over, just right, you'd know what I mean.

'My sex drive isn't going anywhere, Josh, feng shui fountains, hippie smells and all these plants everywhere or not. But I'm freaking the freak right out.'

'Lorelei's Twitter spats getting to you?'

'No. Well, yes, but I can handle her.'

'You're an old pro, Decima. You got nothing to worry about.'

'You know what they've come up with for my latest promo tag?'

'*The Bitch's Hour* says it all, don't it?'

'Gwynneth Paltrow with guts.'

Josh purses his lips and nods thoughtfully. 'I like that. A sexy woman with guts. Who's not afraid to say it how it is. That's you girl. Through and through.'

'They want me to up the conflict in my interviews.'

'So what's that got to do with lightweight Gwynnie?'

'It's not only the TV show they're talking about, Josh but a whole wellness brand. They're bigging up the perfume launch and then where? Natural make-up, health supplements, *gym* wear...Tell me honestly, Josh. Can I pull this off?'

'You're the Queen of Conflict, Decima.'

'Yes but all the natural beige bitch they're pushing on me is fake. I'm a flirt, a slut, Josh.'

'They're not stupid. That's what makes you so special., You can't stop your sex appeal oozing out of you no matter what you wear. Course you can pull it off or those guys wouldn't have hired you. Talking of which...' He leans in and drops a kiss on my neck. 'What did your father add to my job description when you joined the team?'

I feel his breath on my skin. Hot kisses on my neck and little nibbles on my ear, his beard tickling me exactly the way I like it until I give in to that glorious moment of helpless submission.

'I love these early morning business meetings,' he whispers huskily in my ear. 'You're the real witch. You know that.'

'I do need to talk, Josh,' I manage to say.

'It can wait.' his breathing is short and heavy.

'Fabienne's had this idea.'

'Forget *Fabienne* for a minute will you,'

'She's got this plan for Alice.' I pause.

'Oh yes. I heard.'

'I thought you would.' I don't even ask how. Josh knows everything that's going on in every corner of this Tower. From the top secret closed Zoom meetings with Dubai to the companies who rent the offices from Dad on the lower floors. I wait for him to continue.

'Co-presenting, right? Well, I didn't see that one coming, I'll give you that! It's a bold move. Left field. But she'll rise to it. She's one special woman…' his voice trails away and, for a second, he's lost in thought. But then he picks up again quickly. 'Hey, you're not worried about her upstaging you are you?'

'WHAT?'

He backtracks but it's too late.

'Get out. Get yourself away from me. NOW!'

Before I can take another breath he's moving in on me again.

'Now now, Decima. You're the best. You *know* that.'

What I do know is that his body is with me as much as his mind is elsewhere. I hate what the mere sound of that girl's name does to these men. It's elemental. *Weird.*

'No. Tell me. What is it?'

I feel myself responding but shove him away.

'Get out. Now.'

Any qualms I had about what's in store for Alice are forgotten. She's going to get nothing less than all that she deserves.

10

Dark clouds gathering

Alice

I was planning to visit my folks on Sunday, but Astrid called and told me not to come. She wouldn't say why, only that it wasn't convenient, but she didn't sound at all like herself. Like she'd been crying.

She never cries.

I'm going now.

I **Broomstick** out to the Brent Flats, and stare in horror at my mother's garden. Every plant has been torn up. All her beautiful roses are chopped down, a tangle of branches, petals and stems. It's a scene of total devastation.

She's sitting on the step, her head on her knees, sobbing, and my father is going around raking up the debris into a pile.

She looks up at me. 'Why are you here, Alice? I told you not to come. I didn't want you to see this.'

I go and sit beside her, and put my hand on her knee.

'Astrid, I am not a child. I don't need protecting. I'm perfectly aware that something strange has been going on here, and it's time you told me. And as it's very hot, and I'm hungry, I would like something to eat and drink.'

I hold out my hand and pull her to her feet, steering her to the kitchen.

'Talk to me, mother. What is this about?'

Silently she hands me a piece of card. Written on it in red paint are the words: 'YOU HAVE BEEN WARNED. THIS IS JUST THE START'.

'They're determined to drive us out, force us to sell. I don't know what to do. I didn't tell you before, but all our neighbors sold up because they were threatened. How can we possibly move, even if we wanted to? Where could we go, what could we do with the Screechers? What are we going to do?'

'Let's have a lemonade, then we'll talk.' I take the biscuit tin off the shelf and find some brownies.

She stares at me as if she's looking at a stranger, and then places a plate and glass in front of me.

'We,' I say, 'are going to find a way to fight this. That's what we're going to do. We're going to fight.'

'How do we even do that? These people are so powerful and ruthless. They'll stop at nothing to get us out.'

Give me a moment. I'll be back in a minute,' I say.

Out in the garden my father has piled all the broken plants up to burn.

'Stop,' I say. 'We can save them.'

'Alice, go back inside with your mother.'

'I may be able to save them.'

'By magic, I suppose,' he says sarcastically. 'You're going to cast a spell and they will all mend and throw themselves back into the ground. Is that it? For goodness sake Alice, this is no time for abracadabra.'

My normally taciturn father is showing he's seriously rattled.

'Not quite, but just don't burn them. Let me at least try to take care of them.'

He throws down the fork and shakes his head. 'This is the last thing I need.'

I say: 'I know you don't have a lot of confidence in me, but give me a chance, father. I can't make it any worse, can I?'

'What would you like me to do? Collect up some bat wings and toad eyes? Light a black candle? Recite the Desiderata backwards?'

'Get as many containers as you can find and fill them with water. Trust me.'

I go back into the house and call my mother. 'Come out here and help. We're going to save your plants.'

'Don't be so silly Alice. They're ruined. We can't save them. I don't have that level of power.' Her voice breaks.

'Come. We can try,' I say gently.

I lead her back to where Patrick is collecting buckets.

'Fill these with water. I'll be back in a few minutes.'

I **Broomstick** home and take the little book of spells Lorelei gave me from where it sits on my bedside table.

Three minutes later I'm back.

'Listen.' I tell them how I forgot to water Decima's Chinese money plant and it was almost dead, and how I used one of Lorelei's spells to revive it.

My father says 'Pff'. Astrid takes the spell book from me and thumbs through it.

'Hm. I'm doubtful. There's a big difference between a wilted pot plant and shrubs that have been chopped down and uprooted. There's no harm in trying though.'

I give her a spontaneous hug, which comes as a bit of a shock to both of us because we are not a family that demonstrates affection. But I'm feeling overwhelmed with anger, and concern for my mother.

'Go back inside. I'll be in a little later, and we'll talk. Keep your fingers crossed.'

With my father I place all the damaged plants into the buckets, and persuade him to help me gather the necessary ingredients for the spell. He's huffing and puffing, but says: 'I don't think this is a good idea, getting your mother's hopes up, but if it makes her feel any better for a little while.'

When I have what I need I prepare a potion following Lorelei's spell and quietly say the words of the incantation. Then I sit with my eyes closed, silently repeating the incantation seven times. I add seven drops of the potion to each of the buckets. A wisp of mist arises, giving off a strange smell that is both sweet and bitter.

I've done everything I can. Now we have to wait.

Back in the house my father says: 'Well, did it work?'

'It will take time, I don't know how long. Now, do you know who these people are? Why are they buying up the land? What would they want the Brent Flats for?'

'It's some billionaire who wants to develop the land to

build a leisure center with a country club and golf course,'
says my mother. 'One of those people who think because
they have money they can do what they want, buy
anything and everything and never mind who they hurt.
They've been cajoling us for months. We've told them we
are not going away, and we don't want their money. Now
they're threatening. That's why everybody else has sold
up. These people are bullies. I'm so afraid of what they'll
do next.'

'This is protected land. They can't build on it. They'll
never get permission.'

'With their money, permission won't be a problem,'
she says bitterly. 'Look at how many dodgy deals have
been done at City Hall over the last few years. They're a
bunch of crooks.'

She's right. There have been so many scandals, and
rumors of bribes and corruption among the counselors.
Several of them are regularly seen dining in the top
restaurants, their wives dressed in designer fashion and
wearing a fortune in jewelry. They drive top of the range
vehicles and live in the most exclusive areas, and you
don't get there overnight on a counselor's wages. While
they can always find funding for the wealthy eastern side
of Hawk Bay City for new malls, playgrounds and parks,
and some truly ugly multi-storey buildings have shot up
in the last few years, on the west side the broken
sidewalks, potholes and closed shops keep getting worse.

'We will find a way to fight them, somehow. In the
meantime, please take care, mother. Stay inside when

you're alone.'

Before I leave I give her another hug and am rewarded with a smile. She strokes my hand and says: 'Thank you for trying to help Alice. You're a good girl and we both love you very much. We'll get through this one way or another. Don't worry.'

But I do worry, of course I do. For all my brave words, I have no idea what we can or are going to do.

Zylch trots along beside me when we go out to walk in the cool of the evening. He doesn't appear to be listening while I talk to him, because he's humming and chasing butterflies, catching them in his paws, inspecting them and then tossing them softly back into the air. He's unpredictable and I really don't know what to expect next. He'll not speak for a week or more, and then without any warning he'll chatter away, or sing. He picks up a lot of stuff from Alexa. I love him.

I don't know what wakes me that night. Whether it's worry about my parents, worry about Sean, excitement about work, but something has disturbed my sleep. I hear something rattling outside, and a terrifying snarling sound. Moving my legs I am surprised to find Zlych isn't there in his usual place. The clock beside the bed shows 4.00 am, and as I reach to put it back I notice a shadow on the curtain, something large, moving past slowly, silently. I gulp, wondering if it's anything to do with the threat to my parents. I cautiously slide out of bed and creep to the window, peering out from the side of the curtains. A huge black creature, the size of a bison, is slinking past the house. The moonlight bounces off its shiny scales. It stops and turns, staring at me from eyes that hold a dancing flame at their center.

I scramble back into bed and pull up the covers, lying rigid with fright, shaking so hard the bed rattles. There are spells to ward off danger, but I can't recall them, my mind has gone blank. A few seconds later there's a click as the door opens and Zylch's soft fur brushes against my face as he jumps onto the bed, strokes my face gently, curls up at my feet and starts snoring quietly. My fear drains away, and I sleep again.

Tomorrow *The Bitch's Hour* goes live for the first time. A huge day. I can't wait to see the new Decima in action.

11

Not according to plan

Decima

I rip off my microphone and stand over Alice. 'Rehearsal is over, sweetheart, off you go.'

She swivels slowly around on her toadstool and glances over to Cameraman 2. He mutters something through tightened lips as he hangs up his headphones.

'Speak up, man!'

He dips his chin. 'This is low, Decima, even for you,' he shakes his head in that slow-motion sign of disapproval.

I want to tear him to shreds with a string of verbal put-downs, but that wouldn't be wise to do to your main cameraman a few hours before transmission.

'Oh she'll be fine,' I bend down to look into her pretty blue eyes. 'Won't you Alice?'

She stares back at me calmly and nods.

I admit it was random to spring it on her, but if she'd had any pre-warning that she was going to be in vision with me, she'd never have slept, and then what? What if my first coffee of the morning had been late? Today of all days? I could have been put right off my stride.

Alice perches on her toadstool, in her rather baggy

frock, rolling her eyes at Cameraman 1. She looks as if she wandered in off the street and onto the set by mistake. Ha ha!

I was worried that the toadstool might be taking it too far. But now it's here and she's sitting on it with her knees up somewhere near her chin, looking so pathetic, I have to say it's another of Fabienne's masterstrokes. She will always be looking up to me. It sends my 'bitch in charge' message out loud and clear to the viewer.

'Go to lunch, Alice.'

She ignores me.

'Come on, chop chop,' I wave my arms above her head. 'Artistes need to be back on set in good time before transmission.'

Cameraman 1 goes over to her and offers her an arm. 'May I have the honor of escorting you to lunch, Ma'am?' he smiles, crooking out his elbow.

'Thanks.' She takes his arm and heaves herself up.

'Come on girl, we'll look after you.' He leads her away, a hand resting lightly on her shoulder.

I look down at the now slightly slithery, sweaty toadstool. Low seating is a classic power game tool. Oldest trick in the book. And this is off the scale. Masterly, Fabienne, masterly. We don't want her getting any on-screen ideas above her station. It's got to be crystal clear to my viewers that she's my slave. It is on the low side, though. It's almost a floor cushion! A very uncomfortable cushion at that. That raised point in the middle must dig right in. She'll never get comfortable. A quiet giggle rises in my throat.

All is as it's meant to be.

In Fabienne's words: in this show, Alice will be the yin to my yang. Or in my words, the punch-bag to my bitch. She's got to look naturally, genuinely fed up. All part of the plan. Getting Alice in vision was a quickfire, perfect solution. I'll not only *be* a bitch, I'll be *seen* as a bitch.

Now that everybody has gone, I have an important job to do.

I whisper into my Hermes bag, 'It's time, Digby. Come on out, boy.'

I cup him in both hands and lift him gently from his bag.

'What do you think of this then, eh?'

In yet another example of Fabienne's clever twisting of a problem into an advantage, she switched 180 degrees on her Digby ban and got the designers to make him part of the set. And how.

'It's time for you to shine too my boy.'

I take Digby over to his cool Jeff Koons-style, precision-engineered, magenta and yellow stainless-steel statue. It shines magnificently on its own pillar, glistening and sparkling beneath the studio lights, contrasting with all the natural beiges and greens.

Digby has always had to be present at every show. Not even Fabienne could persuade me otherwise. I had to beg. He's not simply a good luck symbol but the only thing I have left of my real mother Graciela Mazellini. That's right, Graciela Mazellini, the prima ballerina. I may not be one for Feng Shui, ghosts and witches, but I know that Digby holds my mother's love in every strand of fur still left on his balding body.

On the shelves behind his statue is his new, refurbished throne. Surrounding this on each side is a selection of my first-edition signed books. Unlike my bear, Fabienne was really excited about these. Signaling, it's all about subtle signaling she breathed excitedly. Whilst Digby hints that there's a softness to me (allegedly), my books show off my intellect and good taste, she says. So I've allowed a select few to be brought from home.

Truth be told they're all birthday gifts from my adoptive father, trying to buy my love back in the days when he still had those delusions. Not as sweet as it sounds either, between you and me, but a money laundering scam with some crooked auction house. But my fans don't have to know any of that. Fabienne has picked out the Jane Austen (100% forgery, but who around here would know or care?), a couple of Zadie Smiths, and those two Brit Zodiac girls (reverse harem romances – real treasures I can truly identify with). All of it, a useful focus, she says, if the conversation slows.

Not that it ever has.

But we can't take any chances. My new guestlist isn't taken from the Hawk Bay City entertainment PR swamp but is a collection of the most gutsy high-achieving women in the world. Women like me. Our first guest today, Bethany Al Falasi, won't ever know that we're only on Tier 2 of Fabienne's 10-point publicity plan. i.e. this show is little more than a pilot. In less than 2 weeks' time, we'll be streaming coast to coast from New York to LA and around the world from Australia to Dubai and Europe. But today it's our old Hawk Bay City local transmitters.

Time races forward and slows down at the same time. Before I know it Sean is putting out the call.

'Ten minutes everybody, ten minutes.'

I take a last look in the mirror.

'Where's Alice? WHERE'S ALICE?'

She pops out from behind me, making me jump.

'Ah there you are. Let me look at you.' I stand back. 'Hmm, yes, make-up has done the best they can I suppose. Cheer up, will you? Millions would kill for the opportunity. As it's your first day, you can walk out onto set with me.

'OK', she says. Can you believe it – she starts walking off ahead of me.

'What do you want me to do?'

'I've told you. Nothing.' I push ahead of her and set off again across the studio floor. Everybody is in position. Everybody is watching us.

'What do I have to say?'

'Don't you dare say ANYTHING. You hear me. NOTHING.'

'Whatever you say,' she chirps.

'Oh shut up you fool and keep up. Waaah!'

'What is it, Decima?'

'One of my eyelashes has come unstuck. Make-up. MAKE-UP to the floor NOW.'

'They're already waiting for you, Decima.'

'Keep up there, keep up.'

When we reach the set I feel instant nostalgia for my old Passion Pit. I step up on a kind of tatami mat platform surrounded by smooth, white beech shelves, bamboo and ferns. Thank goodness for Digby's magnificent statue and Alice's toadstool, that's all.

'Five minutes, FIVE MINUTES now everybody.'

I settle into my seat. The make-up girl is ready with the eyelash glue held high between her fingers, ready to squirt. The air is crackling with hushed importance.

That addictive thrust of adrenaline that powers you out of the fear and into the Zone as you go on air will happen, I know it will, but that knowledge doesn't make a jot of difference. I am freaking right the freak out right now.

Alice is hovering.

'Sit on your toadstool and look interested,' I snap. 'That's all you have to do.'

She raises her eyebrows slightly and lowers herself in slow motion.

'And don't, whatever you do, speak.'

'ONE MINUTE NOW.'

I take in a few deep breaths of Fabienne's sage smoke that is being wafted around everywhere. It's not only the air. Every part of the studio has been Feng Shui'd to bits. All tosh, but Fabienne is a nut job in that area.

I feel a little like Alice looks. But I'm a real bitch and a good enough actor to turn the confidence volume up high here.

'Counting down, stand by everybody. TEN, NINE…'

Fear. All perfectly normal.

At FOUR the countdown goes silent. I watch Sean's fingers go down from THREE, TWO, ONE. His hand goes up, he steps back and the light on top of Camera 1 turns from red to green. At the very last moment, I snap into my smile. The nerves will go, they will go. The guest is… what's her name? Where's the teleprompter? If you're not scared before transmission there's something wrong with you, but this is mad. It's turned so hot in here I can barely breathe.

I get through the introduction. Start-up CEO Bethany Al Falasi from Dubai, a slim, slight wisp of a woman in a hijab scarf, takes her seat and I wonder if there's been some mistake.

Has this child just got out of bed? She seems to have forgotten to get dressed.

They must be letting me in gently, I think. She'll be easy to handle. But as soon as she starts talking about her Dubai Energy green growth company I realize that I have been mistaken. I take in the detailed tailoring of her striped light blue pajamas with concealed buttons and the hang of her matching trousers that fold onto low-top soft leather trainers. This is a young, modern rich bitch in full European designer.

The nerves haven't left me and I race through my list of questions far too quickly. As slick as the oil her country is heaving with, she soon picks up on this.

She fixes me with her big, black eyes. 'Maybe there's something else you'd rather talk about, Decima?'

For a second I'm speechless. Then I go for it. My viewers want to know exactly the same gossip as I do.

'How old are you again?'

'I'm 21, Decima. How old are you?'

I waffle. Then I get a lecture from her on how a woman's age doesn't matter anymore and I should be ashamed of myself for being so cagey.

I turn to Alice. It's time for her presence to be useful. 'How old are you, Alice?'

Her eyes widen, she gets the message and her lips stay sealed.

'Perhaps I'm not the only one.' I return Bethany's gentle, patronizing smile and forge on.

'So, your little start-up turned a profit of $14 million last year? What do you spend it on?'

'Alice, can I ask you something?' she says, completely ignoring me.

Tilting her head and smiling, Alice looks from Bethany to me and back to Bethany.

'How do you put up with this?'

'Did you not read your contract?' I butt in. 'This is *The Bitch's Hour.* She loves her job. Don't you Alice?'

Alice nods silently.

'But why haven't you given her a proper chair?'

I turn the questioning back to her until we're both batting backward and forwards, asking each other questions without answering anything. The studio gets hotter and hotter. I'm holding my own, enjoying the conflict, but sweat is pooling in my armpits. I think I might faint.

Something bites me on the leg. I have to itch it. I rub my ankle against it. Now it's creeping up both legs. It must be an allergy to something in Fabienne's new set-up. It's unbearable, I'm rubbing my legs against each other and against the chair to try and relieve the itch, but it gets worse until I have to scratch with my fingernails. Bethany pulls a face and shifts her seat further away.

Somehow we get to the end. Bethany thanks me for a fun time.

'You really are a bitch aren't you! That made a refreshing change,' she says. 'Ask me back any time!'

I'm stunned.

She hugs Alice, whispers something, and leaves. Annoying, but at least they're not going to be needing the Green Room anymore.

'Sean.' I march off to make good use of it. It's never going to replace my Passion Pit but old habits die hard. A quick, sweaty time with Sean, followed by a cold shower will set me to rights again. I don't hear him following and turn around. He's helping Alice up from her toadstool.

'Sean NOW!'

Alice falls into his arms. The whole studio floor goes quiet.

Sean darts me a quick look. 'In a tick now, Decima.'

'No ticks, Sean, NOW.'

12

So near but so far

I help Alice up from her seat and try to get her standing but her legs are so weak, she slumps forward into me like a rag doll. A weird guttural noise, like an asthmatic bleat, is coming from somewhere deep inside her throat. It's a bit of an amdram noise I have to say. Is she acting this way? I can't be sure she's not.

'You're alright now, Alice, let's get you away from here.'

Decima is yelling at me but I ignore her. I might pay for it later, but you know what, I'm glad of it. Decima may want me but Alice needs me.

No brainer.

The very last thing *I* need right now is a one-on-one with Decima, to tell you the truth, so the longer I can leave it the better. There's always the hope she'll get bored of waiting for me and call in one of the others. I'm having to work twice as hard with her lately and it's not fair. Not fair at all.

She's so self-absorbed she thinks I've had my new Prince Albert, my little fellah's ring, done for her. Unfortunately, this has made her want my solo services more and more. The tattoo there is another thing. She'd go crazy if she ever discovered my fellah saluting Alice in the middle of a quickie. . But, the truth of it is the job of keeping it hidden from her kind of turns me on. It gives me something to fix my thoughts on, and what's better to think about than the love of your life? I'm not going to lie, there have been some near misses, even though it's on the underneath side, but it's not as tricky as you might think. You see, me being a grower not a shower if you get what I'm saying, hides the evidence of her name. The letters distort, like the writing on a balloon as I rise to attention.

I grip Alice's hands firmly together around the back of my neck and half-walk, half-drag her across the studio floor. I can vaguely hear Decima shouting at me but it's like it's from another world. Alice is hyperventilating right into my left ear and choking me as it happens, but that's fine, I'm still breathing, near enough, and I'm not proud of this I'm telling you, but I can't help myself. My heart has risen to heaven high at being so close to such perfection in a woman, and not only my heart.

My new ring pushes against me, begging to be out there and finding its rightful home with this soft perfumed flesh before me. We're both struggling to breathe. It doesn't help that those wondrous breasts I have admired from afar for so long are heaving against me.

'Now, come on, Alice you'll be fine now,' I whisper. 'Keep a hold of me a little while longer.'

I tuck my chin into her cleavage in as good a disguise for my own breathing as I can, for it's fast going out of control, and we set off across the studio floor to her office. Thankfully it's on the far side of the building because I don't want this to ever end.

I swallow hard and breathe through my nose. I'm not perving on her. I'm not. Truly I'm not. The smell, oh goodness the smell of her. Like sweet powdery violets mixed with rich, burnt, caramel.

We reach her office, I kick the door open and get her inside.

'All right now, you're safe here.'

As soon as the door is closed behind us, she collapses into my shoulder, wailing and sobbing.

'Now come on. It's only natural, what you're feeling, Alice. You did good there. You looked a treat on the screen so you did. Bethany there really liked you didn't she.'

She looks up at me, tears streaming down her face.

I have to avert my gaze, or I'd be melting right into those sad, sad eyes. 'Slow down now and get your breath back. It'll be alright, Alice. You'll be fine.'

And so we stand in a blissful hug for as long as I dare stay. Oh Alice, Alice. I look down at this wondrous creature in my arms. This is so meant to be. I raise a hand to stroke her hair but stop myself just in time. I look out of the window to the whole sweep of Hawk Bay City spread out below and say a silent prayer for our future together. So near but so far.

My down below is like a heat-seeking missile and I have to keep adjusting the way I'm standing. But every time I do that she only leans into me more, groans a bit and sets me soaring to an even higher plane of ecstasy.

I'll say this. I won't have trouble rising to the attention stakes with Decima in a moment. That woman needs it several times a day, she truly does. As long as I carry out what's stated in my contract, I'm clear.

My commitment to Alice is serious, that's what matters. We'll be together soon, I know it. As soon as the buzz gets going on my *Symphony of the Stars* and I'm truly on my way as a musician, I can leave the Tower. Servicing Decima will be a thing of the past. Talking of which, I'd better be going now before I'm in trouble.

'Now Alice, I'm going to sit you down over here.'

Slowly slowly I ease her into her office chair. It keeps swiveling away across the room, like the thing has a mind of its own, but eventually we get there. She immediately slumps forward onto her desk, sobbing harder, her shoulders heaving.

'You rest there, OK?'

With a loud sigh, she buries her head in her folded arms. She snuffles something I don't catch.

I take a box of tissues from the windowsill and place it beside her. I pull one out and, as best I can, dab dry my shoulder, wet with her tears, before hurrying off to the Green Room.

13

Doing what I'm told

Alice

Decima had been pleasant to me, chatting about the new show, asking my advice on certain things and putting me at ease. I was beginning to like her and knew she'd be very good at *The Bitch's Hour* because let's be honest, nobody is as bitchy as her when she wants to be.

So I was completely off-guard when she sprung it on me without any warning that I was to appear on the show at a couple of hours' notice. I wasn't even dressed for it and very nearly went into panic mode. I ditched the idea of **Broomsticking** home and changing into one of my new outfits. Nobody would believe I could have got there and back so quickly. It would be impossible even with the fastest car. No, I'd have to make the best of it. I used a staple to fix the hem of my frock where it had come undone.

Decima didn't seem at all sympathetic. It was almost as if she was deliberately trying to upset me. Silly me to think that I wasn't a target for her bitchiness. But I bounced it back at her by loosening one of her artificial eyelashes.

As it turned out, the interview didn't go too well for

her. You could see she was nervous, and Bethany Al Falasi, the young entrepreneur from Dubai, who looked like a child, was completely in control. Patches of sweat were forming under Decima's arms, and there was actually a slight whiff of perspiration mingling with her deodorant.

I could see her giving me sly looks as I tried to perch on the stupid toadstool which is like something you'd find in a kindergarten. Bethany picked up on it, and she and Decima had quite an argument. I took the opportunity to flick the *Itch* spell at Decima to get back at her and watched her struggle not to scratch. The harder she tried not to, the higher I turned up the power so the irritation on both her legs became unbearable and she was furiously rubbing them. The cameraman zoomed in on them as they became red and blotchy. She'll be livid. I hid a small smile of satisfaction.

Before Bethany left she gave me a little hug, and whispered: 'Don't let the bitch get you down. Fight back!'

Oh, I'm going to. I really am.

When it was over I almost collapsed from the cramp after crouching on the stool. Dear Sean came to my rescue.

He grabbed me and almost dragged me from the studio. My legs weren't working properly and he propped me up and made sure I was OK. He was holding me a bit too tight and sniffing my neck but I was so grateful for his kindness I didn't try to pull away.

After a few minutes the circulation returned to my legs.

I thought back to when Decima first felt the itching, how she tried to ignore it, rubbing her leg with her other ankle. And then how the little red spots kept popping up on her legs and she couldn't keep them still until she was clawing at her skin with both hands. The patches of sweat popped out under her arms. Best of all was the way Bethany wasn't the pushover she expected and turned the interview on its head. As instructed by Decima, I sat without speaking a word. Under different circumstances, I could have stepped in there and helped, but she'd told me to sit and do nothing, so that's what I did. Well, nothing she knew about. There's plenty more of that to come if that's what she wants. Plenty more. Altogether a most satisfying first time on the show for me despite the toadstool.

The more I thought about it, the funnier it became. Funniest of all was that while Sean was hauling me out of the studio he thought I was crying, while really I was helpless and shaking with laughter.

14

Worried about Sean

Alice

Poor Sean. Decima won't leave him in peace. She keeps telling me to call him up to her office, then he's in there for ages. He comes out looking so unhappy, refusing to catch my eye. As if he's ashamed of what they do. He doesn't need to be, I'm not judging them. I always give him a little wave when I see him and try to put him at ease. He's so kind to me and I hate to see him looking so miserable.

Decima summoned him four times today. She kept putting her head round my door and saying, with a big smile: 'Be an angel will you and tell Sean to come up.'

As I'm leaving the office for the night, I find him outside leaning against a wall. His normally pale skin is red and blotchy and there are tears rolling down his face. His jeans are almost falling down. He's always been skinny, but now he looks skeletal. When he sees me he turns and starts to limp away, but I run after him and take hold of his arm. He feebly tries to shake it off, but I hang on.

'You look terrible. Let me help you.'

'I'm OK, thanks, leave me alone.'

'You're not OK, I'm not leaving you alone. I'm taking you home. Where do you live?'

I force his address out of him, and we walk slowly, silently. I link my arm through his and hold him close to me.

He has a small basement apartment in the boho district. I lead him down the steps and wait while he unlocks the door.

'Thanks,' he mumbles, 'just leave me now.'

He tries to squeeze through the door and close it behind him, but I push my way in.

The mess and smell hit me. Sean stands just inside the doorway with his head hanging.

Thinking quickly, I say: 'I don't know about you, but I'm famished. I haven't eaten all day. Could you go and pick up a few things for me? You know that bakery down in Burton?'

It's a 15 minute bus ride to get there.

He nods miserably.

'Get half a dozen sourdough rolls from there. Around the corner there's an Italian deli. Buy some nice cheese, and some cherries. The black ones. We're going to have a picnic. Have you got any beers?'

He shakes his head.

'Then pick up half a dozen Bud Light. And anything else you can think of.'

I push him out of the door and close it behind him, then I throw open the windows and look around. The furniture is all over the place. Two chairs are turned over.

There are dirty clothes on the floor, dirty dishes in the sink, half-eaten containers of food on every surface, unopened mail lying behind the door. The sofa is stained with grease, My feet stick to the floor. The place smells of stale beer, sweat, and fried chicken. It will take half a day to clear it up and clean it. I have an hour at most before Sean returns.

I have a quick flick through my mental directory and flash the **Muckless** spell around. That takes care of the general mess. **Launder** cleans and tidies the clothing, **Spruce** washes the furniture and floor, and in less than 15 minutes the apartment is sparkling with nothing out of place. **Fresh** chases the smells out through the window.

At times like these I do love being a witch!

When Sean returns he stands in the doorway with his mouth hanging open. Taking the shopping from him I sit him down at the table and spread out the food.

'Eat,' I tell him.

'But I'm not…'

I tear off a piece of bread, spread it with cheese and hold it out to him.

'Eat it. Just for me.'

He starts to chew and keeps eating. He looks around.

'Alice, I don't understand how you've done all this,' he says.

'You don't need to,' I reply. 'Eat.'

I finish two of the rolls. Sean eats the rest, and all the cheese. Then all the cherries. Who knows how long it's been since he last had any food?

When every crumb has gone, I open a couple of beers
and sit on the sofa, patting the seat beside me.

'Talk to me Sean. What's wrong?'

He hangs his head.

'I can't keep doing it. The thing with Decima. It's not
right.'

'After all this time? What's changed?'

'I don't want to do it anymore. I don't care for her.'

He gulps.

'Alice, what must you think of me?'

'I think you're a great guy, Sean. A really great guy. To
me you are a friend. A special one.'

'Really?'

'Yes, really.'

He goes to stand looking out of the window

'I could be more than a friend, Alice, if you'd let me.'

'I'm not looking for a relationship, Sean, because…'

'I'll quit! I'll tell Decima first thing tomorrow morning.
I'll go straight there and tell her I'm leaving, and then…'

'Sean, it isn't anything to do with your job, and
Decima. There is somebody else in my heart.'

He spins around, shouting. 'That stupid Scorpio! He's
nothing. He doesn't care for you! I'll kill him.'

'Sean, it isn't Scorpio.'

He stares at me 'But?'

'It isn't Scorpio. It's somebody else, nobody you'd
know. We're not together any more, but I'm not over him
yet and I'm not ready to move on. I'm still hurting.'

'Let me take away the hurt, Alice. I will do anything

for you, and I'll die before I let anybody ever hurt you again.'

I go and take his hand.

'It's too soon,' I say. 'I need time.'

'Then I'll wait. I'll wait for however long it takes, Alice. I swear to you I will never stop waiting.'

'While you're waiting,' I smile, 'will you still be my friend? It would mean so much to me, because I do care for you very much.'

It's true. I do care for him. What happened to the cheerful whistling boy of a few months ago, always smiling and shooting about on his skateboard? His eyes have lost their sparkle, and his grin has disappeared. He's become a lost little boy. He's three years older than me, and I want to mother him.

I crack open another couple of bottles.

'Drink up, then we'll go and walk, get some fresh air, while you tell me all about yourself,' I say.

There's a bus stop outside his door. We jump on and get off at the little park near where I used to live. As we wander around, he starts to talk about his life before he came to the US.

He was born and raised in Ireland, in a place called Kilkenny. His father was killed in an accident when he was very young, and his mother never recovered. She left him with her farming parents and nobody ever heard from her again. She's presumed dead.

'I was a wild boy,' he says. 'Life on the farm didn't suit me. My mam's parents had to work hard to put food on the table and everybody needed to pay their way. Even as a small boy, I had to be up before daylight helping in the cow sheds, going to school, coming home and having to get back in the sheds. It felt like I was always tired and cold and dirty. I wasn't built for that kind of life.

'In the end, they sent me to live with my dad's family closer to the town. I had cousins living nearby, tearaways they were. We had many an adventure. It was mischief, you know, we weren't bad, simply high-spirited. Always laughing. I didn't get on at school with books and dates and things, but I loved helping my uncle in his workshop. He was an electrician, and it seemed like magic to me, what you could do with machines.

'That side of the family were strict Roman Catholics. I didn't want to go to church, but the cousins got me into the choir. Father Ronan told me I had a good voice on me, and he encouraged me to learn music. That turned my life around.'

I haven't said anything, just listened and let him talk, seeing him begin to relax and a tiny blush of color return to his cheeks.

'When I left school my uncle found me an apprenticeship as an electrician, but I'd set my heart on music and saw America as the place where I had a chance to make my mark. So here I am, waiting and hoping. I did OK busking, then I saw the ad for working at the Tower to train in production.'

'So you've no family here, then?'

'No, none here. There's only my paternal grandpa and

the cousins back in Ireland. I'd like to go back one day.
I'll take you with me. It's a beautiful country.'

'That's sad, not having family.' I think of my parents.
As undemonstrative as they are, I know they will always
be there for me. Sean has nobody.

'I've stood on my own feet since I was 18. My music
is my family. As long as I have that, it's all I need.'

There's a bench seat beside a small ornamental lake,
and we sit down there.

He tells me of his dream of writing a *Symphony of the
Stars*, how he already hears it in his head.

'I want people to close their eyes and listen, and feel
themselves floating up there in the night sky, among the
stars and the moon and all the planets.'

We sit in silence for a while.

'Alice, do you mind if I say something?'

'You can say anything you like.'

'It's only that I can't help noticing some strange things
about you. You seem to disappear sometimes, and then
there's the way you cleaned up my mess so quickly. And
that night at Decima's – it looked like you walked through
a wall. And then you were down there in the garden, and
somehow got out of there.'

'Don't remind me,' I shudder. 'I'm a woman of
mystery, Sean.'

'You are that,' he laughs. 'And I think I'm making
progress with you, because you do at least remember my
name now. That gives me hope. Remember you used to
call me Spike!' He chuckles.

I stand up. 'I'm going home now. I'll see you tomorrow. And listen: I will never think any the less of you. We are buddies forever, Sean, no matter what. Nothing can break that. Whatever happens in the future, you will always be precious to me.'

He jumps up and pulls me into a long hug, rocking us back and forwards as he hums the melody of this new song he's been working on. It's very catchy. I close my eyes and smile. When he finishes I open my eyes and see my old apartment. A figure is standing at the entrance, looking up at the window. I blink, and when I look again they have turned around. Our eyes meet, and I feel myself collapsing. Sean drags me upright, laughing.

'If a little croon and cuddle makes you weak at the knees, what would it be like if I kissed you?'

I laugh weakly, and when I turn around the figure has vanished. Or was it ever really there?

'How will you get home?' Sean asks. 'Shall I walk you to the station?'

'No need,' I say. 'I'll jump on my broomstick.'

'You be careful then. I wouldn't want you falling off,' he smiles

I watch him walk away, turn and give a little wave. I look back at the apartment again. There's no one there. It must have been my imagination.

15

Under fire

Decima

Needing some action to calm my nerves, I call an early morning meeting at the top of the Tower.

When the boys are all in, flexing and preening for our session ahead, I page Alice. 'Where are you? Get in here now.'

We wait. I look around. Are they truly not interested in her or am I seeing a bunch of poker faces here?

Cory is perched casually next to Josh on the hospitality table. Next to him are rows of coffee cups and glasses, neat lines of canned drinks and bamboo bowls stacked with fruit and every kind of health bar. He looks as inscrutable and broody as ever. Dressed all in black, he's got one leg swinging in his expectant, ready-to-go signaling. That fidgety leg is as close as that one will ever get to a 'take me now' position with my Coryboy. Sean stands to one side of him next to a giant cactus, squinting against the sun. He looks pale. Even his freckles seemed to have faded to nothing and his clothes looked like they'd been slept in for a week.

Why is Sean's shabby, don't-care, attitude so attractive? I'm looking him up and down and shifting on my feet as I do so, letting him know I'm thinking about that golden ring of his hidden away down there. He doesn't look too pleased about it. Which only makes me want him more.

But then my Boy #4 gets my attention. Ramon leans against the back wall, almost hidden behind a cheese plant, his arms tightly crossed. That sexy sideways smirk says it all. He's so ready for me he can't hide it. He could be acting, but we haven't been together for four days now, I've been so insanely busy. Now it's time to release the tension we're all feeling. It will calm us all down, but first, I will up the jitters before the blessed release.

Alice saunters in.

'What is it?'

'It's too hot in here. Close the blinds.'

The Tower might look like a cool block of ice from the outside, but, like everything of Dad's, it was built on the cheap. The morning sun beating in through the glass wall has already turned the place into a furnace.

'As if I haven't got enough to do,' she slaps her iPad and phone on a table and, humming to herself, proceeds languidly along the wall of vertical blinds, closing them one by one with a noisy, belligerent snap.

'Hurry up and lose the attitude. It's not a hot yoga class we're waiting for and we need to get started.'

Avoiding eye contact, she strolls off.

'Er. Not so fast, Alice.'

She freezes, mid-pace.

'One more thing.'

At the door, she turns in slow motion and raises an eyebrow. I let the silence hang in the air.

'Not *that*,' I say eventually and she almost smiles. I smile back, letting her know that no, she's not going to be offered a complimentary session with my boys. And never will be. Ever again. That's a situation I read wrongly back in the dark days before the big changes. The boys are still each giving me the 'she's a friend' line and I'm forcing myself to believe it. For now.

'Come back in. I've not finished.'

She shrugs and stands next to Sean without looking at him. I give them a long hard stare. What's going on there?

I swat at my neck, it feels as if there's some bug crawling on me. Eventually I speak.

'Before we get going…'

Josh looks at me with a pleading expression.

'It's been tough for me too, Josh, believe me. Difficult as it is, work has to come before pleasure.'

Truth be told, these last two weeks have been the most full-on of my life. I'm under fire. A delegation turned up, all the way from Dubai to Hawk Bay City, calling meeting after meeting with Dad on conference lines from the UK, Ireland or wherever he decided to be that day. Anywhere except here. Thank goodness.

I was given 'notes'. Note after note after note on the first few shows. I should rise more to my guests' intellect whilst at the same time making the show more accessible to the audience. Or, in their words, more *relevant*. Exec producer nonsense, right? But nobody gets these megadollar contracts for nothing. They're in charge and I have got to make it work somehow.

'As you know, Josh and I have been locked into non-stop meetings with the delegates over from Dubai. We've been arguing it out. I made it clear to them that the guest casting needed sorting. Success isn't about how much money they've made. That's not what my show is about. *I* need to be the one making all the money. Not my guests.'

'What happened to the 'we'?' says Cory.

'When I say I, I mean we. We're all in this together. It's not all bad news. They've agreed to invest in a few big names to crank up our ratings. Then it's up to us to keep the audience sticky. The on-air bitching is working well. Alice, you'll be staying in vision.'

She holds a hand up.

'What is it?'

'I will need a proper seat. I'm not going to squat on that stupid toadstool anymore.'

Cheeky. 'We'll talk about that.'

'I think it would be a good idea to get it done quickly. To make sure nothing goes wrong,' she says coolly.

What does that mean? Is she making some kind of threat? She needs slapping into place.

'That's about it,' says Josh, rubbing his hands together. We exchange a look. Good man Josh. There were more than a few complimentary comments about Alice, and orders to get rid of her toadstool immediately so that the viewers could see her more clearly. She doesn't need to know any of that.

'I'm super busy this morning as well,' says Cory.

'I'm ready for you, Decima,' Ramon stretches his arms up and flexes his pecs.

'I know I know, nobody is more ready for you all than me. It's been some kind of a record for me, boys. I've missed you.'

I unbutton my blouse.

Alice heads off. I let her get as far as the door.

'Oh one more thing, Alice.'

She twists around and puts her hands on her hips. She actually puts her hands on her hips. Since she's been in vision, the attitude is springing out of this once-compliant little creature.

I hitch up my skirt and look from Alice to Josh to Alice.

'Get me a coffee.'

Alice grins. 'Sure. I'll leave it outside the door here so I don't disturb you. Now I'll leave you all to it. Bye!'

She closes the door loudly behind her.'

Josh takes me in his arms but then pulls away.

'What's up with your neck, Decima? It's very red and weepy. Doesn't look too good.'

Did that bug bite me? My skin feels like it's burning.

16

Letting go

Cory

I sacrificed a lot when I left the UK but gained the greatest prize of all. Freedom. Non-possession has always been my thing. That's why it works so splendidly with Decima. She gave me a fresh start in a new career I adore, regular sex, a good bunch of friends, and all the time to myself I need. Now my own emotions have done the dirty on me.

I'm not proud of myself for suggesting a beer with Sean. Ulterior motives can be as shameful as envy itself, but, to be frank, I will do anything to get some clarity on how far he's got with Alice.

Below a boarded-up window in a dark, smoky corner of Jerry's, his favorite bar, we drink in silence. Nothing awkward about that, we've known each other long enough, but unsaid words are gathering. *Alice. Alice. Alice. How are you getting on? Have you kissed? She likes you. You have the best chance. Everybody can see it.*

He finishes his beer, knocks back his vodka chaser in one, and slams the glass on the table.

I go to get him another. I've lost her before I could have her. I know that. But if I hear him say it, maybe I can start to accept it. Acceptance is everything. If you can't run from a situation, if you can't change it, you have to make peace with it. I've learned that the hard way. The will they/won't they speculation is destroying me. Because they will. I have no chance. They're both so pure in heart, they're made for each other.

'Thanks for coming, man,' Sean says when I sit back down. 'I know this isn't your kind of a place.'

'No worries.'

After another too long silence we talk about the bars back home. I'm not a drinker but my old local was special, with all the character this dive lacks, from the old oak beams you have to crouch under to get around to the old black lab, Bovril, dozing by the log fire always on sleepy alert for the stray sausage.

'I'll take you there one day, Sean.'

'When our fortunes are made,' he says with a dry laugh.

When we're old and my brother is dead, I think.

'Your music is good, Sean, you know that. So cut the modesty eh? With the right breaks, you can make it.'

'Thanks, man. If Decima cottons on to me and Alice, I'll be kicked out of The Tower with nothing, nothing to my name at all.'

So they are an item? The disappointment is physical: my throat tightens, my stomach sinks. I manage to hold back a choke.

'She's keeping you very busy lately.'

Sean shrugs, 'She's probably picked up on me and Alice, hasn't she.'

Like a fool I don't grab the chance to dig further. Maybe I can't bear to hear it after all? Instead, I say, 'But she's working you hard. Too hard.'

'She'll move on to one of yous soon enough.'

'I guess so,' I shrug. 'At least we have each other.'

'For now.'

I feel a tightness in my chest. There's another long pause whilst I wait for him to explain, but he sips his drink staring into space. Eventually I say it. I have to know.

'What do you mean, for now?'

'You're the philosopher around here. Nothing lasts forever.'

'Except love.'

'And hate.'

'She truly does get off on being hated doesn't she.'

'It's an act, Sean. She's so good at it, it's become a part of who she is.'

'I guess so.'

'There's a lot going on underneath she's probably too scared to even think of thinking about. Imagine having Gauld for a father?'

'Damaged goods, eh. But then who isn't?'

'Some more than others.'

We're both skirting around now. Why are we talking about Decima and not Alice?

'You seem to have it worked out, Cory, happy in your own company. I wish I was so happy being on my own, it'd save a lot of problems right now.'

'It works for me. You're a better person than me, Sean.

You're naturally kind. Everybody loves you.'

'Except.'

My heart thuds. 'Alice is falling for you too, man. We've all noticed it.'

There. I've said it. It's out there, but we both sink back into silence again. It feels too dangerous. But… here goes. I must speak my truth.

'I love her, too, Sean.'

'How can anybody not?' He smiles to himself and stares into the distance. Memories. Of what?

'Don't do anything rash to spoil your chances, Seany. Keep it nice and cool and everything will be fine.'

It already feels like I've said too much. I get another beer in for him, make my excuses and leave.

17

Acceptance

Cory

We all know love is a chemical trick your body plays on your mind. An intoxicating high that turns people anything from a bit daft to stupid crazy. Eventually, as two become one, it all settles down. Or if it doesn't work out, what might have been is mourned and, in time, forgotten and on to the next. If only I was at that stage. Acceptance is the key, but I'm nowhere near that.

I put the roof down on my rusty old VW bug and take the east coast highway out of town. I park up and climb down to the beach. There's a sharp breeze that whips my hair into my eyes. I can't see a thing but it doesn't matter, I let the roar of the wind and the waves take me.

The healing force of nature. I jump down onto the beach, strip, and run in. I swim out and float. Sensing the depths below and watching the sky above, the motion of the waves takes me. I'm outside of my comfort zone – again. This is where I find my soul. Water is soothing, cooling, free, abundant, the force of all forces that makes life possible. Water helps me think, water remembers everything, knows everything, it can solve any problem if you give it a chance.

When it comes to happiness and peace of mind, I've learned the hard way that less truly is more. Now the universe sends me Alice! She will marry Sean. Two sweet, kind people, with everything going for them. He'll have to do something about his drinking, but he's got real problems right now, that'll settle down. A wave comes and lifts me high, too high, and then low too fast. Water goes up my nose. I splutter, shake my head, turn and swim for shore. I *hope* that'll settle down.

Back at the car, I pick some daisies and grasses growing by the verge and make a posy. I take my time. I'm in no hurry to start my shift.

The whole vibe at the Tower is toxic. The closer Sean gets to Alice, the more Decima wants him. Decima is so disturbed, she spreads it around. So like her father. But then, what does she have in her life beyond that flea-bitten bear and nasty parrot? Work, hate, work, repeat. She needs a shock. Unexpected and out of the blue.

I tie the posy with a final twist of grass and lay it carefully on the passenger dash. A posy for Decima? She'd hiss and throw it in my face. A posy for Alice? I wish.

Driving to the Tower, it comes to me. In a flash. I know what I'll do. It's a risk. But something in my gut is telling me it just might work.

18

Kooky

Decima

Sean called in sick last night. I let him off with a phone session and made do with a Saturday night foursome at mine.

After I'd dismissed Cory and Ramon, Josh asked if he could stay. Now Josh never ever stays over. But, hey, my win.

We wake up to the sound of rain. A cozy morning twosome makes a nice change. He's in no hurry to leave so I run one of my giant bubble baths.

'You got enough foam in here?' he says, his cute great backside disappearing into a puff of bubbles.

I follow him in, lean back and yawn contentedly. His big bear hands are all over me. We're soon away again. I imagine Sunday morning couples all over town doing much as we are now.

Afterwards, he says, 'Do you think you should see somebody about your neck, Deccy? It doesn't look too good. Kind of scaly, and it's going down your back.'

'You're so romantic, Josh.' Now we're not lovers in that *in love* way, that's no way the deal here, but all the same, after all our coziness and one on one, I feel hurt, and, weirdly, a bit used.

He's right though, my neck has been getting worse and the irritation is driving me insane. I've never had skin problems before and nothing will stop the itching. I lean back and try not to let yet another of my many worries take over one of the best starts to a day I've had in a long time. Maybe there's something to this marriage business after all? Josh is hot and always ready to go, but that comment stung.

Perhaps I'll get Sean to stay over for next Sunday. I can't get enough of his cute new ring, what does he call it? Sergeant Pepper or something.

Trevor could join us. Sean loves my bird as much as he freaks Josh out.

'So. What's this about?' I say casually.

'What's what about?'

'What are you doing here, Josh?'

'What do you mean?'

'Why are you here? You're always with your kids on Sunday mornings.'

I feel his body stiffen, and not in that way. 'Has Dad put you up to this?' I feel the heat of deep exhales on my neck.

'Kind of.'

'What does that mean?'

I wriggle free and scramble out of the bath. He starts to follow but I push him back down. He lands with a splash. He grabs the side of the bath to get up again but, seeing me poised to go for him again, stays where he is. I pull up a stool and take my time settling myself, crossing my legs, picking at my robe and arranging it faux-bashfully over my knees. 'Don't mess with me Josh. Out with it.'

He scratches the back of his neck. I stare fixedly at the scummy bubble residue swirling around his waist.

'Look, Deccy…'

'What is it? Did Dad have a meeting without me?'

'No. Well, not exactly.'

'That's it, isn't it? What did they say?'

'He asked me to take it.'

'You and Dubai? Behind my back. I knew it.'

'He's got so much going on with that journo sniffing around. He couldn't be sure his line wasn't being listened in to, could even be the, you know, the Italian connections homing in on him. '

'Oh yes. Bring the Mafia into it why don't you. Stop making excuses for him. What's this about? Tell me straight. I can take it. I take all the rest of the lies from my family, don't I.'

'Alright. The thing is, you must have noticed, Alice is…'

I jump up from my stool. 'Oh it's about *her* again is it? I might have known.' I start pacing, change my mind, fold my arms and stand stock still with my back to him. 'Carry on.'

'The fact is Decima,' his tone has changed. I have to take this, whatever it is, on the nose.

'Alice is killing it. The sponsors love her presence on

the screen. They, er, they want her to have equal screen time.'

'*What?*'

'Like a double act, they said. They call her the kooky girl. You'll still be leading, but they want her to say more.'

'The *what?*'

'Look, your father's whole empire, and our survival, Decima, rests on this show being a success. All his businesses are in trouble, not least that issue with the land out at Brent Flats. That could bring the city counselors down with him. That journo Tillman has got TV seed money for a full exposé. Then there's the Mafia on the other side, threatening the devil only knows what.'

'Yes, and doesn't he owe me.' I pause, mid-sentence. What did you say they called Alice?'

'Er, Kooky.'

'Kooky! What's *Kooky* when it's at home?'

'I'm only saying what they're saying.'

'And what did you say to that? Yes sirs, no sirs, ten bags full sirs, sure you'll speak to me.'

'I said I'd…'

'Does Fabienne know about this? What about agent Gwendolyn?'

'No way, Deccy. I'm talking to you privately. I'm only the messenger here, so give me a break eh.'

I shake my head. 'And I thought Lorelei Thornheart was enough to be dealing with.'

'Let me finish. I'm on your side, believe me! Nothing's going to happen. Yet. I played the teething troubles card.

I offered some ideas.'

'What sort of ideas?'

'New visuals, Get Cory to shoot more cool nature scenes for the breaks. All that kind of stuff. They're putting the pressure on, that's all,'

He's out of the bath and I feel the weight of his hands on my shoulders. 'That's their job. Those suits gotta be doing something, they make it all up mostly to impress their bosses.'

'You think so?'

'Empty threats, Decima.' He pulls me up, we stand close and he starts to massage my neck, avoiding the scaly part. 'That's how they work. You know that.'

'Imagine. Alice getting equal airtime,' I huff.

'Yeah right.'

We laugh.

'We got to do something about her toadstool, though, Dec.'

'Why?'

'Bring her up a level.'

'She's gone up enough levels! It's already like she's rising up like Saint Theresa before my eyes.'

'She's coming into her own now, that's all. She'll never, ever upstage you.'

'So I've got nothing to worry about?'

'Hundred percent you're the star, Decima, you know that.'

'Hmm, well, yes I do know that.' Our hands are all over each other again.

'Give Alice a seat and it'll show Dubai you're not worried about their stupid idea.'

'My performance isn't what's worrying them is it. I'm killing it after all. That argument with the Belgian diet beer CEO last week was the best yet.'

'You had her right on the back foot.'

I pull away. 'Hang on a minute. I know what this is about.'

'What?' He is close again. I let his hands go where they want.

'It's Lorelei isn't it?'

'What? Hedging their bets? Getting Alice ready in case they have to publicly fire you, you mean? I don't think so.'

I go cold.

'But you said it!' I scream. 'I hadn't thought of that! It's that Witch Queen of LA, Lorelei Thornheart, that's what's going on here.'

'Now come on, Decima.'

'No, listen to this. Gwendolyn told me only yesterday that her lawyers have been in touch with Dubai. 100% she's on a sabotage mission to ruin me.'

'What legals has Lorelei got on you? Nothin'!'

'Copyright.'

'Of what?'

'The name.'

'But her show was called *The Witch's Hour*. Nothing like *The Bitch's Hour*.'

'Her lawyers say 'The', 'itch's' and 'Hour' together are her copyright.'

'*The*?!'

'Crazy, right? It doesn't matter, lawyers write what they like to get a rise out of you. You know that *real* magic she's threatening to do on her show to prove she's a *real* witch? She gave them details. Says she's going to throw the book at me when it's proven.'

'Oh?'

'She has a new ghost interview, coming, she says. A celebrity ghost.'

'Hey, that's clever.'

'Don't sound so keen.'

'Who?'

'She hasn't said. She's stretching it out. Her YouTube stats are going crazy. Somehow, we need to be bigger and better than the ghost of Michael Jackson.'

'Holy crows, Michael Jackson! Really?'

'I don't know, Josh. Hey, you're really falling for it already aren't you. *You're* the one who faked her first ghost. Remember? You're not in cahoots with Lorelei behind my back are you?'

'Calm down Decima. She's desperate. Can't you see that? You're the one on track to make a killing out of that perfume line. All we have to do is keep Dubai sweet. I'm not saying give in to their orders. Keep the respect. Keep your cool and do your job. When the perfume launches it'll be your picture on a Sunset billboard the size of a truck, not Lorelei's. And certainly not Alice's.'

'Animated!' I scream.

'Awesome!'

'And Times Square,' I yell. 'One of those 3D billboards. *#To-Me. Say It Like It Is.*'

'Imagine Lorelei driving down the Boulevard and seeing it for the first time.'

'I am!' I scream.

'If she's not in jail for fraud by then.'

I laugh my head off. 'No deceptions. The truth hurts, bitch. No lies.'

'And no petty fights with the Witch Queen of LA, OK!'

We high five and he follows me into the lounge.

'What's the time, what's the time?' I let Trevor out of his cage and he flies straight to Josh.

'Get that nasty bird off of me.'

'Get off, get off,' shrieks Trevor, jumping up and down on his head.

I grab my phone and put on The Divine Comedy's *National Express, Explicit Version.*

Trevor shrieks with glee and starts flying circuits around the room.

'What the?'

'It's his favorite song. It has to be the explicit version. Like mother, like child.'

Josh is crouching, like he's in a war or something, covering his head and his privates with his hands, not knowing which to protect more, and I'm laughing my head off. I find fear of Trevor very funny.

The buzzer goes.

'Security Ma'am. The English guy in the white bug

convertible is here for you.'

Josh and I share a confused 'Cory? What is *he* doing here on a Sunday morning?' look. Josh dashes off to the bathroom to get dressed with Trevor in pursuit.

'Let him in.'

19

An unfortunate accident

Alice

Since we had our talk, Sean has brightened up. The color is back in his cheeks and he's put some weight back on.

Every Saturday morning he comes out to the house to see if I need any help. He's offered to plant flowers for me, but I like the yard as it is, a bit wild and overgrown, where Zylch can dig around and play. He's so smart! When Sean arrives he goes and curls up on my bed, or lies down in the long grass. My funny, sweet, clever little Screecher. He gives me so much pleasure.

I keep refusing Sean's invitations to go out because I don't want him to start believing we are having a relationship. Sometimes I feel a bit mean, so I'm going to ask him if he'd like to come with me to see *West Side Story*. I know how much he loves music and I want to give him a treat to thank him for everything.

He answers my text: 'Yay! But it's on me!' Heart emoji.

I reply with a head-shake emoji, 'No way Jose', and a laugh emoji.

Saturday evening I catch the bus downtown and meet Sean at the theater. I almost don't recognize him. He's wearing a smart suit, polished shoes, and he's had his hair cut, nothing like the scruffy guy I'm used to. His face lights up when he sees me, and he hands me a red rose. Nobody's ever given me a flower before.

The film is so beautiful. Sean is tapping his feet and hands to the music and we're bumping shoulders. Then it turns sad, and my eyes start filling up, and I think of Jai and my nose starts running and I'm sniffing. Sean hands me a tissue and puts his arm around me, and after I've wiped my nose I rest my head on his shoulder.

When we come out of the theater we go for a drink. I ask for a soda, but Sean says, in a funny Irish accent: 'Will you not be trying this, begorrah. It's the Irish national drink – a Shamrock cocktail'. It's bright green and slightly salty, not to my taste but I sip it because I don't want to offend him. I make my glass last, but Sean keeps ordering more. The more he drinks, the funnier he gets. He stands up and starts singing: "Alice, I jusht met a girl named Alice," and the other customers cheer and clap. When he sits back down he misses the chair and ends up on the floor. He climbs back up and waves to the bartender, who comes over and says: 'Sean, you've had enough for tonight. Be a good lad and go home now.'

I help him totter out, still singing at the top of his voice. He's in no shape to be left alone, so I get him on the bus with me and take him home to sober up. He topples onto the sofa. I take his jacket and shoes off and put a cushion under his head, then I take Zylch out to play in the yard.

Two hours later Sean's beginning to move. He sits up,

rubbing his face, and says: 'Where the feck am I then?'

'You had too much to drink, Sean. I've brought you to my place to sober up. You're with me.'

He stares at me groggily.

I say: 'You'll have to stay over tonight. The last bus has gone. I'm going to get you some coffee.'

From the kitchen I hear him get up and grope his way to the bathroom.

I pop a couple of waffles in the toaster while I'm making the coffee.

When I take them into the living room he's sitting back on the sofa with a goofy smile on his face.

'Alish,' he says. 'Alish.'

'Yes, that's me. Eat this, it will help you feel better. The coffee's coming. Here's a throw if you get cold.'

I wrap it over his shoulders and go back to the kitchen to finish brewing the coffee.

When I take it into the living room, Sean is lying down again on the sofa, covered with the throw.

'Are you awake?' I ask, quietly.

'Woo! Shurprishe for you,' he yells, tossing the throw into the air. 'Look! It'sh all for you! I love you sho much."

He's pulled his trousers down and is holding his dick in his hands. There's something shiny stuck on the end, like a gold ring, and some black wiggly marks underneath.

For a moment I'm paralyzed with shock, and then I scream and throw my arms up in the air. The coffee flies out of my hands and lands in a scalding stream on the horrible sight.

'Waaaah,' Sean yelps. 'Waah, what the feckin hell. Waah!'

He's curled up in a ball, rocking and squealing and shrieking with pain.

I stare in horror as he topples onto the floor and squirms around with tears rolling down his face.

Rushing to the kitchen I fill a pan with cold water, then I run back and throw it at his lap. His cries get louder as he writhes about clutching at himself.

I kneel beside him. 'Let me see,' I say, trying to sound calm while my heart is racing. I pry his hands away and push him back. The lower part of his stomach, his groin and thighs are scarlet and blistering, a red mess, and his eyes are rolling back in his head.

'I'm going for help,' I tell him. I don't know if he hears me, he's in shock.

Grabbing my phone, I click **Broomstick** and arrive at my parents' house seconds later. It's after 2.00 am, and I bang on the door then imagine myself inside. My father runs down the stairs with a baseball bat in his hands, then stops open-mouthed when he sees me.

'Quick, I need Mother.'

Astrid appears, looking startled.

Before she can speak, I say, 'I need healing lotion, there's an emergency. It's for a friend.'

Exactly one minute after I left him, I'm back beside Sean who is curled up sobbing. I kneel down and stroke his head. 'Sean, listen. Open your eyes. I've got something to take away the pain. Take it.' I push the bottle of

Salvheal lotion into his hand and lift him into a sitting position.

I take the stopper out of the bottle. 'Pour this over your… pour it onto your burns.' I say. 'Go on.' He doesn't move, so I push him onto his back and guide his hand and say 'Pour it on now.' I really can't bring myself to touch that.

His hand is shaking so badly the lotion splashes everywhere, but immediately it touches his skin he relaxes and gives a long sigh.

'Oh shweet mercy me,' he moans, 'what have I done?'

I heave him back onto the couch and cover him with the throw. Within seconds he's asleep, snoring noisily.

20

The morning after

Alice

I'm woken by the sound of a door opening and closing downstairs. Zylch stands on the bed, his crest raised and his teeth showing. For a moment I'm startled, then I remember what happened last night. I drag on some clothes and go down to the living room. The sofa is empty and Sean's clothes have gone. From the window I see him walking towards the gate, so I run after him and call his name.

His nice suit is all crumpled, and when he turns to look at me his face is white, his eyes red and he's hanging his head.

'Hey, what's up Sean? Where are you going?'

He shakes his head and keeps walking away, so I skip in front of him and take him by the shoulders. He smells of stale alcohol and sweat.

'What's happened? Is something wrong?'

'You know what's wrong,' he mumbles. 'The way I behaved last night.'

'Being drunk? You're sorry for being drunk? What's the big deal?'

'You know – after.'

'After what? You're talking in riddles,' I laugh.

'I know what I did.'

'You were drunk, I brought you back here. You slept on the sofa. That's OK. Did you get up in the night and steal my cheese from the fridge? Let me go and check.'

'No,' he says, 'the other thing.'

'Honestly Sean, I really have no idea what you're talking about,' I lie. Thanks to Astrid's healing lotion there will be no scars, nothing to see, no evidence.

'But,' he stammers.

'It sounds as if all that alcohol gave you a bad dream,' I chuckle. 'What you need now is something to eat. Come on.'

I link arms with him and guide him back to the house.

While I'm cooking eggs and brewing coffee, we chat about the film we saw last night. He's looking bewildered and confused, and relieved, and slowly he unwinds.

Zylch strolls past on the window ledge and peers in.

'Is that your cat?'

'Not really,' I reply, putting the eggs down in front of him.

'I feel better after that. Thank you,' he says when he's finished eating. 'What do you do over the weekends?'

'I'm quite a homebody. I like to read, listen to music, walk. Relax and recharge my batteries for the week ahead. I usually visit my folk. What about you?'

'Uh, well, skateboarding, a bit of surfing sometimes, mostly writing my music.'

'You working on something?'

He hesitates. 'Yeah, well, uh, I've got something going.'

'Go on then, tell me.'

'It's long term. I've been writing it for a few years now. I believe it's going to be big. I'm calling it *Symphony of the Stars*. The idea is that you close your eyes and it carries you up into the night, flying among the stars and planets, looking down at the earth, leaving all your cares behind, floating in peace and happiness. It's different from anything I've ever written. I like to think it will become a classic, like *Dark Side of the Moon*.'

He's forgotten he already mentioned this to me when I was at his apartment, but I let him carry on because he really comes alive when he's talking about it.

'How long do you think it will take to finish it?'

'Maybe years before I'm happy with it. It's all planned in my head. The trip around the stars is related by the planets. Each planet is a different instrument. Jupiter is a cello. Saturn a sax...'

'Er...' I break in gently, because Zylch, who is getting cuter and smarter by the day, is fidgeting, and also I've invited Shelly and the girls for lunch.

'Sean, it sounds so beautiful. How about you come back next weekend and let me listen to what you've got so far? I'd really love that.'

'Really? You mean it?'

'It's a date. And I'll see you at the Tower before then.'

A shadow crosses his face and he glances away. 'Yeah, I guess so.'

'Come on, I'll walk with you to the bus stop.'

I steer him out of the house and we walk through the field, down the little dusty lane. Out of the corner of my eye, I see Zylch hopping around and throwing stones then chasing after them. I give him a warning look, and he whistles and chuckles.

'What was that? Is somebody out there?' says Sean, looking round.

'Probably some kids,' I say.

I wave him away on the bus and walk back towards the house. Zylch bounds in front of me, crouches down, and momentarily turns himself into a large lizard.

'Like it?' he asks.

'Yes, very clever Zylch. Now behave yourself.'

'Hungry!' he laughs, bounding back towards the house.

Shelly turned down my offer to send an Uber for her. She said she and the girls would enjoy the bus ride out here, and then walk through the fields.

She's unusually quiet today. While the girls are playing with Zylch, she says:

'I thought I passed Sean going back to town on the bus.'

'He came by this morning,' I say. I'm not going to tell her that he stayed the night, or about his behavior. I would never tell anybody about that.

'Last night we went to the cinema.'

Shelley's eyes light up.

'So you are going out with him? Great!'

'I'm not 'going out' with him. We went to the cinema

once. I'll probably go somewhere with him again sometimes. He's a friend, that's all. Good company. He's funny, and kind. Sort of like a brother.'

'Whatever you say, Sweetie.'

She's usually a chatterbox, but she lies back on the grass, gazing up at the sky, and then closes her eyes with a big sigh.

'What's the matter? You're very quiet. Is everything OK?'

'Oh yeah, fine. Really enjoying the quiet. The girls and I love it out here. I could live here forever.'

When they leave I have the feeling she's been keeping something from me. I guess she'll tell me when she's ready.

'And Zylch kept saying 'Hidey hidey' and running away to hide from us,' I hear little Jessie telling her mum.

'Yes, he did,' adds her sister Patty.

Shelley laughs. 'You kids have the wildest imagination.'

That night I lie in bed awake for a long time, wondering what to do about Sean.

The other thing is that I need to try to find a way to help my parents, so I'm going to call the office where Jai worked. Their mission is ecological and environmental research and protection, and the Brent Flats has some of the rarest plant species found anywhere else in the world. I'm going to talk to them about what's happening there, about the threats. The thought is making me feel sick, but I have to do it.

<h1 style="text-align:center">21</h1>

<h2 style="text-align:center">Cory's surprise</h2>

Decima

'NiNar, NiNar.'

Trevor is on the top bookshelf freaking the freak right out.

'Trevor, get down from there *now*,' I grab the plant sprayer and fire. He doesn't budge but gets more hysterical.

'Manyana, manyana.' He only talks in Spanish when he's stressed.

From the hallway, come childish whooping noises from Josh. I asked him to let Cory in on his way out, not share a long leisurely chat. And what are those weird scratching sounds, like they're both attacking the parquet with knitting needles? 'Picolita picolita, NiNar NiNar NiNAR.'

'What is going *on* out there?' I slam the sprayer down and go to investigate. As I reach the door Josh pops his head in.

'Er, you might want to get that wretched bird in its cage.'

'What's going on?' I push him to one side and go into the hallway, slamming the door behind me. The scratching sound gets frantic.

Cory is leaning backward, like he's in a tug of war. At his feet, pulling hard at a leash is a dog. Its pale blue eyes fix on me. Yelping for joy, it runs for me on the spot, its claws scratching the parquet. It looks like it is laughing. That seeing me is the best moment of its entire life and that it would rather die in a ditch than not get to me to say a proper hello.

'What on EARTH is this?'

'This is Roxy.'

'Get it out of here now before my parrot commits suicide.'

By the time we're on the driveway and Josh has left, Roxy has reached her target. Me. She is jumping up at my face and licking me all over, filling my nostrils with vile, meaty doggy breath. I love it.

I tickle her creamy chest.

'She's a husky,'

'I can see that. Whose is it?'

'Yours.'

'Don't be idiotic.'

'I'm not crazy, Decima, I do know you're too busy to have a dog. But, well, look, why don't you lock up, we'll take a quick walk and I'll explain.'

I go back inside and change into a trackie and trainers. Trevor is still on the top bookcase, picking at his feathers. He's not coming down anytime soon. I leave his cage door open for him and throw in some banana.

Roxy squeals at the sight of me, she actually squeals,

and pulls at the leash. 'You *again*. How lucky am I? How has life been so kind to me to have you in my world?'

Feeling like a kid at my first pony riding lesson, I rush to greet her.

After many licks, hugs and tickles, we take the cliff track beside my house. Cory lets the leash run long and Roxy leads the way, zig-zagging along the narrow tracks going every which way through the bracken and grasses. It's overcast and spitting with rain and I couldn't care less.

'This is cruel, Cory. Are you trying to distract me, is that it?'

'It's fun, no?'

'Yes, but I don't have time for fun. You do know we have reached the most crucial time in the show's life? That we have the most important guest ever coming in this week?'

'Who's that?'

'Michiko Kim, she's got close connections with our sponsors, Josh tells me, I'm not sure how he knows. Some spy I guess. That's all you need to know.'

'Here,' he gives me the leash.

I feel Roxy's pull. My heart leaps. I forget about the spy and start listing all the reasons why I can't have a dog. The more I think, the more reasons come to me. Not least, Trevor, who would be dead from a heart attack in days.

'...and then there's Digby.'

Cory gives me a look, 'Now you're making excuses.'

'He would sense betrayal instantly.'

Roxy veers right on an almost vertical, rocky path down to the cove. Cory takes the leash, reels it in and unclips her. She's off like a bullet until she's a dot on the shore down below.

'You shouldn't have done that.'

'Ah see, you're talking like her owner already.'

Certain she's lost, I am freaked out, but when we get to the beach, she's back, bouncing around our feet telling us how amazing it is to be alive on this incredible day.

Despite myself, I laugh. I laugh and laugh at the sight of this crazy cream and gray ball of joy. She rolls onto her back and I tickle her soft, downy tummy.

'Cory, this is cruel. My life is crazy. I can barely look after myself.'

I think I'm going to cry.

Cory crouches down and puts an arm around me. A tear escapes and drops onto her fur.

'But you can!'

'I can't!' Choked up, I sniff noisily.

He holds me tight.

'You're under a lot of stress right now. You must give yourself some downtime or, one day soon, that pressure valve inside you will blow.'

'SHOWING ME WHAT I CAN'T HAVE ISN'T HELPING, OK!' I snap.

'All right, all right.'

'I'm being attacked from all sides at once.'

'You're keeping all of us afloat, Decima. And we're all grateful to you, hey?'

'Don't be nice to me, Cory. I can't take it,' I sob.

Roxy jumps up, gives my nose a tiny lick, and bounds away.

We sit on a rock and watch her play with a piece of seaweed. Leaping up on her back legs, she tucks her front paws neatly in before pouncing down, over and over.

'The pressure you've got would kill most people.'

'I thrive on it,' I lie, wiping my sleeve across my snotty nose.

It turns out Roxy belongs to a group called The Dog Borrowers. Owners sign up, and the dogless sign up to walk them. Roxy's owner loves her. But Roxy has so much energy, Pam needs all the help she can get.

I say goodbye to Cory and Roxy at the front of my building, planning to download the Dog Borrowers App fast, before another borrower gets hold of Roxy, but as soon as I open the door I can tell something's horribly wrong.

22

Missing

Decima

'Trevor?'

Silence.

'Trevor, where are you?'

I run to his cage. The door is wide open, the banana untouched.

I race around the apartment. The living room fire is laid. I stand staring at splinters of Lorelei's door leaning up to a neat point. Grant! Oh no. Grant!

I stab at my phone. When he answers, I'm so angry I go into super-calm.

'Graaant?'

'Hello there Ma'am.'

'Hiii!'

'Everything alright?'

'Er what have you done with Trevor?'

'Excuse me?'

'Trevor, my bird, the *parrot*. He doesn't seem to be here.'

Silence.

'Did you go outside?'

'I laid the fire and then changed the water in the hot

110

tub ma'am as you ordered and, and…. Oh? Come to think of it, oh no, oh Lord help me, yes, I did feel something go past my ear.'

I'm too incensed to do anything but click my phone shut and rush to the terrace.

'Trevor, TREVOR.'

It's cold, damp and misty. I keep calling and listen hard but all I can hear is the sea.

Back inside, I search Twitter, Facebook, NextDoor, all the parrot forums. Nothing. I draft a missing notice but stop to think. I hear Fabienne's voice of reason in my ear. Do you want everyone to know your business? Do you want gloats from Lorelei's supporters fuelling your loss? Do you want nasty parrot memes popping up on your phone in the middle of the night? I leave the terrace doors wide open and sleep on the couch. Or try to.

Riding into work the next day, I stare blankly ahead of me, clutching Digby to my heart. I still can't believe it. Twenty years! We grew up together. Twenty years he was with me. A surprise gift from my dear, real, mother. Someone to talk to when she realized I wasn't making friends at school. Even she had accepted that Ornella and I were never going to be close. I named him Trevor after a friend of Dad's who'd been especially affectionate towards me. 'Keep it a secret,' Decima, he'd told me many times, running his hands all over me. And I had.

Now all I have left of my mother and my first love is Digby. I suck my thumb. I bury my misery and click into work mode, planning today's agenda with the boys. Cory deserves a special treat. I've missed Sean and I can never get enough of Ramon.It had better be a group session. I message my order for the three to go to the Green Room after the show. I hope Josh will feel the sting.

Speaking of stings, that red scaly patch on the back of my neck isn't getting any better.

23

A Korean surprise

Decima

Since being pressured into giving Alice more air time, I let her know that she will be on-air live with me today. She turned up dressed in what I suppose she imagines to be style. A cheap outfit that would suit a 40-year-old bank clerk. No clue! She's flustered when she meets me at the elevator.

'They're *here*,' she whispers, shoving my coffee into my hand.

'What do you mean?'

'I mean,' she hisses through clenched teeth, 'they're *here*.'

I can't believe how stroppy she's getting these days.

'But she's not due in makeup for over an hour yet?'

'Do you think I don't know that? They arrived early. I've told Ramon to settle them and keep them happy until we're ready.'

We reach the studio floor and she lowers her voice.

'I got the…' she suddenly stops, her stressed-out expression morphs into a big, nervous smile. Because there walking towards us is Michiko Kim herself. Behind is her entourage, and behind them, a hyperactive Sean hops up and down, darting in all directions like a useless sheepdog, trying to herd them toward the Green Room which is in the opposite direction.

There's a weary kind of wisdom to Kim. A judgemental scrutiny she bestows on anything that happens to catch her cold, narrow gaze. She wears a biker's jacket and black leather jeans, both dripping in silver chains of every size. Below a helmet of black hair, shaved close to the scalp, low, thick bushy eyebrows frame heavily kohled eyes. She looks like she's about to go into a boxing ring. Her entourage of six is dressed in a similar way and, en masse, look terrifying.

At the earliest moment, I beckon Alice into my dressing room to give her a piece of my mind.

'What call time did you give them?'

'What call time do you think?' she spits. 'This is NOT my fault, Decima. Deal with it. Sometimes people are early.'

'This is embarrassing. The guest has got the edge now. She knows she's got the edge. The interview is ruined already. Now get out of my sight.'

Alice clears her throat. 'Er, can I mention one thing quickly?'

'What now.'

'My toadstool. It's still there.'

'And?'

'I had assurances from HR that it would be removed by today's big interview.'

'Oh you *had assurances* had you, Alice? We have guests

in the building. Guests who are waiting. Go and fawn over them. Get a tranquilizer in her drink if you can. I'll see you on set.'

I slam my dressing room door, lock it and go into my phone. I should have spent the morning going over Alice's notes about the Michiko Kim Korean blockbuster film franchise, beating Hollywood's and Bollywood's box office takings together into a pulp, but I found myself googling husky dog care instead. I've connected with Pam and it's all true. It's not make-believe. I can take Roxy out whenever I like. It will make losing Trevor so much easier.

I familiarize myself with the film as much as I can. I mean, how much is there to learn about a CGI group of killer tuna fish who take their revenge on Japanese celebrity chefs one at a time? Shock hit of the year. Shock is the right word. And a profit percentage going to direct action to save endangered tuna and wild salmon everywhere.

It seems Alice has done a good job of buttering up Michiko because she looks a lot less ominous when we settle ourselves in front of the cameras. Smiling and nodding at me, she marches on set with all chains jangling. But then she turns to Alice and BOWS to her. With the yoga prayer hands together stuff and everything. What the actual?

We take our seats.

I am in no mood for conflict. But that's why I'm here. I go in with the charity donations, quizzing her on what the word 'profit percentage' really means. Cheap journalism rehashed from some BuzzFeed crits, but hopefully it'll get her going.

She's a different creature in front of the cameras. Like so many. Fake fake fake. Humble, oh so humble. So smiley, soft hush-hushy voice, full of deference.

I go for another angle but she's not having it.

She suddenly turns to Alice and starts talking to her in Korean. Then, I don't believe what I'm hearing: Alice replies in Korean! What is this? When the ACTUAL did Alice speak Korean?

I get Michiko's attention back to me with a soft question.

'Were any real tuna fishes used in the filming?' or some such crap. But I'm not totally focused because the weirdest thing happens – my chair starts going up and down. One minute I'm below Alice's toadstool. Then suddenly I go up again.

Each time I speak, I go up or down. I catch Alice's eye, and see a spark of what? Mischief? Amusement? Warning? As if she knows something. Despite the heat in the studio, I shiver.

Everybody is keeping a straight face. We're all ignoring it, carrying on in true 'the show must go on' style until there's a stray squeak of laughter from one of the crew. That sets everybody off. The cameramen and floor crew are covering their faces, some are stuffing tissues in their mouths, others their fists. Sean is crippled. Bent over double, his ears glowing red. Cameraman 1, lips firmly sealed, eyes watering, has to hold on to his camera lightly with one finger, he's shaking with laughter so much.

'Look. Maybe we swap seat,' says Michiko. 'Here, I insist.' And suddenly she's shuffling us around. Before I can do anything she's grabbed Alice by the shoulders and put her on the guest seat and, when I stand up in protest, she pinches my seat, leaving me to squat on the toadstool.

Then they start talking in Korean again, nodding and smiling and laughing, ignoring me.

'Keep it going, Alice,' I hear Josh in my earpiece. 'We got the instant subtitles up. The LA Korean community will love this. And the Koreans – we're streaming in Asia too, remember.'

The second we go off air the whole place explodes with repressed laughter. Michiko and Alice join in. I somehow keep my equilibrium, smiling broadly. My, I can act when I need to. When it seems to be dying down, someone squeaks and it all goes off again.

Michiko thanks me profusely, she's never had such a fantastic interview. CGO TV is the best in the world. Alice asks if she'd be up for filming a short CGO TV promo for our social media. Yes she'll be delighted. Whatever we want. She'll be in touch with Dubai who, it so happens, are one of her film's key partners, to tell them how successful my interview has been. She and Alice go off arm in arm to do the recording, with Sean and Ramon following close behind.

I heave myself up off the toadstool. Nobody helps me. I take a quick look underneath my seat, trying to work out what happened there. Why didn't it go up and down for

Michiko when she sat there? Is even my *seat* against me now? What is going on? Who is messing with me? My neck is stinging really badly now.

I go back to my dressing room, cancel the boys and call my father before he can call me.

24

The Biggest Shock

Decima

'What kind of crapshow was that? Subtitles! Really? Michiko Kim speaks English better than any of us!'

'That was out of my control, Dad, you know that.'

'You can say that again,' he fumes. 'Is this a comedy show we're putting on here? If it hadn't been for…'

'Alright, hold it right there. I've got a question for you that needs answering straight if you're capable of that.'

I hear a sharp intake of breath. Ornella. Listening in, of course she is.

'Josh told me about the secret meeting. What's that about, hey, HEY?" I shout. I suddenly remember where I am and lower my voice. 'Why did you and Josh meet with Dubai behind my back?'

'To talk about you, of course. You know that now. And it seems they're right on the nail. You looked like a fool today. A complete idiot going up and down in that seat. Alice handled the guest magnificently.'

'So you're in with Dubai on the Alice lovefest are you?'

'For the time being, yes.'

'What does that mean?'

'That means I'm three steps ahead of you as always,

Decima. You might be pleased to hear that Alice won't be there for much longer.'

'Oh she's not going anywhere, of that I can assure you. She's an ambitious little madam. It's the quiet ones you got to watch, that's what they say isn't it? She'll be taking over your job next.'

'The way things are going, that sounds like an attractive proposition right now, but it won't be happening. Now shut up and listen to me for a moment will you? Yes, Dubai wants her on screen more. They're flexing their muscles. And, frankly, I've got bigger issues to deal with right now. You know that problem family at the Brent Flats?'

'Don't change the subject.'

'Shut UP and listen. That's her parents' place. We are *stuck*. They are digging their heels in, they're never, ever going to sell. With that journo Tillman sniffing around I have to stay legal, but I have to get them out. Those two things do not add up, will never add up. Stalemate. Therefore I'm going to have to go the other way.'

'What do you mean?'

'I'm going to have to give that family the biggest shock of their lives. A shock that will see them run for the hills and get out of Hawk Bay City for good.'

'That won't work. Like I said, Alice isn't going anywhere.'

'She's not going anywhere for much longer, no. Not in this world anyway.'

'What do you mean?'

'Like I said. They need a big enough shock to see them out of town for good.'

I know enough about phone records to not say what he's thinking. But *get her killed*? Really?

'What about the show?'

'You'll get your show back to yourself. And when the shock of her "accident" goes public, the ratings will go through the roof. We'll get some repeats. In tribute. Wind the viewers up all over again.'

I'm stunned into silence. Alice gone? *Dead* and gone. My first thought is for all the work that she does so well. Who else would know that getting my coffee exactly right and into my hands the second I get out of the elevator sets my mood for the whole day?

25

Crazy day

Ramon

Oh man.

Where do I even begin?

I was in the basement on my own, sorting out some of the equipment, when Security phoned down and told me to find out if there's a dominatrix convention in town. Apparently there's a gang of freaky women in black leather, biker boots and rattling chains marching around Reception like avenging angels and jabbering in some foreign language.

Nobody knew anything about it, and I didn't know what I was meant to do. When I went up and tried talking with them, they were all shouting at once, at each other, at Reception and Security, and at me. The only word I could pick out was 'Decima'. This kind of thing is above my pay grade, so I called Alice in her office..

Since she moved up from the basement to her office on the top floor, she's gained a heap of confidence and she's not letting Decima push her around any more. Despite her attitude, I do have quite a soft spot for Decima, but bullying is not a good look.

'Decima's guest and her team – too early. Stand by for

freakout! Bring them up and settle them in the guest lounge and keep them happy until we're ready for them.'

I herded them to the elevator and followed them up, then shooed them along the corridor into the lounge. I said very slowly: 'Do – you – want – coffee – drink?'

The main woman stared at me for a long time, and said in perfect English: 'No thank you.'

I didn't know how to entertain them, so I stood there grinning and feeling uncomfortable while the woman continued staring at me. She was talking in her own language to the other women. I couldn't understand what they were saying, but it felt like it was about me because they all kept looking at me like I was a freak.

Longest fifteen minutes of my life trying to appear nonchalant and hanging around with this bunch of aliens. What are they even going to do – some kind of martial arts demo? Mahoosive relief when Alice comes to collect them.

I go up into the studio to watch the interview, and it turns out the main woman is a film producer in Korea, wherever that is. Who knew they even made films there? To get a slot on CGO TV she has to be pretty hot. Who'd have thought?

A quick search on my phone finds that Decima's guest is Michiko Kim, who is crazily successful and has just produced the film of the year in the Asian market. Goes to show, never judge someone by their appearance.

The interview is so funny, none of us can stop laughing. I have to say that Decima is not on her best form. She isn't in the zone and doesn't connect at all with Michiko. You'd think mentally she was miles away.

For the first time I'm actually bored watching her, and I never thought I'd say that. She is notorious for her sharp, cutting questions and getting her subjects to open up. Today it's so dull I'm heading for the door when I see Sean doubled over with silent laughter, pointing to where Decima's seat is going up and down like a carousel horse. One minute her feet are dangling in the air, next she's almost on her knees. From the expression on her face, it doesn't look as if this is something she was expecting, it's not part of the setup. She's trying to ignore it, while everybody's falling about laughing. Then the Michiko woman takes control, playing musical chairs so Decima ends up on Alice's stupid toadstool thing. There's been a lot of talk among us all about how mean it is to make Alice sit on that, and now there's Decima trying not to slide off onto the floor.

I go and stand next to Janelle, the make-up girl, who says quietly: 'Hold on there a minute. Alice is speaking Korean.'

'How do you know it's Korean?'

'What else would it be? The woman's Korean. And it sounds a bit like Japanese. I had a Japanese boyfriend once.'

'You have to be kidding. How the hell would Alice be speaking Korean?'

'Don't ask me bub, but speaking Korean I'm pretty sure she is.'

Michiko is all but ignoring Decima who's tipping backward off the toadstool, and chatting away with Alice. After the interview they go off together like best friends, and Decima storms out of the studio banging the door behind her.

I'm back down in the basement when Alice calls and asks me to go up to her office.

'So,' she begins, 'I have something for you, Ramon.'

She's twiddling a small card in her hand.

'Oh?'

'Michiko asked me to give this to "that very handsome boy who look so funny when he waiting with us in the lounge". I guess she meant you.'

She has a huge grin on her face.

I reach for the card, and she skips around her desk waving it in the air. I dart in the other direction and lunge at her, but she dodges, and we end up chasing each other round her office laughing until I finally catch up with her and wrap her in my arms.

The door flies open.

'Ah do forgive me,' spits Decima. 'I had no idea I was interrupting lovers having fun. It sounded as if somebody was slaughtering a pig.'

We disentangle ourselves and both say, at the same time,

'No! We were just… ' But she's already gone.

'Oh dear,' sighs Alice, but she's grinning.

I pluck the simple white card from her.

It says: 'Michiko Kim', followed by a load of squiggles

that mean nothing to me.

'Turn it over, Ramon.'

On the back is written in English: 'Contact me.' The business number has been crossed out. Written beside it is: Private: +82 02 315489.'

I stare at it dumbly. A film producer has given me their private number. My heart is thumping like it's going to leap out of my chest.

26

She's the one

Sean

Ramon hasn't stopped, has he. He stares at this piece of card with crazy squiggles on it for hours on end saying stuff like 'Did that really happen?' or 'I'm going to be famous!' followed right after every time by a frown and 'Will anything come of it? Will it? Will it? Am I dreaming, Sean?' He should get it laminated before he wears it out by looking at it, I tell him.

Like Josh and Cory, I'm making all the right happy noises, but I can't help but add a few stings like, 'So you're going to learn Korean then, are you, Ramon?' But then Josh adds, 'Get Alice to teach you,' and then I have to pretend to laugh.

I've had a bad week one way and another but I'm pulling myself out of it as best I can. Ramon's good fortune isn't helping, but there are more important things in life. Like, it's not Ramon is it, all polished and booted on his way for a cozy night with Alice right now.

I'm taking the longer skateboard route way out East past Elk Neck Swamp and the shooting range. Then I'll double back downhill all the way through the forest trail and across the river back across the fields to the smallholdings. It's been a hot day. The bins are full and there's a fair bit of litter about. The trail isn't a place to be after dark. Even though the muggers leave us skateboard dudes alone, we're not much good for thieving, I keep my wits about me.

I breathe in the cooling scent of fresh pine. The forest shade soothes like nothing else. This is my place. Where I come to write my music. I glide along full of hope but also worry for the night ahead. Alice'll want to talk about the Koreans and Ramon, and I'll have to pretend to be as happy for him as her. I must show her what a generous spirit I am or she'll never fall in love with me

I've finished the lyrics to *She's the One* and I'll be playing it to her in full later. First she'll hear my *Symphony of the Stars*, as she asked for, then there's a short pause at the end of the recording and on it will come. She'll know it's for her and we'll kiss. And I'll be floating up to heaven on a pure cloud of joy.

She stands back to let me in with a peck on the cheek. I see she's made an effort too with the make-up, and her hair is clipped up and to one side with a sparkling slide. Good sign.

But then I sit on the sofa and she sits opposite. In a chair that says 'we are *friends*, Sean, and nothing more'.

We're soon talking about the Koreans. We laugh about Decima getting a taste of the toadstool, and the craziness of her seat going up and down. What was going on there then? I hear all about Decima's latest nastiness towards her. Alice seems to have the ability to sail through any put-down with such a beautiful grace. She often says how sorry she feels for Decima, having a father like that and all after losing her real parents in that terrible fire. Her freakish, sad attachment to that toy teddy bear, Alice reckons says it all.

She suddenly changes the subject, 'Ramon's news is tough for you Sean, it must be.'

Her concern makes my hurt ten times worse so I change the subject back fast.

'How did you ever speak Korean anyhows?'

She blushes and dips her eyes. 'It's a gift I have, Sean. I don't know where it comes from. I can, kind of, tune in. Do you know what I mean? I imagine it's the same with your music. Doesn't it, sort of, simply *come* to you, you were saying once?'

'Something like that. Especially when there's trees around for some reason. It turns up in my head. Then I get home and write it down before I forget.'

'You make it sound so simple and I know it's not! You've got so much talent, Sean. Don't beat yourself up about Ramon too much.'

'Did I ever say that I did!'

'You're only human. It's all about contacts. I'm going to try to help you. I may know someone. Did you bring your music?' She tops up my beer.

I nod.

'Oh Sean, I can't wait to hear it. Do you want to go to the table and I'll be right back with our spaghetti.'

I sit there at her little fold-up card table, fiddling with

the cutlery, with my thoughts going into overdrive. It doesn't help that her peculiar cat is sitting on the windowsill, giving me the evils. It's like it knows my intentions and it's not too pleased about it.

What does she mean by contacts? What if she's seeing Scorpio? Unlikely but I don't know that she's not, do I? The thought of him takes me back to that dark, dark day. The day we all watched innocent Alice being seduced by YouTube star and predator Scorpio in the kitchen – and that's not a euphemism. We saw bits of it on the security camera, we all did. That's traumatic enough, it broke my heart. My big plan to drop Scorpio a dongle with one of my songs came to nothing and I ended up smashing his face in instead. Not the kind of contact I had in mind. Well, to be fair, it was a few well-aimed punches in the gut, and I have wished forever more that it had been lower down as well. So here I am sitting in the friend zone, reliving all my failures.

The only saving grace on that sorry day was the sudden clarity of my feelings. It was, like they say in the poetry, instant. One moment love wasn't anywhere to be seen in my closed mind, the next moment, bam. I *knew*. I knew our destiny to be together was as certain as anything can be in this world. I have to say I've enjoyed keeping an eye on Scorpio's slow decline ever since, too. He's doing nothing but reality shows now, so I hear.

After we've eaten, Alice pushes her plate to one side, clasps her fingers together beneath her chin, looks straight into my soul with her big blue eyes and says, 'So, what's she been up to now?'

Loaded silence.

'Come on, Sean, I've had my moan. Now get it off your chest.'

Despite telling myself I wouldn't, out it all comes.

'She tore into me. Had a right go. Josh told her about Tillman.'

Alice looks at me blankly.

'You know, the journalist who's been digging into Gauld's dodgy dealings.'

'Why's Decima mad at you though?'

'Because I told Josh before I told her.'

'Oh I see. Gauld's dodgy dealings eh. He'll have been busy there then.'

'I found out Tillman knows about the link between his candy stores and his drug deals. That was my intelligence that got that. I only overheard a tiny bit of it in the bar and happened to mention it to Josh in a gossipy kind of a way you know, like you do. Then he only went and told Decima before I could get to her!'

'That can't be deliberate of Josh?'

'You see the best in everyone so you do. Now she's mad at me.'

'Does Josh know it set her off on you?'

Now this is between me and you, I'd never share this thought with Alice, but I cannot work out why Josh dumped me in it like that. What with Ramon, it's like the threads that hold us guys together are coming apart.

Alice shrugs. 'It's no big deal is it? The candy stores

supplying weed to order are an open secret around town.'

'True. I guess if it goes wider, then the FBI gets involved, that's the problem.'

'Not paying tax on his dope sales.'

'A straightforward enough rap. Go to jail, don't pass go. But you know, Tillman was only interested in the Brent Flats thing at first. You know how Gauld has forced everyone to sell except for some stubborn family who refuse to leave their slummy house.'

Alice coughs.

'What?'

'No. Carry on,' she gulps down her drink. What have I said?

'With Tillman watching every move, Gauld has had to keep squeaky clean legal on the eviction. He can't fall back on bribing his district attorney friend anymore.'

'Ahhh.'

'And then this journo Tillman has got some TV backing and is going for Gauld big time. All in.'

'The future's looking more and more uncertain.' She looks me straight in the eye.

'Not? Not…' The Us word is at the tip of my tongue ready to come out. Thankfully I kept it back. I can't blow it now. 'Time for some music! Where do I plug myself in?'

Alice giggles.

'What?'

'Oh nothing.'

I download her speaker App to my phone, move from the table to the sofa, hit PLAY and close my eyes.

I hear the opening bars of the French horns and double bass intro, the staccato choir join in, the trumpet build follows. After a pause come the sweeping strings – that's when I feel the weight of my cushion go up as Alice sinks into the sofa next to me. I'm sweating!

'How did you get all of these instruments to play?' she whispers.

'Keyboards, it's all keyboards Alice. I don't have an orchestra and a fifty-voice choir back in my bedsit.'

'Bedsit, such a cute Irish word,' she giggles and leans back. I stay leaning forward. I'm desperate to sit back with her but I don't want to make any wrong move. Not at this stage. This is crucial. My song will say it all when the right time comes.

27

Love is a special thing

Sean

What a night! For starters, it was Alice inviting me round. Alice wanting to be with me. So the evening was set for a high from the start, but I had no idea. Don't get me wrong. Not in that way. We haven't laid a finger on each other yet. We're getting so close now, anything could ruin it, a wrong move here, a wrong word there. I'm not really sure that last night happened at all to be honest with you.

Too often I've thought I was in love, and I've rushed in and wrecked my chances. Not this time. This time I'm going to play it slow slow slow, handle it like a baby bird fresh from the shell, hold it gently and let it grow. I'm taking no risks. She wants the whole romance deal, so I must wait for the moment when I finally take her in my arms and make her mine.

For so long I have been her shadow, silent and unseen, making sure she is safe. Each day I have followed her home from work, and each morning I have been there to see her safely to work.

There was that Saturday when I thought I'd lost her. I watched her apartment all night, sitting on a bench in the park. When she left her apartment mid-morning I followed her to the train station and hopped onto the next carriage where I could see her through the glass. She got off at the Brent Flats station and I followed her for a while, but then there was no cover when she started walking through the flats, and I had to give up. I waited at the station until after the last train had left at midnight, but she didn't return. I was so scared something had happened to her.

Then I had another thought: she was spending the night with somebody who lived there. I felt sick and felt my face flushed with rage thinking about it. It took me all night to walk home, and my mind conjured up hateful images of my love with another who doesn't deserve her. And then I was angry with her for betraying me. Oh I was so messed up.

But then it was all OK. I saw her coming out of her tiny office as I was going by on Monday. My mouth went so dry, but I managed to croak out: 'Hi, had a good weekend?'

She smiled at me with those bright blue eyes and my knees turned to jelly. I won't mention what it did to another part of me because that would sound disrespectful.

'Hi, Spike,' she said. 'Thanks, I visited my parents out on the Brent Flats. How about you?'

I didn't even mind she got my name wrong. I was so relieved. She wasn't with somebody else.

I mumbled something inane and dashed into the control room. Later, when I think back, I remember seeing a definite spark of interest in her eye. Definitely. We connected. There was a hidden promise in that look, and I made a commitment. Her name tattooed onto my little man and a symbolic gold ring fixed in the end. It will be her wedding ring when the time is right. Did it hurt? Oh yes! The tatt wasn't so bad, only a bit freaky, Tom and me having to stretch it while he was working. But the ring left me sore for days. I had a real problem keeping Decima satisfied.

There was a bad moment way back when I was out on my skateboard and bumped into her with some foreign guy. I saw them together a few times and watched carefully. They didn't touch, he never went into her apartment, so I'm pretty certain there's nothing going on there. Probably a family friend or something like that. I couldn't mention anything to Alice otherwise she'd know I was following her.

Anyway, he's off the scene now. I guess he went back to his country.

What with watching Alice all the time, working, and 'dealing' with Decima, I was knackered. Done in!. There were three nights in a row when she demanded my attention and left me drained and weak-kneed. It felt so wrong, but the tricks Decima knows made me forget about Alice. Decima is an animal and no real man could resist her. You both become animals.

The same time the foreign guy disappeared, Alice was ill. She didn't come to work for four days. When she came back you could tell how sick she'd been; she lost a whole lot of weight. Could be she ate something really bad? She changed her hair and clothes, too, and she looked so frail, my heart ached for her.

I let her know that I was there for her in any and every way, and I think our relationship really took off when she moved into the new place. She was grateful for my help and we began to see more of each other. I kept my feelings to myself as much as possible, keeping cool so I didn't scare her off. Her mother and friend really like me. They can see how I am so right for Alice.

Even her creepy cat likes me.

My love for her inspired *She's the One*. I played it to her and she really liked it. I gave her a copy of the lyrics. My soul, written down for her to hold.

In the crowd, she stands alone
Shining brighter than a diamond stone
Her smile lights up the bleakest day
She's the one to take my breath away

CHORUS
She's the one, she's the one
The only girl for me
She's the one, she's the one
My heart, my life is hers
When you know, you know
She's the one for me

Her love is like the warmest snood

Healing even my darkest mood
Her eyes light up my heart, my soul
We truly are just one true whole

Yes she's the one, the one, the one
My love for her outshines the sun
Her eyes light up my heart, my soul
We truly are just one true whole

Alice loved the song. I didn't say anything stupid, I didn't need to. It was all happening in the air around us. It was as if it wasn't us at all, something was happening TO us, to us both. And we both knew it.

'Don't say anything,' I said as the closing chords faded away.

She looked grateful. 'You're very sweet. You know that?' and she gave me a look that said it all.

It was too fragile to speak about except in song, I wanted to say but that felt too dangerous. I had always heard that love was a special thing, but who knew! Who knew it did that?

Then she calls me AGAIN. I cannot believe it. I drop everything and skate round.

28

Pushed?

Alice

I finally called Jai's old office, the International Ecological Protection Organization. I felt sick dialing the number, in case he answered, but it was a woman. We had a long talk. She was shocked when I told her about the way my mother's garden was trashed and the threats from the developers who want to knock the house down. The woman said she would get her colleagues onto it. Their organization fights the unauthorized development of protected areas like the Brent Flats. Nobody should be able to get planning permission to develop them for any purpose.

Four days later the *Hawk Bay City Herald* published an article written by local journalist Rex Tillman. He interviewed my parents. My father stated that he would not sell his house, he would not give way to threats and he would not allow anybody to drive his family away from the Flats. Tillman wrote about and took photos of my mother's mangled plants stuck in bins and buckets of water.

Two nights later he was mugged and badly beaten outside his house. He has two broken ribs and will probably lose sight in his right eye. Shocking. What are the police doing about it? There's so much violence in this town.

It's a beautiful Wednesday evening when we're all leaving the Tower after work. Decima has been driven away in her limo, Josh has jogged off, Sean is clacking down the sidewalk on his skateboard, and Cory is somewhere behind me.

I'm standing waiting for the traffic to stop so I can cross.

Feeling a hand on my back I turn to smile, thinking it's Cory. The hand pushes, hard, and I lose my balance, staggering into the road. Brakes shriek as I land in front of a car and feel the wing knock me to the ground.

I'm lying face down on the hot surface. I can see feet all around me, and hear sounds of cars hooting and people screaming. Somebody is calling for an ambulance. I try to stand up, but there's no strength in my limbs. The sounds are fading out, my eyesight is blurring and I'm feeling very cold.

Far away I hear a voice shout 'No! Alice!'

I feel myself lifted from the hard surface and pressed gently against a soft fabric, strong arms cradling me.

There's a gray veil coming down over my eyes. I'm very sleepy.

'Stay awake, Alice. Stay awake.'

I force my eyes open and look up into Cory's face.

'That's my good girl, my lovely girl. Keep your eyes open, you're going to be OK.'

I'm aware of the fragrance of his aftershave, the mint on his breath and the faintest smell of sweat. His long black hair brushes against my cheek.

'I've got you. You're safe Alice. You're safe. I'm with you.'

I hear a siren and am aware of hands lifting me onto a gurney and sliding it into an ambulance. I sense people moving around inside, touching me, a machine bleeping, low conversation, and Cory is holding my hand. Then nothing.

I wake in a hospital room. When I open my eyes Cory is sitting in a chair beside the bed smiling at me.

'The sleeping beauty awakens.'

A nurse comes in, adjusts the pillows, helps me to sit up.

'You've no broken bones, honey, but you got a lot of bumps and bruises. Going to be sore for quite a while. You staying in tonight 'cos you had a bang on the head.'

I can't stay in. There's nobody to feed Zylch.

I hear running feet coming down the corridor.

Sean knocks open the door, red-faced, panting, his chest heaving.

'Oh Jaysus, what happened? Who's done this to you? I'll kill them.'

He notices Cory sitting beside me, and scowls. 'Thanks for letting me know. What happened?'

'It was an accident. I was there when Alice fell. I wanted to make sure she was OK and came with her in the ambulance. I'll be on my way now you're here, Sean.'

He comes over and kisses me lightly on the forehead.

'I'll come and visit tomorrow. When you can go home, I'll drive you.

'I'll stay here with her tonight,' Sean says.

'Ah no, really, I'll be fine. There's no need,' I protest.

'I'm staying anyway,' he says, giving Cory a friendly pat on the shoulder as he leaves, and sinking onto his knees next to the bed.

All I can think of is Zylch, waiting for me, hungry.

'Sean?'

'Yes?'

'I'm worried about my um, cat. Zylch. He needs feeding.'

He jumps up. 'I'm on my way, Alice. Leave it to me. Is there some cat food at your house, or shall I pick some up?'

'He's fussy, Sean. He won't eat cat food. There's a piece of Parmesan cheese and left-over pasta in the fridge. If you could put it in his bowl, that will keep him going until I get home tomorrow.'

Please, Zylch, I say silently, don't do anything crazy.

'I'll be back soon, Alice. Don't worry, I'll look after him for you.' He squeezes my hand and gives a thumbs-up as he closes the door.

It's almost dark outside now. I'm applying a healing spell to my arms where they are scraped when I notice, from the corner of my eye, a movement at the window, which is tilted slightly open. I know immediately what it is, even before it flops onto my bed and shuffles up to my pillow.

'Zylch, what are you doing here?' I whisper.

His small hands stroke my face as he rubs his head on my chin.

'It's alright, Zylch. I'm OK and I'll be back home with you tomorrow. Be a good boy for me. Sean is on his way to feed you, so PLEASE behave.'

He pulls back from me, looks into my eyes for a moment, winks, flaps his little wings and vanishes as quickly as he appeared. Did he always have wings? How did I not notice that?

Two hours later Sean is back.

'Your cat is fine,' he says. 'He was curled up asleep on the couch so I didn't disturb him.'

'Thank you so much, Sean. You're an angel.'

'You know I'll do anything for you, Alice.'

My head aches and I'm feeling drowsy. Sean is talking too much, so I close my eyes and manage to summon the **Husshh** spell, which sends him to sleep.

A nurse gives me a couple of pills to swallow and turns out the light.

I'm almost asleep when I recall Cory's words: 'It was an accident. Alice tripped.'

But it wasn't an accident. Somebody pushed me. I clearly remember that hand on my back.

When I wake up Sean is asleep, crumpled up in the chair. Bless him, he looks so young and innocent.

He jerks awake when the nurse comes in to say I can go home once the doctor has seen me.

I'm sent home with my right arm strapped to give the torn ligaments in my shoulder time to heal. The doctor says at least a week, but I'm sure I'll find something in the little spell book that Lorelei gave me which will help to heal it quicker. Cory drives me home, with Sean warning him to go slow and mind the bends and bumps.

I'll have five days off work, and since I haven't had a holiday for two years, I'm enjoying sitting outside, watching Zylch playing in and around the pond, listening to the birds and feeling the breeze.

Josh arrives with a box of fruit and chocolates, and a 'Get-well' card signed by all the staff at the Tower. He brings a copy of the Hawk Bay Herald reporting on my 'accident'. The driver of the car that hit me was cleared of any responsibility. Witnesses confirmed that I had fallen in front of his car and there was nothing he could have done to stop. He was treated for shock.

As Josh is leaving I'm very surprised to see my parents driving up.

'Why didn't you call?' my mother shouts angrily. 'You're in hospital and you don't tell us?'

'It was nothing, and I didn't want you to worry. See, I'm home, I'm fine.'

'We had to find out from your father's colleague, who saw it in the paper? How do you think that makes us feel?'

'I'm sorry, really. I should have told you, but you would have worried unnecessarily. I did what I thought best.'

My father is staring at me, his face grim.

'What happened?' he asks.

'I tripped.'

'But you didn't, did you. You were pushed.'

'How do you know?'

'How I know, Alice, is because since the article about our property appeared, the journalist who visited us was supposedly mugged and suffered serious injury, the Hawk Bay Herald was firebombed two days ago, the International Ecological Protection Organization offices received a letter bomb, and you 'fell' in front of a car. None of that is a coincidence. I want you to move back home. You are not safe here alone. The people behind all this are ruthless, Alice. They are determined to force us out. We don't know what they may do next.'

I have never known my father talk so much. He never normally says more than a couple of sentences at the most. He hasn't finished. He clenches his fists by his sides and shouts:

'How dare they hurt my daughter! How bloody well dare they. You could have been killed, Alice.'

My usually mild father is shaking with rage. 'Put some things together and come home now.'

'No, I'll be safe. I have Zylch. He'll take care of me. I'll be OK.'

'Zylch! Zylch! What do you think that thing can do if somebody turns up here with a gun?'

Zylch, who has been lying on the branch of a tree apparently asleep, slides down to the ground and stretches. He walks a little way, and then stops, with his back to us.

'Alice, it's just a fighting cat. It can't protect you.'

Slowly Zylch turns towards us. He crouches with his head bowed down. Then he looks up, and his face starts changing. His beautiful fur begins transforming into thick metallic bronze scales over his entire body. As he rears up on his hind legs, the armor-plated scales shake and rattle like war drums. He grows to the size of a buffalo, with a thick spiked tail that lashes slowly from side to side, and muscular limbs ending in razor-sharp curved claws. Huge scaled wings grow from his back, casting a monstrous shadow on the ground. His eyes glow red, like laser beams. He points them at a fallen fence post and it explodes with a bang, then he opens his mouth to show a double row of fangs, blasting acrid-smelling flames up into the sky.

My father sits down on the ground with a thump, shaking his head slowly from side to side. 'Good lord,' he gasps.

'Awesome,' whispers my mother. 'I had no idea.'

Zylch shakes himself. There's a slight rattling as the scales shiver and vanish, and in a second he has returned to his silver-furred, cat-like self, winding himself around my legs. I pick him up and nuzzle him.

'Alice is safe with me,' says Zylch.

My father shakes his head. 'Did that thing speak? Did I hear right? It talked?'

'There are more things in heaven and earth than are dreamt of,' replies Zylch.

My mother stares open-mouthed.

'Tell me I'm not hallucinating? It's quoting Shakespeare?'

'As I said, I am perfectly safe here with Zylch. You don't have to worry. Nothing is going to harm me.'

My parents stand there, silently, looking from Zylch to me, to each other. I put Zylch down and wrap my arms around them and usher them slowly to their car.

'I'm sorry you were concerned. But please stop now. It's yourselves who need to be careful. I'll give you a call every day to make sure you're OK. Off you go.'

It's funny, but at the moment I'm feeling more like the parent than the child. They looked so bewildered.

I'm feeling tired now, so I share a couple of boiled eggs with Zylch, glug a large glass of ice cold lemonade, and curl up on the bed. I sleep for 12 hours, dreaming of flying toadstools. When I wake, Zylch is sitting on the end of the bed.

'Coffee, you can't make coffee can you, Zylch?'

He sits up and raises a paw to his face, then he shakes his head sadly.

'No fringers. Sorry.'

Sean comes twice every day to ask if I need anything, and I'm trying not to get irritated with him fussing over me because I know he means well, but I would really like to have some time to myself.

29

Move or die

Decima

Alice returns to work today. I'm pleased. I've been down to three lackluster partners all this time. And some mornings, I even had to make my own coffee! Now, at least, the boys should start performing properly for me again.

Cory is my favored one. I treated him to a special pleasure last night. We were both working late. I led him through the welcome back banners, balloons and trays of cakes to the Green Room and closed the blinds against the rain.

He came up behind me and stood very close with his hands on my hips. 'What weather, eh.'

We stayed like that for a while, listening to the wind howling around the Tower like a banshee. Now Cory is a zen guy. I let him build up slowly for what was coming.

'How's Roxy?'

'Pam wouldn't let me take her. Said it was too stormy. We were pleading with her but she held firm.'

'We?'

'Me and Roxy.'

'I'm sure Pam knows best?'

'I know best, Cory. Roxy would have loved it. But I'd die rather than fall out with Pam so I ended up staying for a coffee.'

'You got your Roxy time.'

'I did. Pam's got all sorts of animals there. Horses, more dogs, a cute couple of little terriers, a Siamese cat. She told me about huskies. Did you know they're the most intelligent, independent breed?'

'Roxy is your soul sister then.'

'A lifeline, what with all that's going on around here. We talk for hours. I tell Roxy everything.'

'You be careful there.'

'In my hurry to get away from the studio, I even forgot Digby. Left him behind on his throne. But, you know, Digby really loves his throne. He didn't mind. I think he's missing Trevor, you know. Pam had a parrot once…'

'Er,' Cory interrupted. 'Are we forgetting why we are here?'

'Am I keeping you?'

'It's only I've got to meet the boys soon to put the finishing touches to our little 'Welcome Home Alice' movie.'

I swallowed hard, forced a big smile and turned around. 'I've a special treat for you, that's why.'

'Now there's no need for that,' he whispered. Cory is so laid back he's hardly there at all sometimes.

'My way of saying thanks. See what you think of this.' I took from my bag my new, upgraded 2.0 version of the Zipwire vibrator chamber and pressed the App on my phone.

'This is straight off the production line.' I shouted above the gentle hum. 'What do you think? Good eh? A bit noisy? Hmm.'

He barely heard me speak. Before he left, he gave me a kiss on the side of my neck, avoiding the nasty patch at the back. 'Well, that was different.'

We're getting closer by the day, Cory and I. Sean can get lost.

'Could you record your verdict on the website,' I called as he left. 'I'll WhatsApp you the link.'

I still get sent samples from the Zipwire Fantasy Tools sex toy company where I used to work as a tester. Now guybrators are really taking off and my media profile is on the up, it seems I'm useful to my old bosses again. Who knows? If Dad goes to jail and it all goes belly up here, they may be useful to me again too.

Word goes out that Alice is approaching the building. The whole place erupts. Her favorite song, *Viva la Vida*, plays on a loop through all the speakers. Sean dances around madly, whooping, punching the air, high-fiving anybody near, singing along with Coldplay at the top of his voice. When he comes at me, I give his raised palm a miss.

Every corridor has staff dancing up and down, laughing, pinching and mock-punching each other.

I'm glad she's back because I can't stand hearing any more *poor Alice* conversations on a loop. Blah blah ad infinitum round and round we go.

'SUCH a shame. Yes yes, isn't it the worst.'

'I can't believe it,' I say. 'Can you? I'm in *shock*.' 'Will she recover? Did she trip over? What could she have tripped on? How did it happen?'

'I don't know, I don't care and I wasn't *there*, OK?' I don't say. I'm an amazing actress, did I ever tell you that? I join in with all the awws and ahhs and yes isn't it terrible, simply awful I know, noises. Well, I wasn't there, was I? Dad's mission failed. This time. She's had a stay of execution. She will be destroyed soon enough. Until then, I'm in *Be Nice to Alice* disguise, joining in with the zeitgeist.

But in the meantime I am relieved she's back. Tanya the Temp does her best, but Alice's research is spot on and the admin runs like clockwork. Tanya needs more training before Alice's next 'accident' sees her gone for good.

How will I feel when she's gone? Don't waste energy on speculative thoughts, my life coach would say. My one and only shot at the big time is right now. Period. Same for Dad. He's not going to give up on his Golf and Country Club at the Flats when he's gotten so far, any more than Alice's parents are going to let him knock their house down. So there we are. Something's got to give.

Sometimes simple messages are the only way. Alice will be killed first. If that doesn't get them out, they'll be next. Move or die.

From every office come the squeaks and breathy huffs of yet more balloons being blown up. The girls from accounts arrive, trailing behind them whole silver helium balloon sentences like WELCOME HOME, WE LOVE YOU ALICE. HR is unpacking cake tins full of brownies and fairy cakes; the desks are piled high with poppers, ready to launch as soon as she appears.

I tag onto the end of a passing conga line, kick my legs out side to side and wail out the Coldplay chorus with the rest of them.

There's a commotion at the elevator, the conga line comes to an abrupt halt, everybody crashing into each other, shushing and giggling.

The elevator pings to a hushed silence. Alice walks out looking a million dollars. Bouncing back like a kangaroo on steroids. I rush forward with everyone else. I must be nicer than nice and not draw attention to what's really going on here.

'FIVE FOUR…' silent hand signal 3, 2, 1 ON AIR.

I welcome Alice back onto the screen with a gushing introduction. Easy. Fake sincerity is what TV presenting is all about and I have no problem laying it on thick. Alice will be a much more visible presence on your screens I tell the viewers. After all, she's been through so much, the poor petal.

What they don't know is that she won't be around much longer. When she really is dead and gone, our all-important viewing figures will go off the scale. We can play reruns of the newly-dead Alice. Beat that, Lorelei and your fake celebrity spook chasing.

30

Making my own fun

Decima

It's been weeks now and keeping up the benevolent *Be kind to Alice* fakery is killing me. I need to make my own fun.

Today, the Dubai sponsors have booked four women from Illinois. Temperance, Patience, Prudence and Silence want to be recognized legally as a unit. Their campaign for plural lesbian marriage is trending. Knowing Alice will be dead soon, my generosity knows no bounds. I'm teaching her everything I know.

'This is a tricky one. The interview must be conducted within the rules of streaming daytime TV.'

'I get it, Decima. No sex can be mentioned.'

'Keep the rules at the front of your mind at the same time as putting the guests at ease. The more relaxed they are, the more they'll reveal. When you get more advanced, you can move on to the false ease when, 80% in, you hit them with the one killer question they don't want you to ask. There's always some dirt to dig up somewhere but you leave that to me. Got that?'

She nods.

'So, Alice, what's the number one rule?'

'Relax.'

'Relax and everything else takes care of itself. A hint of panic and you're lost. One fluffed line, it's over. How do you fluff a line?'

'Panic.'

'Do you ever fluff a line when you're speaking normally?'

'No.'

'Exactly. And what's the other golden rule?'

'Keep it fresh.'

'You got it, Alice. Over-prepare at your peril. That's why,' I pause at the studio doors, and turn to her with a big, generous smile. 'I've left it until now to tell you the good news. You'll be leading today's interview.' I don't leave a breath for her response. For a split second, her eyes widen, but she gathers herself quickly.

'You should have given me more notice,' she says calmly, adjusting her collar and giving her shoulders a good shake. 'Anybody would think you're trying to jeopardize your own show.'

'It's exciting, Alice. Grab the opportunity. Don't overthink it. You'll start off the discussion, I'll join in at the end with the killer question. You will close the interview on time but not before they respond.'

I heave open the double-thick soundproof door with my shoulder, grab her arm and shove her into the studio.

She keeps her balance, annoyingly, and marches off with her head up and shoulders pulled back. She throws herself into her flashy new cream vegan leather presenter's chair. It exhales a whoof of air in protest.

I give Digby a stroke and a pat before gently and elegantly settling down next to her.

'The first rule of presenting, Alice, is relaxed alertness.' I say loudly. I want the crew to notice my generous mentoring.

'You've said that already.'

What a little madam she is. I look around with exaggerated impatience. The crew have lost their regular poker faces and are side-eyeing. Sean is jittering about hopping from one foot to the other.

'Five minutes. Five minutes now.' Josh's voice comes through my headphones.

'Five minutes everyone, heaven help us,' Sean calls to the floor.

Alice sits erect, poised and confident. There are strange glints of red in her eyes, she's literally on fire for this.

'What is she on?' Josh says into my headphones. 'She looks so confident, no sign of nerves.'

I glance around the set warily. Can they sense my own nerves?

'Final instruction: forget the millions, forget how many people are watching you.'

'Thanks for the reminder.'

'You look at the camera and talk to it as if you're talking to one person. Your mother, your closest friend, or your lover, maybe.'

I turn to Sean and raise an eyebrow. 'Whoever makes

you feel cozy and warm inside.'

Alice rolls her eyes.

Tanya the Temp, who we've brought in full time to 'assist' Alice, ready to take over when she's dead, brings the guests through from the Green Room.

I hiss under my breath, 'Secret affairs, Alice, is there anything more sexy?'

'I don't know what you're talking about. Would you mind stopping talking for a moment while I recap their names?'

'Follow the teleprompter.'

'I won't be needing that. Besides, I haven't got my contacts in.'

Then, calm as Mary, she lists them quietly to herself. 'Silence, Prudence, Temperance and Patience. Ahh what lovely names. I can't wait to meet them.'

The women arrive. With limp, brown hair tied in ponytails and oval thick-rimmed glasses almost obliterating watery gray eyes, you'd never guess that they were lovers. Sisters maybe. The only difference between them is the shade of their pastel thick cotton shirts, buttoned up to the neck. Celibate sisters. Never have I ever found it harder to imagine anybody having sex than these four.

The green light comes on and Alice is away. She soon has three of the women talking animatedly about their religion, The Sisterhood of Sacred Union, and the global growth of their campaign to legalize polyamorous relationships like theirs.

Alice brings the talk around to their hoped-for wedding and their dreams for their big day. They are looking into moving to the Solomon Islands, where they could legally marry. Silence, I think it's her, lives up to her name and I join her in staying mute to the end, leaving Alice to close the show. (That was unintentional. I think I got cramp when I was about to spring my killer question on them. My back seemed to lock up and I couldn't move for a moment.)

Everybody is smiling. It's a triumph.

As if I didn't need any more proof, Sean gives Alice a delighted hug in front of everyone.

I only see Sean within the group now, and then as little as possible. I stopped our secret phone sessions long ago. Instead, I've started a little secret bathtime schedule with Josh. Bathing and underwater fun together at mine on a Monday followed by a delivery of coffee, juice and pastries as we discuss the list of upcoming guests.

I can kick him out by 10 and get a couple of hours in with Roxy before heading for the studio. Roxy calms me right down. It's a long drive out to Pam's but worth every second.

Today, Josh and I touch on Lorelei's latest trickery. She's still milking her upcoming celeb ghost interview. Clickbait that'll never deliver. It should be the least of my worries but I don't know how much attention Dubai is paying to her stats, now she's on their radar after that stupid, probably fake, lawyer letter.

We go through next month's guest list, fresh in from

Dubai.

'I haven't even heard of any of these women.'

'Nothing new there.'

'True. They'll know who I am, won't they?'

'They sure will.'

'That's all that matters.'

Alice can do all the work.

I run through the list of names.

'There's some tough-sounding women coming up.'

'Bring back Patience, Silence et al, dreaming of wedded bliss eh,' Josh growls in my ear, one hand massages my neck, which thankfully is finally healing up, as he looks over my shoulder.

'This one is a media Goddess in Taiwan,' I run down the list with my finger. 'This one has launched a charity. This one has started her own *bank*. This one breeds Kentucky Derby racehorse winners. This one fronts the biggest meditation App in the Middle East. This one has the fastest-selling cookery book in Indian history.'

The massage stops.

'Carry on,' I order but nothing happens

'What?' I turn around.

He's turned a peculiar shade of puce and is staring into space.

'What is it? Do you know her?'

'No. Not exactly, but I do know something about her.'

'Oh?'

He wasn't going to tell me, but I get it out of him. I cannot *believe* my luck. So Alice thinks presenting is easy does she? OK, bring it on, because I now have a truly massive ace up my sleeve, and I'm happy to bide my time for the joy of destroying her publicly before she's finished off for good.

31

Triumph

Alice

I did it. My first lead presentation on the show. I wasn't ready for it but Decima was quite right to throw me in at the last minute. Since that day when she pushed me on to camera when I wasn't suitably dressed, I always come to work now wearing an outfit that will look good if I have to appear at short notice.

I didn't have any time to worry, I was straight in there! I did have a brief moment of panic, but I am feeling so much love from everybody. I was amazed when I came back to work to realize how popular I am. I didn't even know most of the people who came to hug me and say how glad they were that I was safe. It's given me another huge confidence boost knowing I have so much support.

My first guests were an interesting group of four ladies. The interview went very well. They seemed uncomfortable at first, but once they realized that I was genuinely supportive, and let them explain what they were fighting for, they relaxed and became animated. They are all in love with each other, I know it's unusual, but good for them, we're all different and should respect each other.

Decima was sitting there quietly, and as we reached the end of the interview, I saw she was planning to come in with a killer question to throw them off balance.

She turned towards them, but before she could speak I threw the *Freeze* spell. She couldn't move a muscle, she was like a statue captured leaning forward in her seat with her mouth open. Just for fun I made her nose itch too. I held her there until the guests had left, then I released her. She was shaking her head, looking around, examining the floor and rubbing her face. It was quite funny really.

When the show was over, everybody clapped. Sean ran up and hugged me. 'You nailed it, Alice, absolutely nailed it. You're a natural!'

'Hear, hear,' says Decima. 'That was brilliant Alice. I am proud of you. I always knew you could do it.'

My phone buzzes. There's a message from my father. 'Well done'. It's the first time he's ever sent me a message, so it means a lot.

On social media it seems I'm a hit. "Refreshing, empathetic, genuinely nice, a future star, heading for greater things."

Wow! I mustn't let it go to my head, although I have to be honest and say I'm feeling rather pleased with myself.

When I'm home and having a cuddle with Zylch, a delivery van arrives with a huge bunch of flowers from Decima, with a card saying: "Congratulations, Alice. Your first solo interview was a tremendous success. I knew you could do it. Here's to many more."

With Decima, you never know what she's going to do next. It's like flipping a coin and wondering which way it will fall.

I'm leaving for work on Monday, when a message pings into my phone from HR, saying I'm to take ten days paid holiday. Decima has reported that she's worried about me. Apparently I'm looking very pale and she thinks I may be suffering the effects of my 'accident' and have returned to work too soon. Tanya the temp who stood in for me while I was recovering will take over until I'm back.

I WhatsApp Decima and say I'm fine and don't need to take any time off. She replies that after my brilliant debut as a presenter, she wants to make sure that I don't tire myself out because she has great things planned for me. She tells me to take care, to relax and have fun, and she'll look forward to seeing me back soon.

I'm a bit lost at first, not used to having so much time to myself, but I come up with a way to entertain myself and make good use of my time.

I practice interviewing techniques. There's loads of advice on YouTube, about body language, how to prepare etc., so I've filmed myself interviewing Zylch, a plant pot, my old teddy bear and an assortment of garden tools. Although I know I did OK with the four ladies, that was pretty much due to luck, and I want to keep building my confidence and know that I can handle anything like Decima does.

The rest of the time I play with Zylch, who helps me

in the garden digging holes, but not necessarily where I want them.

I forgot to mention that my father called two weeks ago, with some great news. He was going to throw away all the cuttings we took from my mother's wrecked garden, but when he took them out of the buckets he found they had all grown new roots. My mother potted them up and they have already started to develop shoots and leaves. He said he was so proud, and apologized for doubting me. I'm thrilled, I didn't know if it would actually work.

Anyway, back to my presentation techniques. I think I've really learned a lot and have definitely boosted my confidence. I'm pretty sure I can cope with anything that might happen!

I've been shopping and bought myself a few new outfits – two skirts, four blouses and two jackets. Hopefully they'll look OK. Shelley couldn't come with me, but I'm getting a little more sure of myself and I think I've chosen well.

Sean has phoned every morning to ask if I need anything or any help. I've said as sweetly as I can that what I most want is time to myself, and although I could hear the disappointment in his voice, he has respected my wishes.

Sunday evening he's thrilled when I ask if he'd like to come round so I can 'interview' him. He has to pretend to be a very difficult female millionairess, and I have to coax 'her' to relax and open up. Sean really gets into the role, he's so funny, we end up nearly crying with laughter.

Then we practice the interviewee who freezes; the one who refuses to answer any questions; the one who won't sit down; the one who keeps looking at her watch; the one who keeps answering her mobile phone, and the interviewee who brings her two pet monkeys on set with her and they keep trying to bite me. In every case I have to find a way to take control and keep the interview going.

By the time we've finished I'm certain that no matter what happens I will always be able to conduct a great interview. My confidence is sky-high.

I've enjoyed doing this with Sean. He makes me laugh, he's so willing to do anything to please. He is really good company; I wish I could be sure that we're right for each other, but I simply don't feel it yet.

Yesterday I was reorganizing my wardrobe for when I go back to work. I was clearing out an old purse and found a crumpled scrap of paper at the bottom. I smoothed it out. Suddenly I felt dizzy and had to sit down.

I remembered the piece of paper Jai had pushed under the door, the night of our disastrous dinner. How I'd screwed it up and tossed it in the corner, and how Zylch had found it when we were moving out of the apartment and I'd stuffed it in my purse, meaning to throw it in the trash.

It had been in my purse all this time, forgotten. I stared at it for a while, and then folded it neatly back up, unread. I couldn't do it. I couldn't read whatever he wanted to say. Why haven't I thrown it away? It's nothing more than a meaningless piece of paper, but it's all I have left of him. And despite everything, I am not ready to let go. All the wounds from that night burst open again. My optimism, believing that Jai was going to ask me to marry him. The humiliation of him telling me he was going to marry somebody else. My flight from the restaurant, all the tears I wept, the unbearable pain. It all came back to the surface. It's still there. I'm still hopelessly in love with him.

32

Shock

Alice

I'm not due back at work until Wednesday and had planned to spend today with Zylch. We're playing chess. I explained the moves to him yesterday, and he understood immediately. He tells me his moves, and I position his pieces for him, with him not having any fingers. He beats me every time. I'm just trying to see how to protect my queen from his menacing pawn, when my phone goes. The first time I ignore it, and the second time, but it keeps ringing so I pick up.

It's Josh. 'Alice, get here straight away,,' he pants. 'We have an emergency. You're taking the interview this afternoon. We'll fill you in when you get here.'

We go on air at 2.00 pm, and it's 12.20 am now. I shower and wash my hair, dress, and have to ***Broomstick*** to The Tower to get there on time. I'm rushed up to the studio. Josh tells me Decima has been taken ill at the last moment, and the guest arrived half an hour ago and is waiting in the Green Room. Normally I'd go and meet them and chat for a few minutes before we go on air, but there's no time today. At the last minute I hear Josh running up calling my name. I turn towards him.

'Alice,' he bleats. There's the strangest look on his face. 'What is it?'

'Just that… Oh, never mind.' He hands me a small card that simply says: 'An Asian actress known as Sita. Touring the US promoting a book for a charity she set up. She also donates all her earnings to the charity.'

Weird. He looks distraught.

'Is that it?' I ask. 'That's all the information I've got?'

'You're flying blind, Alice. But you'll nail it.'

He's sweating hard, panting. Josh, the original Mr. Cool, looks like a man in a panic.

An alarm bell goes off in my head. Something strange is going on here. Decima's sudden illness at the very last minute, and no information for me regarding the guest? I get a whiff of mischief. It feels as if I'm walking into the unknown, being set up to fail.

I run a mental list through my head of famously generous celebrities: Barbra Streisand, Taylor Swift, Meryl Streep, Melinda Gates, Angelina Jolie, Oprah Winfrey. None of them would agree to appear on The Bitch's Hour. They're mega-stars. And none of them are Asian. I've no idea what to expect.

I take my place in Decima's chair and put my earphone in. Make-up Janelle dives in with some last-moment powdering and then a quick spray of Decima's cooling, calming face mist. It smells heavenly. I wait for the camera lights to go on, feeling mega-calm. Even the countdown to transmission doesn't phase me. Despite my qualms, I'm looking forward to it. It's truly exciting. This could become addictive. Sean takes over at 10 seconds, until, after 4 seconds it's 3, 2, 1. When I see the green light, I look into Camera No. 1 and smile.

'Good afternoon, and welcome to today's show, brought to you by gremlins. Yes, that's right, I said gremlins. They're making a pretty good attempt at sabotaging our program, but I'm fighting back. So hold onto your hats!

'Decima has fallen foul of the little beasts, who have forced her to have to pull out at the very last minute. She's been knocked out by a nasty bug; but never fear, she's already feeling better and will be back tomorrow. Meanwhile, I've been called back from holiday to stand in for her today, and wait for it – there's been no time to brief me on today's guest. So I know very little about her, except that she is an actress who has come to the studio today to tell us about an amazing book designed to raise funds for a charity she created. If that isn't intriguing, I don't know what is. So let us find out all about this incredible lady and learn why she does what she does. Ladies and gentlemen, please welcome Sita.'

My guest walks onto the set, holding out her hand.

'I'm so pleased to be meeting you, Alice. I've heard so much about you,' she says. 'I hear you're a whizz.'

I'm taken aback. It's meant to be me welcoming her and it feels as if she's conducting the interview. Is this a setup? A tingle of suspicion grips me. I can't begin to even process what she means when she says she's heard so much about me.

Her handshake is firm and gentle.

I gesture her into the chair next to mine.

There is no need for me to relax her because she's completely chilled out, leaning back with her hands resting in her lap. She's wearing a simple round-necked, short-sleeved green dress that falls in soft folds around her knees, and flat-heeled sandals. Her only adornment is a pair of small emerald earrings. Her ink-black hair is cut in a head-hugging pixie style framing enormous brown eyes and a wide, smiling mouth. She's a perfect picture of effortless grace and elegance.

I'm fighting a small wave of panic working its way up from my stomach, so I take a deep breath.

She takes a glass of water from the table between us, hands it to me and takes one for herself.

'Cheers,' she says, clinking her glass against mine. 'Good health'. Her eyes smile over her glass as she raises it to her lips.

My glass clatters as I replace it on the table with a shaking hand, trying to think of something to say.

'Do you like mangos?' she asks.

'Er, yes, I think so. I haven't eaten them often. Why do you ask?'

'Where I come from they're very popular. But do you know what, I've never found a way of eating them without getting sticky juice all over my face and hands. So messy!'

I laugh. 'Whereabouts are you from, Sita?'

'From the north of India, in the beautiful Punjab.'

Suddenly I know. I think I may be sick.

The last time I saw this woman on YouTube she was wearing a crimson saree and covered in gold jewelry, on her way to marry Jai.

How I hate her. A geyser of jealous rage explodes in my chest as I invoke a death spell. I want to watch her die, curled in agony, her face contorted and screaming with pain. Live on TV!

In that nano-second I look into her eyes, and the hate drains out of me. This is not who I am, and she is not my enemy. She is putting me at ease, helping me to conquer my nerves, and I must focus on my job. I immediately understand that Decima is behind this. Somehow she has found out about my love of Jai and she has come up with this plan to destroy me live, in front of our viewers. She'll be watching gleefully as I fall apart. Well, she can sit and wait. That isn't going to happen. I am going to get through this.

Very quickly I send myself a calming charm and relax back into my seat with a smile.

'So, who is Sita? What can you tell us about her?'

She smiles. 'A little Indian girl once dreamed of becoming a film star. She loved to dress up and put on shows for her friends and family. When she was very young her parents humored her, but as she grew up they told her to leave those ideas behind. They wanted her to become a professional, a doctor, a lawyer or a banker. She'd never make a successful career out of acting, they said, it wasn't a suitable occupation for her.

'Despite her parents' disapproval the little girl followed her dream and began to land small parts in films. Then her big break came when she was spotted by one of Pollywood's top producers.'

'Did you say Pollywood?'

'Yes, it's the Punjab's version of Hollywood or Bollywood.'

'OK! Do go on.'

'So the girl was cast in the role of Sita, a Hindu goddess, in a series of seven movies. She played the part so often that she herself became popularly known as Sita, and the name stuck.'

'What a great story. Tell me, has she ever reconciled with her family?'

'Indeed yes. They are very proud of their daughter now.' She smiles.

I nod.

'Now, I understand that you donate all your earnings to charity. Is that correct? Can you tell us about that?'

'I was a very fortunate girl. My parents were rich and I grew up in luxury. An uncle left me several properties when he died, so I was a wealthy woman in my own right. I had more money than I would ever need, and what's the point of that?

'I was exploring the best way of using it, when a woman threw herself under the wheels of my car on the way to the studio one morning.

'She was seriously injured, but we rushed her to hospital and she survived.

'I went to visit her and asked what had driven her to try to kill herself. Meera was a widow in her 40s, but she looked 80. From her, I learned about many thousands of women like her.

'Although the terrible practice of suttee – burning themselves to death on the funeral pyres of their husband – was abolished long ago, life for many widows in India can be a living death. They become outcasts, or unwanted burdens on their families where they are treated as slaves, and that is how they will spend the rest of their lives, beaten, abused, prisoners of poverty and despair.

'Meera showed me her scars and deformed bones resulting from years of ill-treatment by her husband's brother and his family. She'd endured so much misery that she decided she would sooner be dead than continue living like that.

'I took her to live with me until she had recovered, and she stayed on. She calls herself my big sister. Through her, I met many other women in similar circumstances, and that's when I decided to set up a trust to take care of them, where they could receive medical attention, food and shelter, and where they also have opportunities to learn trades to enable them to become independent if they wish. No woman is ever turned away, and victims of domestic violence are also welcomed. There are currently six Meera's Homes throughout India able to provide for over 2,000 women.'

'I'm proud to call Meera my friend and bless the day she came into my life. I've learned so much from her. She opened my eyes into a world I knew nothing about, and I hope that in a small way I am able to make it a better place for some.'

'What a beautiful story, Sita. You are a remarkable lady.'

'No, not at all remarkable. But extraordinarily lucky. And this story is not about me. It's about women who have survived the worst that life can throw at them. Women whose bodies and spirits have been broken but who fight to mend themselves and each other.'

'I believe you have something rather special to tell us about now.'

'Indeed. I'm immensely proud to tell you about a project the ladies began a couple of years ago, and which has now come to fruition.'

She reaches into her purse and hands me a book with a vibrant, glossy cover in purple and turquoise. In the center is a drawing of a smiling Indian woman. Around her the title is picked out in curly gold lettering: '*With Love from Me to You.*' The sub-title reads: 'Inspirations'.

'You're holding the first copy of the English language version of a book that has been put together by the ladies of Meera's Homes. It's a compilation of true stories, recipes, household hints, prayers, poetry and art. The ladies come from all types of backgrounds, from the very wealthy to the poorest of the poor. While many are highly educated, even more are illiterate. Each home formed a group that went around encouraging and cajoling everybody to contribute something. We wanted to show every single woman at Meera's Homes that they have something of value to share.

'The result was spectacular. The first print run of 20,000 sold out in four days. In one month the book sold 140,000 copies. It was originally printed in Hindi, but as word spread, we were asked for an Urdu translation, which volunteers undertook. Since then it has been published in six Asian languages and has sold over 700,000 copies. For every book sold, all the profit goes directly for the benefit of the ladies of Meera's Homes.

'Readers love this book. It makes them laugh, it makes them weep, they love the recipes, the paintings, the words of wisdom, and we believe it's now time for the Western world to enjoy it too. So here in the United States today we are launching the English language version and hoping we can break through the one million worldwide sales mark.

'However, the greatest success of this book is the pride of each and every woman whose name is printed in it, who know that their contributions are being appreciated around the world.'

'On behalf of them all, may I say a huge thank you for allowing me to be here today.'

'It has been my pleasure, Sita. But before you leave, may I ask you how you chose the title of the book?'

She laughs. 'It was suggested by one of the oldest residents, a huge Beatles fan, as indeed are many of the ladies of all ages. The Beatles' music is very popular, and the ladies were unanimous in agreeing that the title and the lyrics perfectly fitted the book.'

'Indeed,' I reply. 'Viewers, you know what to do. Let's see how quickly we can push this book through the one million mark for these ladies. Because they're worth it.'

Sean is signaling that it's time to wind the interview up.

'It has been a very great privilege having you here today, Sita,' I say, and I truly mean it.

'I know our viewers will have been as fascinated as I am by your story, and full of admiration for what you are doing to help others. And I'm sure they will be putting in their orders for the book '

I stand up to say goodbye and hand the book back to her.

'That is your copy,' she says, putting it back in my hands. 'The very first English copy, which I hope you will enjoy as much as we have enjoyed creating it.'

She opens her purse and takes out a small package wrapped in tissue paper.

'I have a small gift for you.'

I peel back the tissue and take out a silken scarf.

'It's the exact same blue as your eyes,' she smiles and walks away as gracefully as she walked in.

I turn to camera with a bright smile to hide the pain tearing my heart to pieces.

'Well, that's it for today folks. I hope you've enjoyed the show. Tomorrow you'll be back in the safe hands of Decima. Goodbye for now, and don't forget to buy this beautiful book.' I hold it up to the camera.

As I walk out of the studio I catch Josh's eye. He

lowers his head and turns away. Of course, it had to be him. He knew. I trusted him, telling him about Jai, and he betrayed me to Decima. Oh Josh.

In the washroom I stuff my fist in my mouth and weep until I'm dry. Then I envisage myself out of here and **Broomstick** home.

Zylch comes and lies beside me on the bed, with one arm over my shoulder, patting me with his soft paws.

'I held it together, Zylch. I didn't break. I'll never break.'

When I wake some time later Zylch is still there, his warm breath on my neck. My right hand is clenched in a fist. I open my fingers and see the sapphire blue silk scarf given to me by the beautiful, gracious, kind woman who is Jai's wife.

I hold it to my face and look in the mirror. It does indeed exactly match the color of my eyes. How did Sita know?

I can't sleep. My mind's a mess. I need to clear my head.

I pick up my phone and call Sean.

33

A trip to the stars

Alice

Sean sounds dozy when he answers the phone, and I see it's after midnight.

'Alice! What's wrong?'

'Oh so sorry, I didn't realize the time. Go back to sleep.'

'No way. You didn't call me for nothing. What is it? In fact, don't answer, I'm on my way.'

He's hung up before I can stop him, and twenty minutes later hurls himself through the door, panting. His hair is tangled up, his T-shirt inside out, and I can smell beer on his breath.

'Alice, Jaysus, tell me you're OK,' he gasps.

'As you can see, Sean, I'm perfectly fine, and I feel terrible for waking you up.'

'But why did you? You didn't call me for nothing. Did you want to celebrate? The press are raving about your interview. The way you knew to sit back and let her speak. It was magical. Did you know that's the first time Sita has ever agreed to appear live on TV? In fact the very first interview she has ever done anywhere? It's a massive win for you Alice. You're the darling of the media, and they're saying on Twitter the book sales are going ballistic. Already over one million!'

He's pink-faced and jiggling with excitement, but his words bounce off me. 'I didn't know anything about the Sita interview. I just felt lonely,' I reply. 'Tired, and flat, and lonely. I thought about your Symphony of the Stars, and wished I could listen to it again.'

'You can do that!' Sean yells. 'I've brought it with me!'

My heart swells, seeing his joy. He is so very sweet and caring. Well, loving, in truth. If only I could return his feelings. I wish I could, but I'm still not ready. But there is something I can do.

'Tell you what. Let's go outside and listen to it together, and watch the stars. Shall we?'

While he sets up the speaker, I make us a warm drink. In the kitchen cupboard, on the top shelf, is the bottle that Astrid gave me to use if Decima became too difficult. **Dorm** is a sedative that creates beautiful hallucinations. I've never used it until tonight, when I squeeze three drops into Sean's cup.

We sit side by side on the swing bench, rocking back and forwards slowly, silently, looking up into the night sky. Zylch jumps up beside me.

As we sip our drinks, Sean starts playing his symphony. I try to pick out the different instruments as they warm up, like an orchestra preparing for a concert. There's the deep-throated double-bass, the trilling flute, the melancholy cello, the passionate saxophone, rippling guitar, all intertwining, weaving around each other, interrupted by booming drums, the twanging of a harp and a high pitched sound I don't recognize.

'What's that one?'

'Sure and isn't it the tin whistle, a nod to me Irish heritage,' he smiles.

As the instruments take their places and work together, the result is hypnotically beautiful.

'Sean, did you really create this all by yourself?' I ask.

He nods slowly. 'It's my heart and soul,' he says. 'My pleasure and pain, my sadness and joy, my hopes and dreams. It's how I imagine it would be to fly up into the sky and touch the stars.'

I feel tears pricking my eyes. As he puts down his empty cup, and leans back, he gives a small sigh and closes his eyes, resting his head on my shoulder. The drops have worked, now it's my turn.

'Hold tight, my sweet friend. We're going on a trip,' I whisper, wrapping my arms around him.

'Be good, Zylch. I'll be back soon.' He blinks at me with golden eyes.

Holding Sean as tight as I can, I chant the ***Weightless*** incantation. Nothing happens immediately, but after a few minutes I feel the floating sensation of rising up, and up, and up.

I focus on the Milky Way, and we begin to climb through the night. The city lights below shrink into pinpoints until they disappear entirely as the stars move closer, and I'm astonished to see that they are all different colors, like jewels.

The higher we float, the more vivid the colors become, and it feels as if we are inside a kaleidoscope. The black velvet of the sky is soft and warm and so very peaceful.

Tonight I feel, for the first time, the full power of my magic.

I release my grip on Sean and link hands with him, as we fly next to each other, and the sound of his beautiful symphony follows us as we dive and spin at will among the stars and planets.

Free from gravity, our bodies react to the music. Swirling and twirling as the tempo accelerates, floating and drifting when the softer notes take over.

Who knew how many stars there are? Not a few here and there, but uncountable numbers, glowing green, orange, yellow, red.

The symphony roars and we are on a roller coaster; as the sound fades we are floating on our backs; the tempo increases again and we are in a whirlpool. One minute somber, the next hopeful; hauntingly sad and teasingly lighthearted. The notes slowly fade away until the only sound is the tin whistle.

During the time we have been there among the stars, I have felt every known emotion from the depths of grief to the heights of joy.

As we drift back down to the garden, my face is wet with tears and my fingers are tightly linked with Sean's. I feel as if I know everything there is to know about him. He's kind, funny, generous, loyal, uncertain, gentle, passionate, patient, brave. He's not Jai, but I realize that it's time for me to let go of the past. I turn his face to mine and softly kiss his lips.

34

Proposal

Alice

The moment I touch his lips, Sean opens his eyes.

'Alice, oh Alice,' he whispers. 'Oh Alice.'

Then he begins to cry. Tears roll down his face and his body jerks with sobs. He burrows his face into my shoulder and clings to me.

I'm a bit taken aback and don't know what to do, so I pat him on his back and say 'There, there,' until he stops and wipes his face on his sleeve.

'What is it?' I ask. 'What's wrong?'

'I'm so happy, Alice.'

He bursts into tears again.

'Um, it doesn't seem like it, Sean. Let's go in.'

I pull him up from the seat and put my arm around him, and lead him into the house.

He slumps down at the kitchen table, with his head in his hands.

'It's all too much. I don't know if I'm hallucinating, dreaming, crazy or what. Alice, tell me I actually flew through the night sky with you, and that you kissed me. Tell me it really happened. Or tell me I was imagining it all, except your kiss. Tell me I wasn't imagining that.'

'Does this help?' I ask, lifting his face and kissing him again.

He stands up and pulls me against his chest, crushing me in his arms and shoving his tongue into my mouth.

I push him away gently.

'Come on,' he pants, 'let's go to bed.'

'Please, Sean. Slow down.'

'Marry me, Alice. You are my whole life. I swear you won't regret it. I will do anything and everything to make you happy.' Say 'Yes'.'

'Yes, Sean. I will marry you.' I pull him into my arms and bury my head in his shoulder. His heart thumps against mine, and we stand like that for a very long time

I feel a great sense of calm washing over me, as if all the tension in my body and spirit has been swept away. I'm at peace with myself and know I've made the right decision. Sean is a good man. I do love him and believe that passion will come once we are married.

'Woo hoo! Alice! Shall we go to Ireland to be wed? Do you want a big wedding, or shall we go and do it quickly, just you and me?'

'I think I like the idea of going to your Emerald Isle. I've heard so much about Ireland. It will be lovely to meet your relatives there and to see where your family comes from. And I'll wear a big white dress and see you dressed up like a real gent. Can we do the whole romantic thing? Engagement, wedding, honeymoon?'

'We can do anything and everything you want. However you want it to be, whatever will make you happy.'

'Mmm,' I sigh. 'I'm going to enjoy us planning this together.'

The elephant in the room, of course, is Decima.

'Shall I stay tonight?' Sean asks.

'You should go home now. It's very late. We have to be at work in a few hours.' I give him a hug and a kiss. 'Let's wait until we're married, shall we? Old-fashioned way?'

A shadow of disappointment flickers over his face, but then he smiles.

'I haven't even gone yet, and already I can't wait to see you,' he laughs.

I wave him away and climb into bed. Zylch is sitting beside the bed, watching me solemnly.

'Am I doing the right thing? Are you happy for me, Zylch?' I ask.

He hops onto the bed and gazes at me.

'I love you too, Alice,' he says. He bows his head down, and I stroke him between his ears until he curls up, purring.

When I wake I'm feeling groggy from little sleep. I make a huge jug of coffee and take it outside to drink while I enjoy the early morning birdsong and warm breeze.

My phone rings. Who on earth would call me so early?

'Alice,' moans Sean. 'How the hell are we going to tell Decima?'

35

Dream come true

Sean

At last, my patience has been rewarded. Alice is finally mine, all mine. My love for her is so deep it hurts, so beautiful it makes me weep. I am filled with so much emotion I feel I could burst into flames and then melt into ice. I can think of nothing else. I want to shout it out to the world.

I always believed that *Symphony of the Stars* would change my life. I put everything of myself into writing it. I thought it would bring me fame and fortune, but it's given me more than that, more than money could buy, more than I could have ever believed would happen.

When Alice called me and we sat together in the dark listening to my music, something magical happened. We were flying, hand in hand, soaring up into space. The night sky sparkled in wild colors, like the flashing lights of a disco, except it was quiet and peaceful. I could have stayed there forever. It felt so real, and then I woke up and Alice was kissing me.

My beautiful, precious angel is mine. She has agreed to marry me.

I will protect her with my life. When I find out who

drugged her to make her the innocent plaything of Scorpio for half an hour, they will pay the price. That is the only explanation for what happened on that terrible morning. She was tricked into behaving in a way she would never behave. I swear it. The memory makes me dizzy with rage and stabs into my heart every time I think of it. How will I ever erase it? Can they hypnotize you to forget traumatic events? It gnaws away at me like a bug in my brain, flashing up images of the scene, with us watching. They all know. That makes it worse. Do they tell other people? Is it common knowledge? Arghh, I have to stop these thoughts. The past is the past, now is now and the future lies ahead. Alice will be my wife, we will make beautiful children. With each other, our lives will be complete. There are tears running down my face, tears of happiness.

I see the moment when at last I take her into my arms and lead her to the bed as we look into each other's eyes. Gently, so very gently laying her down and lying beside her. I reach out with shaking hands to stroke her perfect skin. She turns to me with the look of love in her eyes, and a fire in them that urges me to...

Oh no.

My phone rings. It's Decima.

'Hi Sean. I want you to talk to me,' she whispers.

'Tell me the things you want to do. I'm here, all alone, in front of the mirror. Tell me what I should do. Tell me what you'd do if you were here,' she gasps.

I despise myself for reacting to her, but her call comes

at exactly the right moment.

'Not now. I'm too busy,' I say.

'But I really need you Sean.'

'I'm going to hang up,' I say coldly.

'Don't hang up. I'll do anything you tell me. Anything.'

I keep silent.

'Sean! Please!'

'Put your phone on video,' I whisper.

Her face comes up on the screen. Her mouth is slightly open, the tip of her tongue showing.

'Now this is what I want you to do, and I want you to watch me while you're doing it. You are to do exactly what I tell you. Do you understand?'

'I understand. Tell me what to do now.'

This is the most explosive session we've ever had. I close my eyes for a moment, imagining this is Alice. I avoid looking at Decima's face. It won't be like this with Alice. It will be pure, gentle but passionate. With Decima it's total exquisite lust. There are no boundaries.

It's over quickly, leaving Decima screaming and roaring as she clicks off her phone.

I stand in the shower, weak-kneed and begging Alice to forgive me. How long will I have to wait until she is the one, the only one? How soon can we be married? I think again of our wedding night, and am ready for action once more. I pick up my phone and call Decima.

36

Unreal

Ramon

Somebody pinch me.

Am I dreaming?

It took me a couple of weeks before I had the guts to call the Michiko woman. I was pretty sure it was a wind-up and she'd have forgotten she gave me her card.

I couldn't get through to her; some guard dog PA who said Michiko would call me back. Yeah, sure she will.

And so she does, right when I am 'occupied' with Decima, so Michiko actually leaves a message.

'Call me back.' My heart misses a beat. This is real.

Decima scratches my balls. Hard.

'Oi, concentrate on what you're doing.'

I concentrate as hard as anybody ever concentrated, to finish quickly.

While I'm pulling on my jeans, Decima asks: 'Who was that? Are you two-timing me, lover boy?'

'Of course not. I will never do that Decima. I swear to you on my mother's life, you are my only woman.'

'So you're telling me you don't go sniffing around the blonde, blue-eyed babe who's the latest media sensation?'

'You mean Alice? You're kidding. She's a sweet girl

and I like her, but she doesn't heat my blood. She's a kitten, and I'm a man who wants a tigress, with sharp teeth and claws. A tigress called Decima.'

'Ha, I'll believe you, you gorgeous creature. I'd sulk if I had to share you.'

'Well, you don't. I've told you once, I'm telling you again. Now I gotta go.'

'Ciao,' she says, climbing into her hot tub and waving me away dismissively.

I can't get out of there fast enough, and call Michiko's number. This time she answers.

'You come on Tuesday night, 8.30 pm. I send you the address.'

She hangs up. My message box pings, and sure enough there's a map. It's in California, the other side of the country. I'm going to have to get a flight there and back. My worst nightmare. Flying, fearing a crash. The best part of seven hours trapped on a plane. But it's the only way to get there. This is too big a chance to miss.

I take three days leave, and fly out on Tuesday morning, doped up to the eyeballs with Valium so I sleep most of the way, except when the man next to me jabs me in the ribs because I'm snoring. When we land mid-afternoon I overdose on coffee then book into a hotel and take a very long shower and sleep for a couple of hours.

Not knowing my way around, I take an Uber to Michiko's office address and arrive at 8.25. The security guy points me to a chair and picks up the phone. At 8.29

Michiko walks into the lobby, holds out her hand and asks me to follow her.

Her office is out the back. It's basically a large glass box, four glass walls and a glass ceiling, surrounded with plants and white sand that's been swept into patterns. The only thing on her desk is a phone. She gestures me to an angular chair, that is a whole lot more comfortable than it looks, and takes her seat behind her desk in a similar chair.

The next hour is surreal. She's telling me that I'm going to play a leading role in her new film series. I don't understand if I'm to be a hero or a villain. I think maybe both? Maybe something like James Gordon in Gotham?

Tomorrow we'll be meeting to discuss my contract. Her English is near-perfect so while I think I understand, I'm not totally certain. Also I have a throbbing headache from a combination of Valium, too much coffee and too many thoughts swirling around in my head. I'm a simple Mexican boy who dreamed of becoming a film star but never really believed the dream would come true. Everything is happening too fast,

'But, screen test?' I stammer.

'No need. You are just what I want. And I always have what I want.'

Suddenly her rather scary face breaks into a smile. 'Don't worry, pretty boy, you going to be very fine. Trust Michiko.'

Holy mackerel!

She sends me back to my hotel in a limousine, which returns next morning and delivers me to a swanky building, where a doorman opens the limousine door, calls me 'Sir' and leads me into the lobby, where I am knocked backward to see my agent Maggie waiting.

'What the? How did you get here?'

'Yeah, I know, crazy, eh? When I told you you'd break into films one day I truly believed it, but not like this. This is THE big time. Korean movies are huge, and Michiko Kim is regarded as the hottest thing in the film world. You are going to be a very, very big star, Ramon. Michiko called me yesterday afternoon, and I flew in on the red-eye. That lady does not hang around!' She leans forwards and tweaks a bit of my hair down over my forehead.

'She's so right, you're the perfect Presley look-alike. Quite uncanny.'

An elevator door opens and a leather and chain-draped girl marches up and says: 'You come, please.' We shoot up to the 58th floor, into a room the size of a football stadium, where a group of men in suits are sitting at a conference table on top of which Michiko is stalking around dressed in some kind of military uniform in pink, with matching pink patent leather thigh length boots with 12 inch platform soles, talking Korean and pointing her finger at where I'm standing. Forty people turn and stare at me.

'This is my new star,' Michiko announces. A young guy with rainbow-colored hair down to his waist, wearing a mini-skirt and what looks like a collection of knives and forks dangling from his neck runs forward and makes a bow. The knives and forks jangle. I sort of nod my head in reply and follow him to a waiting chair, accompanied by Maggie.

Michiko talks, the men listen, their heads tilted back so they're looking up at her on the table. As tiny as she is, she wears the authority of a woman who is at the top of her game, knows what she wants, and knows how to get it. The men show her the utmost respect. Most of the talk is over my head. Maggie sits quietly, nodding from time to time. I whisper to her, asking what is happening. She tells me to relax.

'I'll deal with the contract,' she says. 'I'll walk you through everything step by step. You can trust me, and you can trust these people. You are going to be a big Hallyuwood name very soon.'

'Hallyuwood?'

'Korean equivalent of Hollywood, Bollywood or Pollywood.'

Well, why have an agent if you're not going to trust them? There are so many questions I want to ask. Will I have to learn to speak Korean? Will I have to live there? How much will I earn? And also, what the hell am I going to tell Decima?

I fly back to Hawk Bay with Maggie. She's working on a pile of papers. I've taken Valium to get me through the flight, but too much coffee has kept me awake, and by the time we land I've become a total zombie. I grab an Uber to take me home and crash out. Not for long though, because I forget to turn my phone off, and it rings. And rings, and rings until I groan and snatch it up.

Sean's yell almost breaks my eardrums.

'Man! You're never going to believe this,' he hollers. 'Alice flew me into the sky and around the stars, and then she kissed me. We're an item! What do you think?'

Privately I think he's lost the plot, but I say 'That's great Sean, I'm real happy for you. Real happy. I've got a bit of news, too.'

But he's not interested. He burbles on and on about Alice and the phone drops out of my hand as I crash into a deep sleep.

37

The golden goose

Decima

Alice's sweetness and light to my mean bitch is adored by the sponsors, guests, viewers and, yes, me. There's less for me to do and think about. The viewing stats are all good and Dubai have greenlit the *#ToMe* perfume distribution 'with a few changes' agent Gwendolyn says vaguely. The perfume money, serious money, is in my account and there's more, much more, on the way.

Happy days? Well, no.

I'm trying to persuade Dad to call the Mafia killers off Alice and go for one of her parents instead. She *has* to be in vision now. She does all the heavy lifting with the interviews, giving me time to work on the brand. For 'work on the brand' read 'walking Roxy'.

I'm not sure what's going on with Fabienne./ My own link to Dubai has gone from being best friend, in my face 24/7, to major ignore. 'Busy days, Decima. Busy days,' is all she'll say. Dubai will only communicate with me through my agent.

Then I spot quote marks in an email I'm cc'd into. Perfume has become 'perfume'. When I demand clarity, Gwendolyn tells me it will retail in Hawk Bay City area only, 'to test the market'.

'What is US brand ambassador about *that*?' I scream. 'What about the rest of the wellness brand?'

'You've been paid, now zip it,' Gwendolyne says sweetly. 'Don't make waves that aren't there.'

Before the money has time to settle, I'm bombarded day and night with demands from Dad to hand it over. He can smell it I swear. For weeks now he has been behaving like a president at war: in his plane 24/7, landing only for fuel stops. One night I forget to mute my phone.

I open a slit in my eye mask and hit loudspeaker.

'What NOW?'

'Decima! This is urgent. DON'T hang up.'

He's setting my sister onto me.

'You have got to step up, Decima, and twansfer the money NOW.'

'Yeah right in the middle of the night.'

'YES.'

'He's got millions stashed all over the place, Ornella. Now get OUT of my hair. I earned it the hard way. Not floating around the skies ripping people off.'

'But, he hasn't got it, Decima.' Her breathing is strange, almost gasping. 'You've seen the financial pwess. I don't believe you haven't. And, and, and,' she pauses for an extra-long gasp. 'That's the least of his pwoblems, our pwoblems. By our I mean you, too, Decima. We're all in this together.'

'Haha, only when it suits you.'

'No for weal. That botched killing of the Bwent Flats

daughter.'

'My PA you mean.'

'Whatever. They want double the wate to do it again. Dad's refwusing to pay for the first one. But the twuth is the banks are foreclosing all over the place, now he weally can't pay *anything*. We're all in danger.'

'It's the middle of the NIGHT here Ornella. I have a SHOW tomorrow.'

'You do?'

'What does THAT mean?'

'I see your little pwotegee is getting on weally super well. Doing all your work for you.'

This may be true but I don't like hearing it. 'Sister, get LOST.' I smash my phone down on the side table. It rings again.

'We're gwounded Decima!' she shrieks.

'Oh, on the ground like mere mortals, how unfortunate for you.'

'They punctured the tires on the plane, Decima. We almost cwashed on take-off. It was only thanks to Towin's skill that we didn't die then, and then we had to cwash land. They're twying to kill us all.'

'Where are you?'

'In the Qantas hanger.'

'*What?* Put Dad on.'

'I can't. He's in the gents.'

'What's he doing there?'

'Hiding of course. Won't come out until we're weady to fly again.'

'Are you in *Australia*?'

'Don't be stupid. Of course we're not in Austwalia. How would we get *there*?'

'Er. *Fly*? So where are you?'

'To be honest I'm not quite sure.'

'Oh yeah.'

'But that's the twuth Decima. And anyway, if I did know it's better not to say.'

'But you said?'

'Oof whoopsie so I did.'

She's so thick this girl. I'm not sure how much of this Mafia turning against us story to believe. Dad is a paranoid nut at the best of times.

'Please Decima. Twansfer the cash. We need to get back to the safety of the skies.'

Even for Ornella, this sounds weird. Like she's been transported into an old black and white war movie.

'Hang on a moment. Are they *holding* you there?'

'I didn't say that, I didn't say that, OUCH OOFFF.'

Another long silence is followed by a squeal, a crash, a groan.

'Decima HELP US! PLEASE HELP US.'

THUMP.

I roll my eyes to the ceiling. More sound effects. 100 per cent fake. The lengths these two will go to. But it goes on. And on. Then I hear Dad's voice bleating 'stop, stop' over and over. A high, shrill death scream is followed by silence. I swallow hard.

'Ornella?'

Nothing.

'Ornella, answer me this minute.'

Silence.

Guilt.

I'm not a fan of my family. But hearing their murder on my phone? I could do without it. I think about them gone, wiped off the face of the earth. It's tempting but the next thought isn't. I sit bolt upright. If the hitmen don't get their money, I'll be next.

'Listen, now listen to me, Ornella. Ornella are you there?'

I hold my breath for what seems like forever. I hear a squeak.

'I'm cutting the line off now because I'm going to log into my bank to transfer the money now. OK. Tell them I'm transferring ALL the money. TELL THEM.'

It pains me to say it out loud but say it I must, 'Tell him to call them off Alice. The show needs her. There's plenty more money where that came from as long as we don't mess the format.'

There. I've said it out loud. My admiration for my protégée doesn't have to be faked anymore. As long as one of us doesn't get killed, CGO TV will be one big happy lovefest.

My hands are shaking. I get into my bank account and find it hard to remember the numbers and passwords. How weird is it that they know? That those thugs know I've had this massive payment come through? How much are they tracing us all? How many tabs have they got on us? I look at my phone with new suspicion. Suddenly everything feels very disturbing indeed. It really is me who needs 24-hour protection now. Not Alice.

38

Attack

Decima

'She's not for sale.'

'I don't think you heard me. I said name your price.'

'Look Decima…'

'Look *Pam*. This is a life and death situation. I need protection.'

Silence.

I'm cross with myself now. I didn't mean to give that away. I barely know this woman. I must keep my cool. Deep breaths. Calm down. Calm calm calm.

'I had a burglar.'

'At Eagle Heights? Isn't it gated?'

'He didn't get in, but he could have so easily…'

I peter out. She isn't buying it.

'Look, Decima, I know how you feel about Roxy but…'

'Ten thousand.'

'She's a special girl.'

'Twenty thousand.'

'I'll say it slow now. Roxy. is. not. for. sale. There are other dogs.'

'But there aren't, that's the…' My voice cracks. The

truth hits me full-on and I crumble. Every time I recover, images of Roxy fill my mind and I'm off again.

'Give me a moment here,' I garble. 'Don't hang up, please, pl…'

'Listen, I'll find you one, OK? I'll find you a dog.'

One? *One?* She doesn't get it does she.

'Come to me at 6 tomorrow,' she says brusquely.

'After the show, 6pm, I'll be there.'

'No, morning.'

'Morning?'

'Dog walking group,' she snaps. 'Some folk have real jobs to go to.' The line goes dead.

6am? I have to go. I need my Roxy time. My unique, irreplaceable Roxy. What other dog would shake herself all over after a walk and jump right on top of her water bowl, rolling in it before leaping on me, soaking me too? No other dog would know to do that. It's our ritual.

I cancel the boys and take an early night, clambering out of bed again almost before I'm in it. It feels like the middle of the night. Haven't these dog walking idiots heard of Flexi time? I wrap up warm and tiptoe out, forgetting Trevor isn't fast asleep on his shower rail any more. I take the old coast road north towards the mountains. Dawn comes with a low glow. The sea, still as ice, reflects the pewter and pearl sky. The streaks of light get more intense by the minute. I pull over and take some shots.

I send the best image to my Instagram team. I'm surprised when Heather messages back immediately but I shouldn't be. These dudes are at my disposal 24/7. She's a child, this girl, part of my glam team choreographing my every move. Since the perfume contract, I have these remote assistants coming out of my ears. At least they haven't been stood down yet. That could come at any moment, I sense.

But you're not there?

Of course I'm here.

Er, I can't see you, Decima. You're not IN THE SHOT! It's a VIEW!

I'll have to check with Head Office about that.

Oh come off it.

So cool! Do a quick selfie, Decima, and we'll make an awesome post. Well done.

Patronizing or what?

I pull down the car vanity mirror. My hair is all over the place, my eyes are slits. I'm in old sludge green trackies and a big loose jumper ready for Roxy to rub her wet happy body all over me. My new oversized Marni fake fur coat in black/brown and cream, Roxy's colors, and over-the-knee black leather boots are the only giveaways that I'm a celebrity.

Forget it. I drive on. Who knew success was so complicated?

Take that girl Heather. Jumping to the PR rules. To the sponsors' demands against my own. My life is fast becoming nothing to do with me. I'm ruled by PR. Or is it the Mafia?

It's terrifying.

I'll get the urgency of my need for Roxy across to Pam somehow. She'll have to accept it.

I'm kind of missing the days when the show was Alice and me, Alice doing whatever I asked. Now she's got Tanya the Temp working for her full time, who knows what ideas above her station are whirring around those clever little brain cells of hers.

I hear my life coach's voice in my head. 'Ditch the negatives, Decima. If the little voice in your head whines, tell it to go away and get yourself back in the moment. Slow right down and feel your breath. Watch it hit those little hairs inside your nostrils. In. Out. Be in the moment. Feel that life force surging through you.'

Rubbish. But sometimes rubbish works. I put my foot down and, with a deep growl, the Porsche takes off. The G force flattens me back into my seat.

Freedom. My confidence restored.

Who knew this ungodly hour would be so beautiful? The road is empty, all mine and I'm driving towards Roxy. Irreplaceable Roxy.

Screw Heather and *the Team*. Dressing down is the best thing. Forget Instagram. Positive energy works. I'll convince Pam in person. She can get another dog. I'll keep raising my bid to life-changing levels. It'll only go to Dad otherwise anyway.

Pam lives in Mountain View. It's a trashy trailer park area right before the city gives out altogether to open grassland and deep, black lakes leading to mountain foothills. The views are something else but there's not a proper store for miles around here. How do they survive?

A group of women are standing around on Pam's porch. Four of them, three in sludgy raincoats with empty rucksacks sagging off their backs, one in a knitted pink cardigan that hangs below her raincoat to her knees. They're in a circle, chatting amongst themselves, turning to look at me and looking back to each other again. Judging me before they know me.

I hate them already.

I wish I hadn't come. Will I have to *talk* to them? I don't do small talk. I don't do friends. I don't want questions either. I'll escape them somehow and get my one-to-one with Roxy. I hear a familiar yelp. My heart leaps. Roxy has spotted me and is pulling Pam towards my car like she's on a tow rope. As soon as I open the door, her front paws are on my lap. I forget everything and bury my face in her fresh Roxy-scented fur, listening to her rhythmic, happy pant.

'Come on then, Roxy, let's go.'

I spring out of the car and hold my hand out for her lead. But Pam steps back, hauling Roxy in. Roxy resists and pulls against her, desperate to get to me. See that Pam? See that bond? I want to say, but hold my tongue. Actions speak louder.

The group shuffle over. A pale little woman in a brown waterproof with a plump little brown pug with a white face introduces Mischief. A tall, pale, skinny woman with cropped black hair and startling penciled-on eyebrows introduces a fluffball of ginger as Basil. There are three other dogs, a beagle called Daisy, a scruffy terrier thing and a slick little black whippet whose name I didn't catch. These women don't seem to have names of their own. No bother. The less I know about them the better.

I hold my hand out for Roxy's lead but instead, I'm given a different dog.

'Meet Twinkle,' says Pam.

I glare down at the little rat looking up at me, wagging its backside like it was a tail. I open my mouth to protest but they're already off, striding across the trail and chatting amongst themselves.

Twinkle pulls on her lead trying to catch up. I jerk her back. Ignoring them as they are all ignoring me suits me fine. Except, I can barely admit it, Roxy. She's trotting on ahead, looking up to check on Pam every now and then, adoringly, in the exact same way she does me. My eyes bore into the back of Pam. I am so angry.

She keeps stopping and turning around. Every time she does so, the mess of mank at my feet leaps forward, jerking my arm.

When I've caught up, they set off again in their cozy huddle and I linger behind again. I cannot be a part of these sad discussions about compostable poo bags, trash TV and the recipe for kale, whatever that is. These are not my people. Not one of them has shown any sign of recognizing me.

Pam drops back, Roxy is thrilled to see me all over again. Surely she sees this bond? How can she not?

'Have you thought any more about my offer?' I ask,

ruffling Roxy's neck.

'Yes,' she pauses, searching for words. 'Look…'

The sun goes behind a cloud and a cool wind picks up.

'I need her,' I say, pathetically, sensing I'm not going to like hearing what comes next.

'My work shifts have changed. I've taken Roxy off the borrower's register. It's already done.'

I go cold.

'I'm pleased you're going to get a dog of your own,' she continues formally, 'and I'll be happy to help you.' And with that, she strides off to catch up with the others. Roxy trots next to her without looking back at me even once. I stay rooted to the spot in shock. 'You won't regret it,' she calls back.

Within seconds it's raining. Lightly at first but then the heavens open. It's sheeting it. They all stop to put their hoods up. Holding my fur close around me, I have no option but to catch up with them.

Pink cardigan woman fishes in her rucksack.

'Here, put this on,' she unfolds a small pink rectangle.

I take it and reluctantly pull the pac-a-mac over my coat. Mercifully the hood covers my face. If any paps are around, they're not getting a thing out of this.

'Stick together now.' They're off again all in a huddle.

'Shouldn't we be turning back?' I call.

'Catch up now,' Pam says, ignoring me.

So I ignore her and keep my distance. They all stop, turn, and wait for me.

'Why do you think we go out in groups, Decima?' says

Pam.

'This ain't Mason's Park girl. There's no cameras around these parts,' says pink cardigan woman who I think is called Babs.

'Don't be so sure. The paps get everywhere.'

'Eh?' She gives me a blank look.

'*Security* cameras,' says Pam.

'There's no people either,' I point out. 'Except us.'

'Don't be so sure. Not in these parts.'

They set off again, I stubbornly keep my distance.

I should have listened.

Before I know what's happening, Twinkle is squealing like a pig in a slaughterhouse. They all rush back. Roxy is up on her hind legs barking furiously. A great brute of a dog, all muscle and jaw, has appeared from nowhere, grabbed Twinkle by her neck and is now shaking her like a toy.

A boy in filthy falling-down jeans appears. I immediately clock the expensive New York brand.

'Call it off, call it off,' Pam shrieks.

But, with his thumbs hooked in his front pockets, revealing even more of his khaki Klein underpants, and a twisted smirk of satisfaction on his face, the piece of trash stands back and watches like he's at some kind of boxing match. This sends me apoplectic. I let go of Twinkle's lead and I go for him. I land a slap and a punch in his face and raise a muddy boot to kick him where it hurts when there's a sharp pull at my leg. The monster has dropped Twinkle and its great jaws are now latched onto me.

It pulls and rips the leather of my boot and gets to my shin, shaking my leg like a shark. I am so enraged I don't feel a thing. I make a dive to the ground for Twinkle and fold her into my arms, hopping and kicking at the brute all the while. For a split second it freezes before looking up in slow motion to fix its yellow eyes on Twinkle. It lets go of my leg and leaps up, over and over, its great jaw snapping at Twinkle, shivering in my arms. The women are all screaming, the dogs are all barking. The little pug with the white face is giving its all snapping at the brute's feet. The pug lands a bite. This does it. The boy finally grabs the monster's collar, giving Mischief a kick and me a hefty shove as he does so. I stagger and stumble a few steps, gripping Twinkle for all I'm worth.

He swaggers off, killer dog trotting at his heels. I examine the teeth marks on my leg. I'm shivering. My boots are ruined. The women surround us, clucking and fretting, asking Twinkle if she's all right. Examining Mischief for damage. No one seems to care about me. Determined not to cry, I swallow hard. Pink cardigan woman Babs, who has been filming it all, turns her phone onto me. I haven't the strength to stop her.

They're all saying they've never seen him before. It's never happened before. Muggings, yes, all the time. Attacks, never.

That is no local roughneck, I want to tell them. That's why.

This is it. It's happening.

39

Issues

Cory

I let Decima's umpteenth call go to voicemail, put on k d lang, turn her off again, pour a large whiskey on the rocks, and go out to the yard.

It's a night for ghosts all right. Everything I ran away from is coming back to haunt me.

Decima is hopping mad, screaming at me for bringing Roxy into her life, only for her to be taken away again, as if it's my fault. You might find it strange, but I usually enjoy Decima's outbursts. It's a test. I don't let myself react, which brings in presence. When her anger is absorbed into me, there's nowhere else for it to go and she simmers right down. If we're together and not on the phone, she'll usually end up laughing.

But lately I've taken to avoiding her whenever possible. I've got a whole lot of issues happening myself right now. I wish I could share them, but I've been hiding my true identity from everybody for so long, revealing my truth would be a massive extra burden on me right now.

What does 'coma' mean exactly? People recover from them don't they? My brother Jonty has had a terrible accident on the polo field. If he dies, all hell will break loose. The next thing will be executors, lawyers, his scheming fiancée Erica, tax duties, land duties, wills, fights about wills and the whole jolly shamoodle that comes with any death of the landed gentry.

I have such mixed emotions and so many questions.

Why haven't I been contacted as next of kin? Does it mean that Erica has got him to the altar already?

I only discovered it on Twitter via a direct message from Simon, the landlord of The Sportsman, our old local. He passed on the news by kindly tagging me into a tweet from a disgruntled tenant who hopes he'll die. I google coma once more, then close my eyes and listen to the night, searching for the truth behind my mixed emotions of fear, panic and, I must confess, underlying joy.

Do I go back home to see my only brother, my only kith and kin, before he's gone forever? Do I want to see my only relative still alive on this earth? No, no and no.

If only it were that simple. My brain hurts. What an idiot, what a fool he is. Was? Is? What an idiot I've been. I have to go back to the UK. Deep down I know it.

We parted on good enough terms, as much as you can with a functioning alcoholic. There could only be one Lord Cholmondeley and he was welcome to the title and the tenants and all that went with them. The castle, the farms, the trout stream, the forest.

I'm the younger twin by three minutes, the lordship was never going to be mine. Thank goodness. But if he dies... A quick call to The Sportsman, Jonty's second home, more like his first home, has only brought more uncertainty. The rumor is that she's pregnant. If they have married, and then, if a boy is born, my family's line, after 800 years, would transfer out of my hands. The thing is, I don't know how I feel about that. Of course, I'm rising up in indignation. But it's complicated.

When I left, I didn't give a thought to Jonty getting married. He was far too addicted to online dating, innocents and professionals alike. Any female who was more impressed with his four-poster bed than repulsed by his stinking breath would do for a night before he was on with the next. I knew he'd never settle and nobody could be close to him for long. But then Erica came along. The original on-off girlfriend/hooker has made it her life's work to get him.

I call Decima. She's a fighter. Her spirit gives me energy. But I can't say anything. We talk for a long time about one subject only. Dogs. Dogs, dogs, dogs. She has exciting news and needs a lift. It takes my mind off things at least and I'm glad I decided not to mention it. When people find out that you're not as normal as most of the world, they go weird on you. Everything becomes fake and charade-like. Decima and I are in a good place, I don't want to ruin it. No, there's only one person I can trust. Who won't freak out completely. I hope.

40

The price of fame

Decima

I can't stop smiling. I'm in the back of Cory's car with my two fur babies feeling like a kid at Christmas. The roof is down, it's raining again, and I'm holding Twinkle tight, close to my heart. Barney's two great paws are on my lap, his chocolate eyes gazing into mine, his velvety ears flapping in the wind.

'Alright Barney, I love you too, yes I do, yes I do-do-doooo.'

He stops panting and gives my nose the smallest, most delicate, lick.

I well up. I need this. I need this so much. This is real love. Not somebody doing what they're paid to do, not somebody having to pretend, not somebody waiting to be told how wonderful they are. This is the real thing. Love that gives, expecting nothing in return.

Turns out, Roxy isn't the only dog in the world. Who knew? After paying $30,000 for Twinkle's life-saving surgery, and with a little prodding from Pam, I took her on. Twinkle didn't come alone. She and Barney, another ugly reject, have been friends forever at the rescue home.

Cory parks up. The dogs go mad with excitement.

'No comments, now,' I say mock-sternly, taking the

tiny pack of pink pac-a-mac from my bag. With Cory laughing at me, I unfold & pull it on, giving a few exaggerated poses for him. Giggling together, we set off in the rain. Now I feel overdressed, Cory doesn't cover his head with anything.

He wasn't, though, laughing at me, he was laughing with me. It's a good feeling. It doesn't matter!

'You don't mind getting wet, Cory?'

'Some people like to feel the rain. Others just get wet.'

'Cool!'

'Bob Marley.'

'You're still the cool one here.'

We watch Twinkle and Barney sniffing about in the mist up ahead. Little feathery flutters rise from my heart to my throat. I'm choked with happiness and have to hold back the tears. I can't believe that someone has done this for me. That *Cory* has done this for me. Out of the goodness of his heart. Is this what that weird 'love' feeling is like? He *is* the best company. Like a therapist, he doesn't talk but waits for me to let it all out.

We sit on a rock close to the waves. I confide my latest Dad problems. Things I've never told him before. I look out to sea and take a snapshot outside of the two of us with our dogs. We could be any couple, anywhere.

I tuck my hand between his legs. He doesn't respond. I take it away again.

'You know what?' I confess into the silence. 'I dread going on air now. I wish Alice could take over and I could disappear somewhere.'

'You're catastrophizing.'

'I mean it. What I'd love right now is a ranch in Santa Antonio Hill Country. I could sit it out with my animals and all of you boys until CGO TV is toast and Dad is in jail…'

'That won't happen.'

'For many reasons,' I agree. Hoping he doesn't mean the boys' involvement in my fantasy future life.

'Gauld will probably come out of this crisis fatter and richer than before. That's how big business works.'

'How they get their thrills. True. I dread going on air though.'

'It's working well, the chemistry between you and Alice,' he pauses. 'It's magnetic. Mysterious even. You're keeping the audience guessing. They love that.'

'What do you mean?'

'Are you rivals? Is she another of your lovers? Your mentee? Your student? Your teacher!'

'Now hang on a minute!' I thump him. Nothing, not even that comment can alter my good mood.

'And she's… She's…'

He shakes his head, he knows he's said too much. Worship is in his eyes and his voice.

'I'm not in control, Cory, that's the truth of it. Call me superstitious but either the Tower is haunted or Lorelei really is a witch.'

Cory puts an arm around me and squeezes me tight. 'Let's go.'

On our way back to the car, I unload my suspicions

about Lorelei. We walk arm in arm, the dogs running ahead. Barney turns every now and then to check we're still following. Like Roxy used to do. My heart lifts. It doesn't last.

What if her much-hyped ghost interview next week truly works? What if Josh *didn't* fake the door? What if that was all real witchcraft as well. That lawsuit is still hanging around. Who am I to know after all? Cory's calm presence lifts me back into the moment.

'The taste of normality. It feeds my soul,' I say. 'I wish I could give all this fame nonsense up.'

'You might be doing that the way it's going.'

'You know what? I won't really care.'

'I was joking.'

'It's no joke, Cory, it's happening.'

'Then we'll move on. To a new chapter somewhere. That's how life works out. Nothing stays the same.'

'All of us in San Antonio, surrounded by nature, living the simple life.'

'Maybe.'

'What does maybe mean?'

'Sean is getting his feet cozy under Alice's table. They'll marry at some point, don't you think? You've got to see it.'

I barely react. It's not news. I don't pay Sean much attention these days. But that reminds me of something. 'Have you looked closely at his privates lately?'

Cory laughs. 'What? Er, no! Wait, you mean his ring, that's old news, surely?'

'No. Not that. Tonight, later, have a look.'
'What am I looking for?'
'He's got something *written* there.'
'What?'
'Underneath. Take a look.'
We reach the car. He didn't sound surprised at all.
He knew.
I can't trust anybody.

41

The right thing to do

Cory

Through the gently swirling smoke of Jerry's Bar, I see Sean slumped at the bar.

He unprops his chin and twists slowly on his stool. 'What are you doing here?'

'I'm back from walking the dogs. Thought I'd stop by.'

He stares at me, long and hard.

'What for? You'll be seeing me later.'

'I can give you a ride over,' I say over-brightly.

'Lying scheming bitch.'

'Come on, she's mellowing man.'

'Mellowing?' he jerks bolt upright.

The gentle hum of conversation around the bar stops dead. All eyes flick towards us. 'Letting Alice do all the work while she takes the money? It's criminal! I'm starting to hate her so bad. I'll kill her one day so I will.'

The barman polishes a single glass over and over in deep concentration. Even the smoke seems to freeze.

'Keep your voice down,' I whisper, glancing over my shoulder, 'What I mean is, she's turning to mush. Those dogs are a good thing for her.'

'That's why you're here, is it?'

I look back over my shoulder.

Realizing plain speaking is the best option, I take a deep breath.

'She's seen it,' I whisper.

'Seen what?' he screams. 'The light? Ha-le-luuu-lya for the bitch.'

Blast it, I hoped he knew.

'Shush now and listen.'

'If you'd stop talking in riddles?'

'She's not bothered.'

'Not bothered about *what*?'

'Sssh!'

'What?' he hisses through clenched teeth.

'Your tat, Sean, she's seen it.'

He flushes bright red.

'How?' he yells and stops. 'How,' he whispers, 'could she?'

'Come on, we've had enough sessions.'

'You're talking out of your backside, man. I'd know if she had. I never let her eyes down anywhere near there…' his voice peters out like he's remembered something.

'Oh? Hang on. What did she say then?'

'Not a lot. Mentioned it in passing. Here's the thing: I think you've got the green card, man. All she cares about these days are those dogs.'

'And you.'

'We're getting on well, to be honest, and I can handle it. It's my turn. It takes the weight off you guys.'

He nods and takes a long sip of his beer.

'She likes you. Who doesn't.'

'She trusts me. She's listening to me.'

'Instead of her own voice for once? That's something, I suppose,' he softens.

'I put in the word for you and Alice.'

'You *what?*'

'She's cool man. All I'm here to say is she may call you out on the tat tonight but it'll be more for show than any real anger. Don't get too worked up about it, don't rise to it, OK? Now's your big chance. Go all out for Alice, man. She's yours, we can all see it. Even Decima.'

'Even Decima eh?' he gives a sage nod and looks down at his beer.

I'm as surprised as he is. I'd have thought seeing Alice's name spelled out so clearly on that part of Sean's body Decima sees as her own territory would have sent her ballistic. Though maybe that's because tattoos can only stay legible on the unaroused.

'How do I make Alice mine, though?'

'It'll come good for you both in time, Sean. Keep that thought, that truth in your heart.'

'Keep my cool when Decima attacks me later, that's what you're telling me?'

I nod.

'You're warning me.'

'Let's go, I'll give you a ride over.'

With the sigh of a man going to the slaughter, he tucks his skateboard under his arm and shuffles after me.

We drive over in silence. I'm waiting for news from

the UK. Everything has gone quiet for a few days.

It's all very fine with me telling Sean not to overthink it, but that's precisely what I'm doing now.

I feel crushed. The pain is raw but it's the right path for them both. For us all.

I've been in love before. I'll come out stronger. Eventually.

<h1 style="text-align:center">42</h1>

<h1 style="text-align:center">Good bitch bad bitch</h1>

Decima

That scruffy pink cardigan woman Babs who filmed me rescuing Twinkle has only uploaded it.

Who knew? Dogs, it turns out, are even bigger in the TwitTok Insta-verse than witches. The #DogsofTwitter community is going nuts with the RTs. I do the quick double flick to #DogsofInsta and #Dogtok there I am. There *we* are.

Me. Me, me, me and Twinkle. Loved by all.

'Twinkle, look at this!' I hold my phone down to her nose. 'I'm *a badass heroine…* how about that?'

I'm sucking in my newfound status as a 100 percent good person and all-round animal SAINT hero when Fabienne calls. FUMING

'Hello stranger.'.

'What's going on?'

'What's what going on?'

'I got a call from WNER in New York they want you on Jon Slasher's Talk Show next week.'

'Jon *Slasher*! Wow.'

Her voice hardens. 'No no no, Decima. That isn't going to happen.'

'What's NO about it, Fabienne?'

'They want you on to talk about the dog rescue.'

'What's wrong with that?'

'What's *wrong*? You're the bitch! Not a hero! We spend millions bigging up the badass in you and you have destroyed all our hard work. What do you look like in that clip anyhow? What are you *wearing*?'

'A pink pac-a-mac,' I can't help smiling to myself. 'They're so cool over in Paris right now, I thought you'd know?'

'You look like a piece of thrift store tat that's what. And who are those soggy trailer trash *women* with you? This is *not* the image…'

'Oh get lost.'

Snap.

I am LIKING this good me. And I want to milk it. It takes the mind off the death threats.

I cancel Josh's bath night, get up extra early and head over to Pam's. I cannot wait to bask in the glory from all my new best friends.

They all love me now. And you know what? I love them too. That's all that matters. That is reality right there. My reality. My sanity. It turns out we have more in common than dogs. They have a book club. *My* kind of books. I've been invited over for wine, guac and tacos to discuss the latest Steffanie Holmes.

Back home, after a long, leisurely lunch, I finally switch my phone back on. It erupts with every kind of Fabienne message, from cajoling to threatening, on repeat.

I run a cold shower and call her when I'm ready.

She's so surprised and angry she's choking on her words, can barely speak.

'I'm not all bitch Fabienne. Twinkle and Barney knew that. They fished something out of me. I'm going on the Jon Slasher show to talk about saving Twinkle. I'll make a stash of money for the dog rescue charity and you can't stop me.'

Tonight Lorelei drops her big ghost interview & the boys are coming over to watch her dig her own grave. I'm beating her already. Her failure tonight and my glorification on The Jon Slasher Show will be the tip-tapping in of the last nail on her coffin.

She's been flooding everybody's feeds with her trailers. She's so desperate, Fabienne's Twitter team hasn't even bothered to counter it with put-downs, she's doing it all to herself.

43

ICE?

Decima

Cory and Sean pitch up together. Cory is very attentive at first, the perfect English manners as always, but he slips off to make a phone call, leaving Sean and I alone. Sean avoids all eye contact. He opens his mouth to talk but I shush him down. I can't be bothered with him, I truly can't. We sit in silence as I try to listen in on what Cory is saying, something serious about castles and lawyers. *What?* Is he leaving too? To where? Butlering?

When Josh and Ramon arrive Ramon swaggers in, chest thrust forward; he struts about the place like he owns it. The dogs jump excitedly at his feet.

He's wearing a new outfit. Tight black jeans and a jean jacket covered with Bad Boy signs, fox badges, devil badges, stars and stripes, and a silver London brooch.

'Cool or what?' Hips thrust to one side, he poses before me, caressing an old war medal dangling from his collar.

'So your audition came through?'

'And some, Decima. And some.' He wafts off to the bathroom and makes a dramatic reappearance, his Elvis quiff freshly preened. Glamour and success pulse out of him. He's becoming insufferable.

'Be careful what you wish for, Ramon,' I say and leave for the bathroom.

I return naked. Josh and Ramon go for me but I push them away. 'Not in front of the dogs. Strip off all of you,' I fix my eyes on Sean, 'and we'll go outside.'

I sit in the hot tub, listening to the ocean, waiting for my beautiful boys to appear, all ready for me. I take a memory snapshot of the moment. It looks like I'll be losing Ramon soon. Sean's already gone and good riddance. Cory's up to something. Before long it'll be me and Josh and Sunday bath nights and that'll be it.

Josh is the only one not acting strange this evening. Which in itself makes me suspicious. What's he hiding? Ramon can't stop preening. Sean looks terrified. I know Cory's told him. I know he knows I know Cory's told him. He understands exactly what this strip show is all about.

Sean is the last to appear. He takes forever to close the door behind him against the dogs and he's disobeyed my orders. Delaying the showdown.

I am glaring pointedly at his oversized yellow boxer shorts when my phone pings.

What timing. But I can't not look. We're all waiting for Lorelei's big announcement.

'It's out,' I say. 'The celebrity ghost has been named.'

'Who is it?'

'John Lennon.'

Josh shakes his head, 'Tricky.'

'That'll be bad,' says Sean. Cory agrees. Ramon for

some reason thinks she could pull it off. Josh isn't saying one way or the other.

'Whatever happens,' I say, 'the fight between me and Lorelei is over OK. Who got the big contract? Me. Who got the Insta blue tick without paying for it? Who's got a Reddit fan thread speculating on how rich I am?'

What nobody knows is that every cent is going straight across to Dad. Nobody wants to know the reality behind fame, including me. I'm milking this life for what it's worth. Which is kind of heightened when death is tapping at your door, let me tell you.

'Hey Sean,' I climb out of the hot tub. 'I've been googling tats. It seems you can only read what's written when you're not too excited. I see you're nice and relaxed there. Let's have a closer look shall we.'

'There's nothing to see, Decima, only, like, a few marks.'

'Oh really!' I pull his boxers down with one great thrust. With the tip of a fingernail, I lift his *little man*, as he calls it, gently up to see what's beneath.

'I was drunk,' he says looking at the sky. 'It's nothing.'

'But what does it mean?'

'What do you think it means?'

'That you crave gin and tonics, I don't understand?'

Now it's his turn to look confused. They all look at each other. Cory comes over and joins me in front of Sean.

'ICE,' he reads.

'ICE. What does it mean, Sean? ICE?'

Sean wriggles away and covers himself. 'In Case of Emergency, Decima. It's a joke. A kind of viral Irish joke to have it put down there.'

I look around at my naked boys for their reaction. Their minds are elsewhere.

Ignoring the whines of my dogs I give the signal. Josh and Cory step forward. A sudden breeze comes off the ocean, ruffling my hair. For a second, I feel like a goddess, beautiful and desired. The dogs scratch at the balcony doors. The only emotion I feel is for the sounds of those little yelps and paw scratches on the glass doors.

'This isn't going anywhere.' I wriggle out of their clutches. 'Get out, all of you. Go home. *Now.*'

Cory thinks it's a game at first. He looks so crestfallen when he realizes I mean it that, as he's leaving, without thinking, I pull him back and kiss him on the lips.

I lie down on my couch to watch Lorelei with my happy, loving furbabies sprawled beside me. If she pulls it off, I've got all the support and comfort I need right here. But that kiss? Tongue found tongue. It wasn't at all gross. Where did that come from?

44

Go for it

Cory

I drive in silence. I'm more agitated and confused than Sean right now. I was truly ready for her and really could have done with some al fresco distraction. But what was that kiss about? Decima never kisses anybody. It's far too intimate for her. And for me. But that did happen.

'You OK, man?' Sean says, not looking up from his phone.

'Sure,' I lie.

'Thanks for the warning there, man. She's a mean bitch. It could have gone a lot worse.'

I try and keep my equilibrium. 'You dodged a bullet there Sean. Now all your tattoo fears are over.'

'You're joking man. What do I do with ICE? ICE! What'll Alice think when she sees *that*? The A and the L are 100% there, only a tad smaller. Do you know, it's a fine art, Cory, writing sideways on a man's little man.'

Despite my mood, a laugh escapes me. 'You're lucky she wasn't wearing her glasses.'

'It's not funny, man.'

'It could be worse, what if it were LICE?'

'Oh no no no. It could be couldn't it? In the right light.

In the wrong light. Oh no, she'd run a mile!'

'You can get it fixed can't you?'

'Sure I can. There's no hurry anyways. We're saving ourselves.'

'Cool man, you're both ready for it. You should get your proposal in. Make it official.' And put the rest of us out of our misery I don't add.

As it is, I now have to listen and pretend not to mind. It's only a matter of time, he tells me. They're getting on like they're one and the same soul. I know! I want to say. That's Alice! I feel the same when I'm with her! But then he goes on to describe in incredible detail the heights of ecstasy she's taking him to. Lifting him up high and then higher, into the stars.

'*Without* sex,' he adds. 'We haven't gone anywhere near that yet. It's all pure, sweet love.'

'That sounds incredible, man. What a mind you've got.' Envy is eating me. I feel wretched and a fake.

'No, man. You don't understand. It happened. We flew. It truly happened.'

I nod.

'For real, man. I don't expect you to believe me, you weren't with Alice like I was. It *happened*. We *flew*. Hey, it's started.' Mercifully, he stops talking. The tweets about the ghost interview are coming in and he scrolls through his feed, leaving me with my thoughts.

My conversation with Decima replays in my mind. *There's witchy things going on. That's all I know.* All this time, it was never Lorelei, it was Alice.

He gives me a running commentary of the tweets. It's ridiculous and lashback is already well under way.

'It's sound only. There's no John Lennon in vision, no door, nothing more than old interview tracks stuck together.'

'So what's on YouTube?'

'A split screen. Photos of Lorelei and Lennon.'

'That really is a cop-out.'

'Decima will be dancing around, she really has won that battle.'

I invite him back to mine to chill and watch the rest of Lorelei's interview over a few beers.

Sean stretches his legs out and slips his phone into his front jeans pocket. 'Listen, do you mind if I don't stop by? There's really nothing to see.'

An unintended sigh escapes. 'Sure man! I'll take you home.'

'You know what, you can drop me off in town. I'll board it the rest of the way.'

'It's no bother to drive you home, man. I need all the distractions I can get tonight, to be honest.'

He goes quiet.

'I'm, er, as it happens I'm off out to the smallholdings.'

'To Alice's! That's so cool Sean!' a high squeak of insincerity comes out of my mouth.

'To give her a wee little kiss goodnight you understand, I'm not staying over.'

'Sure,' I squeak. My voice goes even higher. 'I'll take you there.'

'There's no need, Cory.'

'Really, it's no problem. No problem at all.'

When we reach Alice's place, I pull up but keep the engine running.

'Do you, er, do you want to come in and say hi?'

'It's OK.' I sit facing ahead. He grabs his board from the back seat and leaps out. He taps on the window. I let it down. 'You sure?'

I swallow hard and nod.

'Is everything alright with you, Cory?'

'Fine. Fine, fine, fine, a bit of stuff going on back home. Nothing that can't be fixed.' Scared I'm going to cry, I pull away. He jumps back and hits the car with a friendly slap. I see him in my mirror, standing there, his head to one side, concerned, watching, getting smaller and smaller. I scream.

It's a night for ghosts all right. Everything I ran away from is coming back to haunt me.

45

Every kind of kind

Decima

I'm at home having some cozy time with Digby and the dogs when life does one of those freakish about-turns.

A truckful of flowers arrives. Ten generous bunches of pink roses and white lilies.

At first, I think they're from the quickie-shag producer I had in my New York dressing room last week, but: no. Surprise surprise. Fabienne. With a *You smashed it* cartoon hippo card and an invitation to lunch.

What's she playing at? She was dead against me going to New York. It's perfectly true. I did smash it. *The Jon Slasher Show* hadn't seen anything like me. Every PrimeTime PR's wet dream show and I went on in my pink pac-a-mac, a naked bodysuit underneath, with Twinkle in my arms and Barney at my feet and I talked kindness. Every kind of kindness.

I went rogue on Fabienne.

I was *real*. All my truths came out on a show that isn't mine.

Bitches can be soppy saps too. We can have no makeup days walking the dogs and not care if we get papped. We can also be Mafia targets. I dropped it in as a passing comment, like I didn't care about getting killed. Like, it comes with the territory. Now, if I do end up in a ditch with my legs and arms tied together, at least it's on the record. If anybody cares, it's out there.

Before I left New York I pitched a new show to my producer conquest, *No Makeup Days of the Rich & Famous* – real bitch celebrities can be tatty and as soppy as well as sassy queens. We'll get our own back on the Paps. Put them out of business. *Own* it.

I'm sad the flowers aren't from my new producer friend. There was a touch of Cory about him. Is that why it was a no-brainer to seduce him? I'm meant to be faithful to my boys after all. I'm not a natural slut but he was irresistible. A gray vibe rather than Cory black. Long but short dark gray hair with an off-white streak running through and that loose Armani charcoal suit so many producers wear it might as well be a uniform. He's the sort who wears a thick gold wedding ring which I see as a big shining beacon that a man isn't getting enough and is ready for it. He smelt like all my Christmases at once. Cedar, woodsmoke, patchouli. Irresistible. A useful conquest to have when my new image is revealed to the Dubai sponsors and they fire me. Or Dad gets arrested. Or killed. Whatever rubbish hits the fan first.

That's what I was thinking. Now this?

I call Fabienne to say my schedule is way too crazy to fit her in. She insists. It's all arranged. She'll have me to London and back before I know it.

Sure enough, after some fine dining and a restful sleep

in Virgin first class, a black cab picks me up at Heathrow Airport and takes me to Claridges right in the center of Mayfair to freshen up.

It's a shock. I'd put this city of my childhood firmly in my past and suddenly here it is again, out of the freaking blue. The red double-decker buses, even larger now, and *everywhere*; the black cabs exactly the same, the lamp posts, the traffic back on the right side, the left side of the road again. History, the past and the future everywhere all at once, and that almost metallic smell of wealth, softened by all the greenery, trees and parkland as if being rich was the most normal, organic, thing in the world but at the same time, aloof, distant, unreachable. Visit me, but don't touch. I could have stayed in Claridges for the rest of my *life*, but before I know it, I'm called down to the lobby.

A black cab takes me back out west, but then we take a left through a shabby Hammersmith street full of fast food cafes, hardware stores and bookmakers. It could almost be Hawk Bay City, until we take a right into a warren of tiny, squat, two-storey red-brick houses with white wooden slat half-blinds at the windows that show that, despite the shabby stores saying otherwise, this is a rich area.

Suddenly the dark streets open up onto an oasis of light. I'm out of the cab and Fabienne pounces on me, double air kissing, dahlings, all the works of fake friendship right there, and we're led to our riverside table.

'Well, this is amazing!' I say, taking it all in.

Enormous white umbrellas and tropical plants throw

puddles of shade over tables, cutlery and glasses sparkling on snow white tablecloths. Waiters in white aprons holding silver trays high dart between the tables. Beyond the terrace, the gray-green River Thames glints in the sunlight.

'The best Italian restaurant in the world, darling. And that's official. Have you seen the prices? Order what you want. We'll have a starter, yes?'

All on Dubai's dollar, I think, and I wonder if they even know about this.

I settle into my seat, nibble at the bread and watch the tourist boats and paddle boarders drift by, waiting for the punchline. *What's going on? Why's she done this?* She's full of apologies for *dragging* me so far, but she simply couldn't find a window to leave London Fashion Week and she simply *had* to see me in person to congratulate me.

'A London institution darling. Jamie Oliver. Takes months to get a table. Trains so many top chefs… Jamie Oliver… did you know Jamie Oliver started here… and really does do Italian better than the Italians…'

All going in one ear and straight out the other. I've *never* tasted food like this.

I suddenly stop chewing, my mouth drops open. I close it again quickly.

She pauses, mid-flow.

'What is it?'

She turns around to see what I'm staring at.

'What? Who have you seen? Everybody comes here, it's celeb mecca, though frankly I think you're the most famous one in here today.'

The olive green sign hits me like a train, transporting me snap back into my childhood. 'That building there. On the other side of the river.'

'That? Oh it was a Harrods warehouse back in the old days. Apartments now, of course, ten million – pounds – each I believe. Starting price. What is it?'

'Oh, nothing!' I turn my eyes away and concentrate on the lobster gnocchi exploding in my mouth. She continues the onslaught of praise, cleverly twisting it, as if the *Jon Slasher Show* was her idea and not something she was so dead against.

She doesn't say it, but I get it. Survival. She's totally misread it. She needs me to believe what she's saying. Her job is on the line and she can't do enough for me.

'Dubai were thrilled, darling, thrilled to bits. And then getting Jennifer Shielman to come on *The Bitch's Hour* next week, well, wow, mega wow, darling. We are ON the money.'

We. Coercion right there. I was the one, thanks to my new producer friend, who met the famously reclusive artist and animal rights campaigner in New York. I invited her onto *The Bitch's Hour* as a joke. No one could have been more surprised than me when she accepted. But now it's Fabienne's idea. All of it. Everything *has* to be Fabienne's idea. That's what Fabienne is. That's all she is. I want her to know I know this without freaking her out, so I say: 'To be perfectly frank with you, Fabienne, if you fly me to restaurants like this you can have anything you want from me.'

The lobster gnocchi is insane. When the dessert menu arrives, I want all of it.

There's a silence as we both scan the menu. It's impossible to choose.

A flutter of guilt disturbs my equilibrium over the backup plan show I pitched in New York. But not for long. It still may go wrong with Dubai. Not despite all of this. But because of it. There's more than a touch of desperation about her. Has the sexy Mr Armani patchouli producer tipped her off about my pitch?

Dessert, the course of truth for every business meeting.

'You have to have the chocolate nemesis, that's an order.'

I get the lemon crostata.

She orders an extra nemesis for me. And then it comes.

'Now,' her tone changes. 'Here's what we're going to do. Keep going with the pink pac-a-mac *be kind* new reality of you, darling, but we want you to up the contrast. Up the bitch side a thousand percent. It's all about extremes. Extremists are the only ones that matter these days. Far right, far left, *that's* where it's at. And you're BANG on the money. We want the Bitch but we also want the Be Kind Bitch.'

'That's the hashtag?'

'You got it. Keep the new you but turn up the volume to 11 on the bitch too.'

'Hmm?'

The simplest target is there right in front of you.'

'You mean Alice?

'Alice. Up the mean and nasty volume on Alice again, darling.'

'Well that's simple enough.'

We high-five.

Before I know it I'm in a black cab traveling back to the airport, leafing through the cookbook souvenir she bought me. It's that book the Indian guest introduced on the show. The woman who's married to Alice's boyfriend. Ha ha. I was hoping she'd fall to pieces. Still, I have to give her credit. She's tough, and not as dopey as she looks. The book cover is actually rather eye-catching, and I'm glad to see it here in London. Anything that helps empower women gets my vote.

Security whisks me straight to the first-class lounge.

I look around discreetly and gleefully join in the charade. Everybody is playing the same game of nonchalant couldn't give a flying fig elegance. Look at me, don't look at me, do. And 100%, not one of us has paid a cent, we're all on expense accounts. Somebody else's dollar. Oh so important business. There's nothing like a free classy flight to tell you that this is *it*. Success. You've arrived. It's happened.

I settle with an obscure brick of a property magazine, so glossy and heavy it's virtually a hardback. I turn the pages without really looking.

It's funny how, when success comes, it's not really there. One of those crazy truths that anybody who hasn't experienced it first-hand would find hard to believe, is how quickly you become used to fame and fortune. Well, I do anyway. It's only what I have deserved all these years. I also know how it plays out. You now reside on this freaky conveyer belt, waiting for the next pat on the back and the next put-down at the same time. Like that card game. Higher or lower. Now it's higher, higher, higher. I can do no wrong. Soon it'll be higher, lower, higher until one day it'll peak and start going lower, lower, lower and my time will be up. I concentrate on sucking in every ounce of this subservient First Class respect I'm getting right now. I've earned it.

46

Flying high

Decima

I call Ornella to brag. She isn't interested in the first-class lounge or The River Café, she's so full of her own news. I guess it was inevitable that she and Torin the pilot would get together at some point. But, *engaged*? Do people still *do* that nonsense?

They're still flying high to lay low, keeping themselves alive on my dollar paying for the new tires for the plane.

She thinks they're out of the woods with the hitmen, thanks to my money, but they aren't taking any chances and nor should I. Will I *get* any thanks for it? Not a chance. She tells me they're getting married in the Maldives and I'll be receiving a save-the-date message soon.

After take-off, I rest my kindle on my lap, even Colleen Hoover can't stop the thoughts whirring. I pick up the cookbook and put it down. It might as well be fiction. When am I ever going to cook fancy recipes? When am I ever going to cook?

I keep telling myself that I'm cool about the money. We're all going to die one day. Nobody knows how or when, do they? Like Twinkle and Barney... and Cory, I live in the moment now.

The Maldives, though. I'm seething. Cory is wrong! The future does exist. Of course it does! Wouldn't it be kind of nice to be settled down, with morning half-asleep sex on tap, long dog walks and getting excited about a drawn-out cozy lunch at a favorite restaurant where the greeter knows you and keeps your table and gives you endless treats between courses? None of that booking three months ahead, being seen at the right table at the right restaurant fakery.

I stare out of the window. It's getting dark. The clouds are streaked with pink and every shade of blue. I take Digby from his bag and hold him close. There is still the faintest smell of smoke on him, and maybe, as I like to believe, Mummy's perfume.

I whisper, 'Look at me, Mummy. Look how well your little girl did.'

London was a shock. That Harrods sign really freaked me out. That shade of green, kind of olive-colored. Sophisticated. Mummy loved that place, she virtually lived there. We'd have family meals at the Food Hall salt beef counter. My real mother, I mean. Before Ornella and I were adopted. Ornella Ornella, bride Ornella. It's been a sad life for her too. Worse. At least I escaped.

Why did they have to die?

I remember the flames, the smoke, the screams, my mother pushing Ornella and me from a window. Then the house disappearing in a blaze of flames and sparks, with Mummy and Daddy trapped inside. The shrieking of the fire engines, the neighbors running out and pulling us to safety, and the cracking noise as the whole house caved in and disintegrated. After an enquiry, it was deemed to be an accident caused by a curtain catching fire from a candle. My mother loved scented candles and had them in every room. The massive insurance payout was in trust for Ornella and me. Gauld was the sole trustee. He was Mummy's agent and a close friend of my real dad. Friendship was his business plan. He knew *everybody*. My parents had named him and his wife as our guardians in case anything happened to them. Eight months later, they died in the fire. A candle? Really? The truth of it is that my real parents' fortune paid to set up his empire. The Tower being the crowning glory of all his crooked property deals.

It's something I have always pushed to the back of my mind. The money isn't something I dwell on because it brings back the trauma of losing my parents. I did once ask Gauld about it, and he said it had all been spent on Ornella's and my private education and the expensive gifts and clothes he had bought for us as we grew up. His wife Petrina was kind and loving, to me in any case, as much as Dad as to Ornella, but she died soon after we went to live with them. As I said, a lucky escape.

Now I wonder if my money is *really* going to the Mafia to keep us all alive, or is it going somewhere else?

At that moment I realize something. The Moët goes down the wrong way and I'm choking and spluttering. A steward is with me instantly, hovering, caring. Like he *really* cares. First-class care care. Who's paying for this

Maldives wedding?

Am *I* paying for this Maldives wedding?

I study the bubbles rising to the top of my glass. Free champagne is one thing. Paying for 50 cases to be shipped to the Maldives for my father and sister's friends to gorge on is quite another. By the time I get home I've convinced myself that that is Ornella's plan. And it goes up to 100 cases. Bollinger. At least 100. A mixture of jetlag and simmering rage, I'm in no state to go straight back to work, but the show must go on. It's the big Jennifer Shielman interview next. I will, I must, find out what Ornella and Dad are up to with my money. But how?

Alice brings me my coffee and gazes at me with loving eyes.

'Alright, alright that's enough now.' She won't stop going on about it. She's as bad as the dog walkers.

'But you were awesome on the Jon Slasher show. The dogs! Your outfit! Sooo freaking *Killing Eve* cool, but original, like, so YOU!'

'I know, I know, OK? You're creeping me out. Now shut it, Alice, you're annoying me.'

Her face drops. She jumps back.

That good enough for you, Fabienne? Despite myself, I feel mean. That was fake.

We settle ourselves onto the set. Cameraman 1 gets his shot lined up on Alice. I get my headphones in and listen to the final preparations going on in the Gallery.

I'm doing the main interview for a change. That was the deal to get Jennifer on.

It's easy to big up her intro.

'The artist, animal rights campaigner, one of America's greatest philanthropists in *history*, Jennifer *Shielman*!'

When she walks on, everybody gasps. This truly is the most beautiful creature you've ever seen. There's like a kind of light around her, you can see it! It goes right through her bones. Her cheekbones are almost transparent.

She tells me how she hates money, won't have it near her and battles to keep a zero bank account. The more she rejects money the more her artwork sells for and the more she cashes in again. Now, at 29 years old she's engaged to be married. There's a lot of this wedding stuff going on, following me around it seems.

'So, who's the lucky man?' I ask innocently.

She opens her mouth. Then closes it again and looks at Alice. I'm about to get it out of her who the scammer is. Who'll be stinging her for every cent she has or hasn't got, when Alice, for some reason, interrupts and engineers a big, clunky change of subject.

'What about your own animals, Jennifer?'

She beams at Alice in relief and goes off on one about her beloved donkeys, lizards and pigs.

I talk over Alice to get the conversation back on track but to no avail.

That's the moment Lorelei decides to join in. Spooking me from afar. I can feel, then literally *see* my dress shrinking around me until I can barely get the air out to breathe, let alone speak. What could have been an incredible exclusive is ruined.

At least it gives me the excuse to sound off on one to Alice. As soon as Jennifer has left the building I lay into her.

In front of the whole crew. It's quite a performance.

47

Confusion

Alice

Sean was panicking about telling Decima we were going to be married. I calmed him down and agreed to discuss our next steps this evening. In the meantime we don't tell anybody.

During my lunch break I **Broomstick** to see my parents to let them know about our engagement, because they are not 'anybody' and have a right to be the first to know their daughter is going to be married. My mother looks a bit shocked to see me. The kitchen is chaotic and she shoos me quickly out into her garden before I can get inside.

'Come and see how it's recovered, Alice! They grew back!'

It's true. After the devastation created by Gauld's men, thanks to Lorelei's magic all the plants grew new roots and are now flourishing. While I'm admiring the garden, at the same time I'm listening to a lot of banging and thumping coming from the house.

'What's happening? All that noise?'

'Ah, that's your father. He's modernizing the kitchen for me. Changing it around a bit.'

'Really? You didn't say anything about that when I was here last? You're not worried by the threats anymore then?'

You know what he's like, always keeping busy. He's making a pantry. You'll see it when it's finished in a couple of weeks.'

'OK. Well, I have some news, I'd like to tell you both. Let's go and find him?'

I walk towards the house, but Astrid catches my arm and says 'I'll give him a shout. Shame to go in when the weather's so pleasant.'

She hurries away, leaving me standing in the garden, in weather which in truth isn't pleasant at all. In fact there's a slight drizzle. Something odd is going on.

A few minutes later she's back with my father. He looks tired and disheveled, his overalls covered in dust, but he greets me with a smile.

'Ah, my clever daughter. You surely did work some magic here, Alice. Your mother's garden restored to its beauty. I'm proud of you.' He gives me an awkward hug. 'But don't you start going crazy with this magic nonsense. What you did was splendid. More than enough.'

I can feel a lecture coming on, so I interrupt and blurt out. 'I'm going to marry Sean.'

'Oh darling girl, I am so thrilled for you. I had hoped… He's such a delightful young man, and he'll make you very happy.'

I've never heard my mother quite so excited.

'When's the wedding?'

'We haven't discussed the details yet. Sean wants us to marry in Ireland.'

'How romantic! Ireland! Imagine that!'

'Indeed,' says my father.

'We are so happy, Alice. We must go out and celebrate.'

'Actually, we are not making it public yet. I wanted you to know, but for the time being, until we've sorted everything out, it's between the four of us. I need to get back to work now. I'm looking forward to seeing the new kitchen when it's ready.'

I **Broomstick** back to work with an uneasy feeling. An updated kitchen? A pantry? Doesn't sound right.

After work, Sean comes round and we share a meal and a couple of beers, talking about our future. He's worried that telling Decima will mean he'll be out of a job. I reassure him that with his talent for music, he'll do fine. I haven't told him yet, but I sent *She's the One* to Scorpio a couple of weeks ago, and he texted me yesterday to say he loves it.

What will I do when we're married? We'll both have to find new jobs, which makes me sad. Even with Decima's moods, I love what I do and I don't know anything else I'd be any good at. But I'll still keep up my project helping people, secretly, and building a network of others to do the same.

Sean is getting himself into a real state about telling Decima. I'm beginning to feel a bit tired of it, because I've told him so many times that I will deal with her, but he's stressed out and keeps going on and on. I stroke his hand. 'I'll do it, Sean. You don't need to worry. I'll tell her, when we're ready.'

When he's left, I pick up Sita's book, intending to put it on a shelf. A white card falls out onto the floor. I pick it up and read:

'Alice, I have to talk to you. There's something you need to know. Please meet me. You can call me any time on this number. 044933201 Your sincere friend, Jasminder.'

I turn the card over, and gasp. On the other side is a painting of a beautiful woman with shoulder-length blonde hair, wearing a gypsy dress in sapphire blue with a ruby red bodice. Sparkly drop earrings swing from her ears, a dozen golden bangles encircle her arms, and on her feet, red strappy high-heeled sandals. Her eyes match the sapphire blue of the dress. The expression on her face is tentative, and she's looking directly at me.

I'm looking at myself on that fateful evening when I went for dinner with Jai.

Every detail is perfect. Only one person could have painted it.

48

Face to face

Alice

I phone Jasminder and agree to meet her at her hotel uptown. I cannot see her as an enemy. She is the woman Jai chose to marry, and she is a kind and decent person. And of course I am curious about what she will tell me. I suppose it will be about her life with Jai, and how they hope that I will find my own happiness. I must dig deep and hide my pain to wish them well.

Giving myself a quick *Calm* spell, I take the elevator up to the top floor, where Jasminder is waiting for me. Her hands are cool and gentle as they take mine and lead me to her suite.

She pushes open the door and guides me in with her hand on my back.

My heart stops when I see a man silhouetted at the window, his back to the room. Oh no, I can't do this. An involuntary cry escapes from me. I can't. I turn to Jasminder with my mouth open, and try to force my way past her to the door. I cannot bear to see Jai. She firmly pushes the door closed, leading me into the room.

'Tom,' she says.

The man turns around, and walks towards us. He's the

same height and build as Jai, but there is no other similarity. He stands behind Jasminder, wraps his arms around her, and kisses her neck. She puts a hand up and touches his face.

I cannot believe what I'm seeing. There is no mistaking the intimacy between them. She's been married to Jai for less than a year. A flicker of rage burns in my heart.

The man holds out his hand.

'Alice, how very kind of you to come. I've heard so much about you. I will leave you two ladies to chat for now, and I hope we will meet again Alice.'

'I'll see you later, my love,' he says.

I stand nailed to the spot as he closes the door and look at Jasminder with all the contempt I can raise.

'Come,' she says, 'let me tell you a story. Please.'

She leads the way to a sofa, sits down, and pats the seat beside her. Drawing a tray towards her from a low table, she pours two cups. The familiar fragrance hits me like a punch.

'Chai,' she says. 'I know you like it.'

Reluctantly, I sit stiffly beside her, taking the cup, bending my head to inhale the familiar spicy scent.

'In my culture, Hinduism, arranged marriages are common. Parents take great trouble to find what they believe to be an ideal partner for their child, based on factors far beyond simple attraction. This often leads to ideal relationships.

'My family and Jai's family,' – my heart flinches when she mentions his name – 'have been friends for more than

50 years. His are manufacturers, mine are traders and exporters. The two businesses are symbiotic.

'Jai and I have known each other since we were little children, and it was a foregone conclusion that our families would see our marriage as ideal. It was agreed between them when we were young teenagers. Neither of us were consulted. That's the way it is in the strict traditions of our families. And who knows, maybe it would have worked out between us. Drink your chai while it's hot,' she interrupts herself.

'You will remember Sita's story from our interview last week. How I defied my parents – it was hard, very hard to go against them, but I was determined, and as you know they eventually accepted my career.

'Jai was expected to follow in his family's business, but he loves the natural world, and couldn't bear the idea of spending his life in an office. His parents agreed that he should come to America for a while, then he would eventually return to India.

'Last year, our families merged their businesses into one, and decided it was time for our marriage to take place. Symbolic of the uniting of the two houses. But by then I had met and fallen in love with Tom, and Jai had met you.

'You have to understand the way our culture works. Respect for our parents is paramount, and so is personal honor. These values are the core of Hinduism. But for myself and Jai, we had found a new way of living. Our relationship has never been anything more than friendship. When we were told we were to be married, it was out of our control. We were honor-bound to obey. Not only that, but my mother was terminally ill and desperate to see us wed.

'Jai and I agreed to go ahead with the wedding for the sake of our parents, and then to discreetly move abroad and continue with our lives the way we choose. Jai was totally committed to his work, until he met you.'

I take a gulp of chai and help myself to a few little pastries.

'I don't need to tell you what an honorable man he is. He tried hard not to fall in love with you, knowing that he was going to have to return to India for us to marry. He wanted to explain to you, and was devastated to think that he had caused you so much pain. He planned to return to America after the wedding and tell you the whole story. He was very much in love with you.

'And that was the plan, until you did not reply to his letter, and he saw that you had found happiness with somebody else. He felt he should not interfere. He would want you to be happy.'

She squeezes my hand.

My head is spinning and my heart is pumping, taking in all she has told me. I'm trying to understand.

But how did he know I had found somebody else? I didn't, haven't. Nobody can possibly know that I have agreed to marry Sean, neither of us have told anybody except my parents.

And then, I remember. In the park with Sean, when he

was hugging and singing to me. The figure I saw standing outside my old apartment, looking up at the window. I hadn't imagined it. Jai was there.

I croak: 'Where is he now?'

'I don't know,' she says. 'He joined another organization studying changes in the ecology. They travel all over the world and he's usually out of contact in remote places for months at a time. I only hear from him very rarely. He'll be so pleased to know that we have met, and I know he'll be happy for you. I hope we can be friends?'

On my way home thoughts whirl around in my head in a jumble, like clothing in a washing machine. Each time I catch a thought it is swept away by another before I can complete it. I need to take my time and think my way through this tangled mess.

'Sad?' asks Zylch, who has chosen to transform himself into a large pink rabbit, with flowery wings and wearing a crown of daisies. He wraps his arms around me.

'Confused, Zylch. So confused. And so tired.' I rest my head on his chest.

I can't sleep, there's something bothering me. I get up and dig around in the bedroom cupboard until I find the purse with Jai's note to me, which I had meant to throw away, but had kept as my last link to him.

I flatten it out and read:

Alice, please trust me. I will explain to you what is happening in India. I know I have hurt you, but it was never my intention and it

I sit reading it over and over again, and then I tear it
into little pieces and flush them away. It's all too late. I've
agreed to marry Sean. I cannot backtrack.

49

Time will come and take my love away

Cory

Saturday is market day at the harbor. By the time I've walked down, I've worked up a real sweat to go with the nerves. I make for one of the cafés lining the waterfront and take a chair in the shade.

The sun is already high and the tables are filling with contented couples and busy families, all seemingly without a care in the world. An illusion I know but the boats tinkling and the smells of coffee and barbequed fish in the salty sea air make for a good energy.

Sean arrives with a spring in his step – another one without a care in the world. Seeing him so loved up is tough. Whatever I tell myself otherwise there's this yearning that's lodged itself in my body and soul. As Sean said, a love this strong is outside of you. A force, messing with your sanity.

My mind gives my heart a lecture. Time will come and take this love away. Time will come and take everything away.

As soon as he's seated, my woes pour out. He stares at me with a glazed-over expression like he's turned into a waxwork.

'…so, as the castle was legally his anyway, Jonty being the older brother, leaving it all behind felt like the best thing I'd ever done. The release of that. The big clear YES that gave me. Let him have it!'

Sean makes a strange noise. I carry on.

'You've no idea what it was like, man. He could have the leaking toilets, the rotting wood panels, the draughts, the crayfish-infested lake, the exploding, freezing heating system, the rats, the ghost, the needy tenants. The title…'

'Now now hold it right there a second,' Sean palm faces me. 'A *title*?'

'Who wants a title? He loved it! Lorded it over the locals like the true fool he is. It all seemed so simple at the time. To leave it all behind. To come to the States to play basketball. Make a living playing the game I love. Loved. More fool me.'

'What's got into you, Cory? Have you lost your mind? You're a sports pro!'

'A failed sports pro, a butler, ex-butler, not lord of any manor. I'm a cameraman.'

'Back then I'm talking.'

'I may have been a little economical with the truth there, Sean. Now it's all coming back to haunt me.'

'So you haven't gone crazy? You're saying this for real?'

'As real as we're sitting here, unfortunately.'

'Cory Chumley? Chumley? Doesn't sound very lordly, Cory. You got a fake name as well?'

'No. I changed the spelling that's all. It's really spelled

C-h-o-l-m-o-n-d-e-l-e-y, but pronounced Chumley.'

'And folk go on about Irish spellings! That sounds crazy enough to be true alright. You gave it all away? Were you crazy, man? No, don't answer that. I know you hate possessions… and conflict.' He nods slowly. 'Come to think of it, it's starting to make sense.'

'If anything happened to him I knew I would inherit. We're twins with no other siblings. I'm the youngest by 78 seconds. It's all there on the birth certificates, no need for lawyers, or so I thought. In my defense, it wasn't total stupidity. Do you know how much genealogy lawyers cost?'

'Do you know what, Cory? I don't recall that I do.'

I ignore his facetious remark and try to explain.

'We didn't have that kind of money, or, to be frank, any money at all. We still don't! Like many aristocrats, our wealth is in bricks and land. Property rich, cash poor.'

Sean raises a hand. 'Now don't give me that.'

'What?' I can't keep the irritation out of my voice. 'This is the first time I've shared this, Sean. Listen. Please.'

'No. You listen a moment. Tell me now, why you rich feckers don't sell off a bit of your *property rich*, if you're so *cash poor*. Like, like one of them oil paintings castles are always full of, or a spit of land, to get, like…'

I grip his arm and pull him towards me. His voice fades away.

'He's *dying*, Sean. *My brother is dying.*'

'Sorry Cory pal, sorry. I'm still taking all of this in. What happened?'

'One moment he was stick and balling with a couple of grooms, the next he was in hospital, his internal organs crushed beyond repair. That's rental polo ponies for you. You never know what wired-up lunatic you're going to be sitting on.'

'Yeah I've heard that.'

'He's still alive I gather, but life support could be turned off at any time.'

'Then you'll inherit a castle? I mean, whoa.' He blushes. 'Sorry I know it's… it's…'

'It's OK. Believe you me there's no love between us.'

'So er what's the…?'

'I never thought he'd find a woman who'd have him. The problem is, he's managed to acquire a fiancée. A money-grabbing escort called Erica who knows her way around a lawyer's office. She's pregnant, you see, or she says she is. I've only got pub gossip to go on, the landlord keeps me updated. It's why I need to get back there fast.'

Sean says something. I have to get him to repeat it.

'Do you care?' he croaks. 'You didn't care about the castle before, like, why the change?'

'It would be theft. On a grand scale. What if I have kids one day? Not that I'm that way inclined, but this kind of situation does tend to get the old brain ticking over.

'Look, he's on life-support. He's at death's door. The rumor is she's planning to marry him before he croaks and take everything. Then she'll sell and it will be the end of my heritage. If I can get back there and switch him off before that happens, it will make my life a great deal simpler.'

Sean throws his eyes in the air, shakes his head, looks away and looks back at me again like he's seen a ghost.

I know the gravity of what I've said. It's early in the day, but I order a couple of shots.

'So, tell me,' I pour mine into his. 'Tell me about that journey to the stars with Alice. I can't get it out of my mind. It sounds to me like it really happened. Is that your genius storytelling or what?'

His whole demeanor changes. He leans forward with a distant look in his eyes and whispers, 'For real, man. I'm telling you.'

'So Alice has supernatural powers?'

Could it have actually happened? Is Alice really a witch? Is that why I'm so utterly obsessed? Why we all are?

'It's all in her phone, man. This App! I'm telling you. Super, supernatural powers.'

'So that means... that means...'

Sean helps me out. 'If I'm getting the events of the past week right, I've realized that Alice is an actual witch and you're Lord of the fecking Manor.' Sean shakes his head again. 'That's a lot for a man to take in all in one go.'

'Do you think she'd take me, Sean?'

'Take *you*?'

'To England, for a little flight to the hospital. To see my brother before he dies?'

'You want me to tell Alice all this then? To get her to take you there. So that you can *murder* him?'

'Well, it's not quite that is it. It's a switch. Like a light switch I believe. Or a plug. Maybe.'

'Switch him off then! So I tell Alice that you didn't used to be a butler but a lord, and now you're planning to murder your only brother. That you've been tricking us all this time.'

'Oh come on, Sean.'

'When we're all working ourselves senseless trying to make it in this world simply to survive, and you have everything on a plate and you throw it away and lie about it?'

He's taking this the wrong way. I manage to talk him down and he eventually agrees he'll talk to her. He needs time to absorb all of this. Then I know he will. Sean's a good, good man. Too good for this world. Like Alice. They're made for each other.

<h1 style="text-align:center">50</h1>

<h1 style="text-align:center">New bestie</h1>

Decima

As the only one with a 9 to 5 job, Joan is the ringleader who calls the shots on the dog walking routes.

'We'll go this way,' she orders, striding off on the longer path around the lake and we all dutifully follow.

Celebrity sucks sometimes. You're banned from normal life. Even knitted pink cardigan bitch Babs is staring at me from beneath her frizzy gray fringe with a round-eyed mixture of adoration and fear – a look I recognize as that uncertain 'you're famous' awe all of us chosen ones have to put up with.

I'd rather be comparing the merits of veggie dog food and diamante collars, but my new friends aren't having it. They all saw me on the Jon Slasher Show. More than that, they saw Pam's bubblegum pink pac-a-mac on TV and it's been trending on the fashion grams ever since. I've become their patron saint. The Adored One. Their Number One Bestie.

This is *not* what I signed up for. Maybe I should have donated my Slasher show fee to the charity anonymously. But where's the fun in that? I'm not *that* good! They're not to know that it would only have gone to Dad and then on to Ornella's Maldives wedding fund.

The coolest thing about these women is that they're so uncool. But I hate this new deference. There's obviously been a lot of googling going on as they've soon moved on from The Jon Slasher Show to my Twitter spats with Lorelei. They know more about me than I do.

'What a mess that Lorelei woman is.'

'A fake. She's finished.'

'Ruined.'

'Nobody is buying it.'

'I heard that darn interview when Lennon was alive and kickin!'

'Come awn, you're never that old Joan.'

'Oh, I sure am.'

I think she is. Joan is ancient! I can't believe she is still working. Some kind of surgery receptionist job. For the medical insurance I guess.

They're all talking at once and the only thing I can do is run with it.

'You girls are too kind.'

'Your life! We had no idea who you were!' says Jacqui. A freakish statement all celebrities are familiar with. A tall, hippyish woman with kind eyes that have never seen a scrap of mascara. I couldn't believe she worked at a big downtown lawyer. She's a part-time translator, it turns out, working from home. Gives her all the time she wants with her dogs, she explained. I nodded approvingly, prickling with envy. How freaking sensible is that!

'Well, we're right behind you, aren't we girls,' says

Babs.

'Lorelei's lost the fight anyhow. Everybody's laughing at her. What a loser.'

'It's not over yet, Joan,' I say. 'She's the master of clickbait, that one. Her interview could turn into one of those ones that's so bad it's compulsive viewing.'

'Oh goodie,' says Babs. 'Then we can all laugh at her some more.'

I smile. Babs is so likable. 'She's raking it in right now. That's the best she can expect.'

'What a way to live,' says Pam. 'She can't be happy can she? Witch or not, having to go to such lengths to put somebody else down. Imagine being her? Poor woman.'

Then something strange happens. I find myself agreeing with Pam.

I need to think. My chance comes when the path twists away from the lake across open land. I pull on Twinkle and Barney's leads and hold back from the others. What did I feel there? But yes, it's true. I do feel sorry for Lorelei right now. I wonder about sending some flowers over to that Malibu beach house but immediately dismiss the idea. She'd take it the wrong way. She'd think I was gloating. Rubbing it in.

My reputation precedes me.

And yes, I've won, but she's still the enemy. Who knows what her next move will be? Meantime who knows where this me-worship will stop? When can we go back to talking about the dogs? They have all but been forgotten on this walk.

What if that Jon Slasher show look really goes viral? I don't think Joan and Babs know what the difference is between a hashtag and an emoji. Before I know it #pinkpacamac will become more than a passing hashtag. An emoji even. That would turn these women crazy. Next thing they'll be on the Slasher show themselves. As fashion influencers.

51

Research

Alice

My emotions are all over the place. I'm such a wreck.

What's happening with my parents? Something is going on there that they're not telling me, and I'm worried.

I don't know if I'm doing the right thing with Sean. I do love him, very much, but I don't know if it's the right kind of love. Can I bring him the happiness he deserves?

After my meeting with Jasminder, I can't stop thinking about Jai, and how things could have turned out for us if he hadn't seen me with Sean, wondering where he is and what he's doing.

I'm excited by my success on the show, but also rather overwhelmed. Decima seems to be pushing more and more of the load onto me as she spends more time with her dogs. At least she seems happier now.

I need to clear my head, and find something to occupy my mind. I remember that I was going to try to find out more about the fire that killed Decima's parents.

It happened before the Internet really became accessible for the public and there's nothing useful there, so I'm going to have to do it the old-fashioned way, going through newspaper archives. I start by following a link to the British Newspaper Archive and opening an account.

For the rest of the day I explore the history of Decima's family.

I start by searching for her mother, Graciela Mazellini.

Her life reads like a romance novel. Born into a poor family in a small village near Naples, from the time she could walk, Graciela loved to dance. She read books and watched films, teaching herself and practicing in front of a mirror in the bedroom she shared with her two sisters. She danced for the local people, until word spread to a local ballet school. Her family could not afford the fees. Realizing the girl had something very special, the dance teacher managed to find her sponsorship.

The article goes on about how hard Graciela worked, the sacrifices she made and her rise to eventually become the Prima Ballerina at a prestigious Italian ballet at the remarkable age of 22.

At the height of her fame she received a phone call to say her village had been struck by an earthquake, killing her parents and sisters. She never danced again.

For a year she vanished from sight, before returning to volunteer for a charity supporting refugees. It was through the charity that she met British racing driver Douglas Marchant, the son of a wealthy English widow.

It's the photographs that fascinate me.

Graciela as a small smiling girl, dancing in the village square.

A group photo with her proud, self-conscious family,

outside the ballet school.

As a teenager dancing in the corps de ballet.

Dozens of photographs of her progressing from the corps to a soloist and then into a principal dancer.

A beautiful portrait showing her black hair tightly scraped back. Those are unmistakably Decima's eyes and her wide mouth.

Graciela as a Prima Ballerina, on stage, surrounded by a sea of bouquets.

That is the last photo of her as a dancer.

Next are several articles about the earthquake, and then silence.

Three years later she's wearing a wedding gown that emphasizes her slender, elegant figure, standing outside a church beside a tall gangly man smiling broadly as he looks down into her upturned face.

I skip through all the articles about Douglas Marchant's motor racing career. From the photos I recognise where Decima's nose came from.

There's nothing more until the report of the fire ten years later, which was headline national news.

Headshots of both parents, photos of an elegant manor house, photos of firefighters trying to stop the blaze, photos of a smoldering ruin, and photos of two small girls. The elder is a pudgy child with blonde curls with a vacant expression, sucking her thumb. Beside her, her dark-haired sister hugs a teddy bear, her face contorted with grief. The caption says: The couple's two daughters, Ornella, 9 and Decima, 7½, are in the care of their grandmother, Mrs Caroline Marchant.

I didn't know Decima even had a sister.

I search the database for Mrs Caroline Marchant and the first article that comes up is an obituary. Two months after the fire, she was found dead at the bottom of the staircase in her house, seemingly having tripped on the hem of her dressing gown.

There's nothing more.

Now I understand why Decima is the way she is. How tragic to lose all the people who loved and cared for her at such a young age. I must be nicer to her, more tolerant. However spiteful she may be, I'm only going to be kind.

52

Telling Decima

Ramon

Telling my mom was the easy bit. She cried and shouted, running around the kitchen and flapping her apron. She didn't know whether she was more happy for me, or more sad that I'd be away a long time. She thinks Korea is a dangerous place and doesn't trust the Koreans.

It took me a long time to reassure her that I'm going to be OK, the food will be fine, I won't be nude, I won't marry a Korean girl and I will be home regularly. She's worried the plane will crash every time I fly. I don't tell her that I share that fear, but try to cheer her up by joking that it can only happen once. I haven't worked out yet how I'm going to manage the flights with my panic attacks. Once she's calmed down she starts planning a celebration feast, inviting all our family and friends. I manage to persuade her not to have a giant poster of me pinned to the wall.

Dad has insisted on walking around the neighborhood with his arm over my shoulder, stopping to tell everybody I'm going to be a movie star, and letting people have their photos taken with me. It all feels a bit corny, but it's fine by me. Whatever makes them happy.

Now I'm trying to psyche myself up to tell Decima. That's going to be a whole different story.

I WhatsApp her. 'Would like some time with you alone.'

She comes right back. 'Come over this evening. Wear old clothes and shoes.'

Huh? What the hell does that mean?

I take the bus and walk the last couple of miles, the anxious sweat cooling on my back in the evening air. Security lets me through straight away, and Decima is waiting at the door.

She's dressed down and unmade up, her hair tangled, holding two scraggy hounds on leashes. I'm not confident around dogs and back away as the bigger one tries to sniff me.

'Hola,' she smiles. She actually smiles, a genuine, warm smile. If she didn't have such a big nose, she'd really be very pretty without all the paint. 'You take Barney, and we'll walk. You'll be OK.' She heads for the path down to the beach with the small mutt tucked under her arm.

Reluctantly I take the leash. The dog almost pulls my arm out of its socket as it lurches after her.

We follow the rocky path that leads down to the shore. She places the small dog – it's called Twinkle, on the sand, and unclips Barney, who chases down to the surf.

There's a chill breeze coming off the ocean, whipping her hair around her face and making her nose and cheeks pink.

She hooks her arm through mine. 'Come on, let's walk

and talk.'

We walk over the sand together, picking up pieces of driftwood and throwing them into the water for Barney to retrieve. She laughs when he returns them and shakes icy salt water and sand all over us.

'So, I'm listening. I guess you have something to tell me.' She sits down and pats the sand beside her.

She's so mellow, so different from how I've known her. I take a deep breath and say: 'Decima, it's something that's happened so fast. I'm trying to get my head around it, still can't believe it's real, but I need to tell you.'

'Let me guess – you've been signed by Michiko. You're going to be her new star.'

My mouth drops open. 'You knew?'

She smiles. 'Michiko's people already contacted me to discuss your contract with the station.'

'And, um, what is the situation then?' My stress level is on overload.

'The situation, my lovely one, is that you are being released from your contract, with my blessing. This is your time, go out and grab it with both hands. You have a great future ahead and I'm happy for you. But I'm going to miss you.'

She's smiling at me, but her eyes are filling with tears. I remember that night Cory and I spent with her, when I saw her tears in the moonlight. Somewhere beneath her brittle shell, there's something vulnerable that touches my heart.

'I won't be gone forever, and I will be coming back.'

'Sure you will,' she says, brushing sand off her legs. 'Sure you will. Let's go.'

We walk back with the dogs and haul up the path to the house.

'Grab one of those,' she says, pointing to a pile of towels inside the door. We rub the dogs until they're dry and the sand has come off. 'Now come upstairs, I've something special for you.'

So it's back to business now.

I follow her up. Instead of the bedroom she leads me into the kitchen and takes a packet from the fridge.

'Ever had English crumpets?'

'I don't think so. Never heard of them. Are they like a muffin?'

'No way! Forget your muffins, a crumpet is something else. On a cold afternoon you can't beat toasted crumpets. I'll show you how.'

She takes a couple of plates and the packet of crumpets, and walks into the living room, where she hands me a long brass fork.

The crumpets are kind of like thick marshmallows, but bread. But not bread. Bread full of holes. She spears one of the things onto the fork. 'Hold it close to the fire.'

This is the weirdest thing I've seen, but I point the fork at the flames and after a few minutes I turn it over the other side. While I'm doing the next one, she's smearing butter on it.

'Taste that!' she says, handing me a plate.

I think she's expecting me to enjoy the crumpet. I bite

into it, and it's chewy and the butter runs out of it and down my chin.

'What do you think?' she asks. 'Isn't that delicious?'

'It's great,' I lie, so she puts a second one on my plate.

We sit silently for a few minutes, munching the crumpets and wiping our chins.

'Cory gets them flown out for me, from England,' she says. 'I've never found them in the States.'

Privately I can understand why.

'When I was a little girl in England, we always had toasted crumpets at home on Sunday afternoons in the winter. It's a very special memory for me. It reminds me of my mother and father.'

I remember something about her folks dying in a fire when she was a young kid. Sad.

'We spread them with Marmite. Cory brings me that too, but I don't think you'd like it.'

How right she is Cory got me to try it once. Nothing can convince me people voluntarily eat that. OMG!

'Er, no thanks, I'm good. They're just fine like this.'

She goes to the kitchen and returns with two mugs filled with English tea. Ugh. I'm a coffee man, but I drink it politely.

The dogs are lying in front of the fire. She doesn't seem to notice they smell, and she lets them lick our greasy plates.

'When are you leaving?' she asks.

'When my work visa comes through. Michiko said probably a couple of weeks. I'll still come into work until then.'

'And then you'll fly away,' she says wistfully. 'Spread your wings and fly away.'

'Yeah, it all feels so unreal. I keep thinking I'll wake up and find it was a dream.'

'It's going to be great for you. I'll be first in the queue to see your films.'

'You won't be queueing, Decima. You'll be coming in with me to the premiere. That's a promise. I'm going to miss you.' And I realize that I will. I'm going to miss her bitchiness, her wit, her unpredictable moods and those rare moments when I catch a hint of something softer, mysterious.

She stands up and pulls me up so I'm standing very close to her.

'I won't see you at work next week, Ramon. I'm going to be too busy, so I'll say goodbye now, and wish you all the luck you deserve.'

She takes my face in her hands and kisses me very lightly on my lips, and then on my forehead.

She opens the door and walks with me to the gates.

'Come on my babies,' she calls, leaving me watching as she walks away with the dogs at her heels.

53

Where's the money?

Decima

I messed up on my closing lines today. Alice had to take over. I might as well have not been there. I'm still sticking to Fabienne's plan and giving Alice a hard time on screen and off. It's not difficult. But she simply takes it on the nose. Cory tells me never to compare. But how can I not? She has so much more of the things that matter. A lover who worships her, stolen from me, a mother and father, a cat, close friends. No wonder she's taking my barbs for what they are. Fake. She's a tough little madam getting tougher by the day and I'm losing the will.

What *do* I have? Digby, the dogs, my books and my boys. Digby is a furry memory stick of Mummy. The dogs are everything to me, but they don't live that long and the boys are all making noises about leaving. Ramon is already on his way to Korea and stardom. Books, at least, will never let me down.

The battle with Lorelei is won. What's annoying me big time is Ornella's wedding. You'd be mad too if you were paying for it. Is the fact that they are using my cash to pay for it proof that the Mafia is off their backs? And therefore my back? Proof that they're not going to kill me? I need to know what is happening with my money. If I don't find out I'll go crazy.

After the show I ask Alice to stay behind with me to do some research on private detectives. She agrees but freaks out. What for? On who? I let her sweat trying to work it out. Then I make an excuse saying my true parents' fortune, that Dad has now lost, all went to him instead of us. He should have held it in trust for us. But the more I think about it, the more I realize that this private detective is going to have their hands very full with their investigation.

Who knew there were so many private detectives in Hawk Bay City? A booming industry. They're all wanting our custom, falling over themselves, suggesting deals, dodgy deals, who can we trust? This must stay secret. All we have is our instincts. We stay so late, I get Alice to call in a delivery pizza. My AmexCard bounces. Dad has cleaned it out again. Alice pays, leaving me fuming and humiliated.

54

Armageddon

Alice

Decima has been very strange the last few weeks. Even more unpredictable than ever. She waxes hot and cold with me all the time. I know that I am adding value to the show, and one minute she's heaping me with praise, the next accusing me of trying to outdo her. It's very wearing but knowing what I do about her tragic history, I haven't reacted. I've tried to be as helpful as possible.

I can't put off any longer telling her that I'm going to marry Sean. He's so wound up with stress that he has started drinking too much. There's never going to be a good time to break the news, but for his sake it needs to be done.

The opportunity comes when she WhatsApps me to ask if I'll stay late, after everybody has left for the night, to help her with some research. Not sure what kind of research, but she says it's something private and personal, not related to the show, and she would appreciate my help. That's new, unlike her normal commands.

I give myself a calming spell because yes, I am nervous about her reaction. Ramon is leaving next week. We are all thrilled for him of course, although I know Sean does feel a little jealous, even though he tries to hide it. Ramon's dream really has come true. Decima seems cool about losing one of her boys, but how will she feel about losing Sean as well?

She's standing looking down onto the city when I go into her office and turns with a smile.

'Hey, thanks for coming.'

She sits at her desk and pulls up a chair next to hers. 'I'd value your help, and I know I can count on your discretion.'

'Of course,' I reply. 'I won't breathe a word. What is it you want to do?'

It turns out she wants to hire a 'snoop' – to investigate a personal financial matter. She doesn't go into details.

'It's a question of finding the right one, who will do the job and be discreet. How do we pick one? There are dozens of them listed in Hawk Bay City.'

I suggest we check them out one by one, and we start out by crossing off those who specialize in divorce, missing persons or animals, or employee records and concentrate on financial matters. That reduces the list down to 18. Next we check out the Google and Yelp reviews for each one, scratching off another 6.

We are down to a dozen possibilities when Decima bangs her hand on the table and shouts 'Stop! Big mistake. These are all too local and I'm famous here. We need to go far away.'

So we bin all our hard work and start again. Focussing on North Dakota.

'I reckon that's a safe bet,' says Decima. 'What are they, peanut farmers, something like that? Do they even have tv there?'

I bite my tongue because a lot of famous people come from North Dakota.

One good thing is that there don't seem to be many registered private investigators there, so we soon find one who, from the reviews, has given nearly all his clients total satisfaction.

'OK, good. Thanks, Alice. I'll call them tomorrow.

It's late, and my belly rumbles.

Decima laughs. 'Somebody's hungry as usual. I'll get pizzas.'

She calls through an order, and gives them her card number, tapping her finger impatiently on her desk.

'What do you mean my card has been declined? Did you take the number properly? Listen carefully while I give it to you again.'

She slowly, loudly, recites her card number, gives the expiry date and verification code and rolls her eyes at me while she waits.

'No funds! Of course there are funds. Do you know who I am? Do you think I'd have a bank account with NO FUNDS, you moron?'

I take my card out and slide it across to her. 'The code is 611.'

She reads out the card details over the phone, slamming down the receiver.

'That's insane, absolutely insane.'

'Probably a blip,' I say. 'These things happen sometimes, no rhyme or reason.'

'Yeah, maybe. It's odd, though. Must be a mistake at their end.'

While we're waiting for the pizzas to arrive, I say

'There's something I need to tell you.'

She sits down on the sofa, kicks off her shoes, curls up her legs and pats the seat beside her.

'So tell me! I hope you're not thinking of leaving? If it's about money, we can fix it for you.'

'It's not about money. It's about Sean. And me.'

She's silent for a moment, and then nods her head slowly.

'Tell me all about you and Sean.'

'We are going to be married.'

'Ah, that's wonderful. So you've finally succeeded. Well done! I wondered which one you'd choose.'

'I don't understand.'

'Of course you do, you silly goose. You've been after him for ages. After all of them in fact.' She gives a little tinkly laugh and now I'm not sure whether she's serious, because she has a big smile on her face.

'I hope you'll be satisfied with Sean, and not try to steal Cory and Josh too. You're too late for Ramon.'

I laugh when I realize she is joking.

'Those big, big blue eyes of yours, the way you look at them. You've driven them all crazy. But,' she pauses, 'when it comes down to it, they'll always come back to me. Because I give them what you never could. And of course Sean, darling Sean, has sent you to tell me, because he doesn't have the balls to do it himself. Which rather surprises me, because as I'm sure you know, he has mahoosive balls to match his mahoosive...'

I gape at her in horror.

'Or perhaps you don't know yet? Marry him with my blessing, Alice. I wish you both every happiness, I truly do. You'll make a fine couple, and when Sean needs to satisfy certain of his, shall we say, more unusual needs, I'll still be here with open arms. And legs. I can see it working out very well for all of us.'

She stares coolly at me, as I sit there, dumb.

'I can give you some tips about what really turns him on, and how to keep him going. He has a tendency to rush things, maybe you've already found that out? Too enthusiastic. What he really goes crazy for is when you...'

I cut across her. 'I'm not interested in what you and he have been doing, Decima, so you're wasting your time if you think it bothers me. Sean and I ...'

Suddenly the building shakes. At first it's no more than a shiver. Earthquakes are rare here in Hawk Bay, they are never very destructive and we usually have a warning. Nobody had predicted this.

The tower shudders harder. The Chinese Money plant slides along the windowsill.

'What the hell!' snaps Decima.

I run over to the window and glance down through the blinds at the ground below. There is no sign of any panic among the traffic and pedestrians. They don't seem to have noticed anything.

'It's OK. Must have been a slight tremor,' I say. The tower has stopped moving.

'Anyway, getting back to Sean and his…'

Then the floor rocks violently. The computer and all the papers slide off her desk. The chairs topple over and crash into the wall as the Tower sways. I'm knocked to the floor. The sofa sails sideways and smashes against the wall, taking Decima with it.

We both try to scramble to our feet but the floor is heaving and we're forced to lie down to stop being hurled around the room.

'Get the phone! Don't lie there, get on the phone and find out what's happening,' Decima shrieks.

I crawl to where the phone has slid into the corner, and stab in the number of the basement. There's a rapid beeping sound, nothing more. I press the buttons again, the same result.

'The phone isn't working. We need to get out of here,' I say.

As I speak, there's a tremendous whooshing, clattering and screeching noise and the room goes momentarily dark as something falls past the window.

'What was that?' Decima yells.

From where I'm lying, hanging on to the desk which is fitted to the floor, I pull myself upright and stare at the window. There's a mass of tangled steel and cables hanging there.

'Oh no,' I gasp. 'The elevator's gone. The whole thing

has fallen away.'

Decima begins hauling herself towards the wall that leads into the hidden door to the Green Room.

'I'll get in my safe room,' she hisses, reaching up and touching the picture, which glides open. She crawls through into her boudoir, and I follow behind her.

'I never knew there was a safe room,' I say.

'That's the WHOLE IDEA. Nobody is meant to know. That's why it's SAFE! To protect me. It's no use you following me, it's only for ONE PERSON.'

'You won't BE safe in there, Decima. The whole building is going to go down.'

The cheval mirrors have all toppled over, covering the floor with broken glass. The bubble bath has tipped on its side and the carpet is inches deep in foaming water that brushes the broken glass backwards and forwards. Decima yelps as she kneels on a shard.

'Ouch, ouch that *hurt*.' She gropes and splashes her way to a panel in the wall and pulls herself upright, pushing the button.

The panel hiding the safe room begins to slide open, but it's bent and jams with only a few inches open. She puts her hands in the narrow space and pushes with all her strength, screaming as her nails break, panting with exertion. Flames burst out through the gap. The light from outside is fading as the sun goes down.

The building is now leaning so heavily it's impossible to stand upright. Through the doorway into the office I see the windows shattering, hear the groaning noise of tortured steel, and screams of people in the floors below. Distant sirens bawl.

Decima has slumped onto the floor against the safe door, her eyes glassy with fear.

'DO SOMETHING YOU STUPID BITCH,' she bawls. 'DON'T SIT THERE LIKE THE IDIOT YOU ARE, DO SOMETHING! THEY'RE TRYING TO KILL ME! DO - YOU - UNDERSTAND? THERE ARE PEOPLE WHO ARE GOING TO KILL ME, AND THEY'RE TAKING YOU TOO.'

The Tower is collapsing. I can feel it sinking, rocking, crumbling. There is only one way out for me. I reach for my phone. It isn't in my pocket. I crawl back into the office, as smoke begins to drift in through the shattered window. I spot my phone in the furthest corner, beneath my overturned chair. It's easy getting to it because the floor is sloping so steeply downwards, but once I have it in my hands I have to haul myself upwards away from the jumble of furniture, pushing myself with knees, elbows and feet.

When I reach the doorway into the boudoir, I grab onto the frame to steady myself. The soapy water swishes around my feet dragging glass fragments with it. I hold the phone out of the water and search for the *Broomstick* app. Pinpoints of flames break through the walls. The smoke is thick now, my eyes are stinging, breathing is painful, burning my lungs.

Decima is screaming, howling, shrieking, shaking with terror. With all her venom and spite stripped away she's a pitiful bedraggled creature. Her hair is singed and flames are licking at her bare flesh. She splashes water from the floor onto her face and arms.

The door into the office slams shut, and we are in darkness. Wet, noisy, smoke-filled, terrifying total darkness. When I stab the torch on my phone it gives off the faintest glimmer.

Now Decima is wailing, as she realizes there is no rescue coming. The Tower is already starting to sink, rocking lopsidedly.

'Mummy,' she whimpers. 'Mummy.'

The corner of the floor drops away, leaving a gaping hole down to 17 floors below. Dust and debris fly around, mixing with the choking smoke. Flames wriggle up the walls.

I must act now. Save myself while I still can. One corner of my phone has melted and the battery is almost depleted.

The **Broomstick** app glows faintly; there may still be enough power left in it to get me out. There's no time. I have to go. I'm almost blinded by smoke, my lungs are on fire, the heat is searing my skin.

I look back at Decima, curled up like a small frightened animal, and through the dust and debris her eyes meet mine. Tears are rolling down her cheeks and she's shaking as she waits for the end. The flames are all around her now. Her shoes are melting. All the spite, the jealousy, the cruel comments, the humiliation she has heaped on me and her guests, the way she has treated the boys, it's all come back to bite her. Karma has caught up with her.

I open the ***Broomstick*** app and face the gap in the wall, putting my finger over the 'Go' button and taking a deep breath, praying there is enough power in the app to get me clear of the Tower.

My finger hovers, hesitates.

I drag myself through the broken glass to where Decima is smoldering and crumpled.

'Put your arms around me,' I tell her. 'And don't let go.'

She reaches out dumbly and wraps her thin, hot arms around my neck. 'Thank you,' she whispers. 'I don't want to die alone. I'm so afraid. Please forgive me for...'

'Shut up. Hold on to me as if your life depends on it, because it does,' I snap. I need all my powers of concentration, all my remaining strength, all my determination if this is going to work.

I clutch the small body to mine and turn to face the wall. Then I tap the ***Broomstick*** app and close my eyes. This is it.

I envision us through the shattered windows, and out into the skies.

For a moment nothing happens. The flames are snapping at my feet. I envision harder and harder, and jab the fading app into hypermode.

55

Aftermath

Alice

I land with a thump in a thicket a quarter of a mile from my parents' house on the Brent Flats. I lie there until I have caught my breath. Decima lies broken a few feet away, her limbs all twisted at unnatural angles. Wisps of smoke rise from her scorched clothing. There's a smell of burnt hair and flesh. I can't feel any pulse in her neck, nor any breath against my hand.

I try to lift her body but I've no strength left. My phone has melted into a blob. I stumble to my parents' house and bang on the door.

My mother rushes out. 'Oh dear Lord, we thought you were dead. We heard the newsflash and tried to call you.'

She drags me inside and dabs my burns with *Salvheal* oil, which brings immediate relief.

'Open your mouth,' she says, squeezing a few drops of fluid onto my tongue. 'That will bring your energy levels back up.'

'Thank goodness you're safe. The fire at the Tower came up as breaking news on all the channels. Your father is frantic. He has gone to see if he can find you.'

'I couldn't call, I only had enough juice left to

__Broomstick__ out with Decima and my phone was wrecked.'

'Is she alright?'

'I don't think so. She's terribly burned and has inhaled a lot of smoke. I got her out, but couldn't carry her back from the Flats. We need to bring her body back.'

Grabbing a rug and a torch, we walk quickly to where I had left Decima, looking like a discarded doll, tiny, battered, lifeless. Vulnerable, unloved, unwanted.

Between us we gently lift the limp body onto the rug, and carry it back to the house and lay it on the bed in my old room.

My mother feels for a pulse, frowning and shaking her head.

'Alice, I don't think she's going to make it.'

'We need to get her to hospital.'

'There's no time. Bring me the med box from my room.'

She opens the box and pulls out a small vial of brown syrup. and smears a few drops on her finger. She opens Decima's mouth with her other hand, and rubs the syrup on to her gums.

Nothing happens, so she does it again. And again. And again.

Fighting down waves of nausea I stare at what was Decima's face and is now a swollen mess of blistered red skin.

'Once more,' Astrid mutters, massaging the syrup into Decima's gums.

A spasm twitches on the ruined face.

'There's life!' says Astrid. 'There's life. She's still with us.'

We peel off the melted clothes and smother Decima's body with *Salvheal* oil, then cover her with a cool white sheet, which rises and falls, almost imperceptibly, as her breathing flutters weakly.

In the bathroom, I rinse my blackened hands and face. I gingerly undress and drop my ruined clothes onto the floor, then step under the shower. The water trickles pink as it runs down my legs, glass splinters from my hair and hands tinkling as the water washes them into the tray. Despite the heat, I am cold and shivering. I find an old tracksuit and some wooly socks, and wrap my hair in a towel.

Then I go back and sit beside my mother as she tenderly wraps the whole of Decima's burnt body with greased gauze and bandages, so she looks like a miniature mummy. 'I think she's stabilized. It's going to be a question of time, and how much she wants to survive.'

There's a flash of headlights through the window, the sound of squealing brakes, a slamming car door, and my father's voice yelling:

'Astrid! Astrid!'

'Up here!'

His footsteps pound up the stairs and he bursts through the doorway.

'I can't find her. She's not…'

He stops when he sees me. His face is filthy, his hair

disheveled.

'Alice!' he pants, bending over with his hands on his knees, his shoulders heaving.

I go and put my arms around his shoulders, hugging him, smelling the smoke on his clothes.

'I went to the Tower as soon as we heard the news. It's chaos there. They're still searching for survivors but the heat is dreadful. They've pulled some bodies out. I looked everywhere for you. Then I went to your house and you weren't there. I was so afraid that…'

He stands up and pulls me into his chest, sobbing.

His tears tickle my neck and for the first time I feel my father's love for me. He really loves me. I catch my mother's eye. She nods and gives a little smile. My heart jumps.

Astrid stands up and ushers us from the bedroom and down the stairs. 'Patrick, go and clean up. I'll make us some coffee.'

I can't see anything to show for my father's 'renovation' of the kitchen. Everything seems to be in its usual place.

'What happened with the work father was doing?'

'Ah, it was a general tidy-up. Checking the woodwork, cleaning up behind the units. You know.'

'I thought it was more than that. Wasn't he building a pantry?'

I find a cake tin on the shelf and start dipping into it absentmindedly. I'm so hungry. I never got to eat that pizza.

'It's there, next to the dresser.'

She quickly changes the subject.

'Does Sean know you're safe?'

'Not yet. I can't contact him without my phone. He knew I was staying late tonight, with Decima. He'll be out of his mind.'

'I have his number. Here, give him a call. He'll be frantic if he's heard the news and hasn't been able to reach you.'

I take Astrid's phone and send him a text message.

'Hi, just to say I'm safe. Can you please let others know. I've lost my phone. Speak tomorrow and fill you in. Love you. Alice. xxx'

I send a message to Shelley too.

'It's Alice. I'm fine but out of contact for a few days, phone has melted! Don't worry about me, catch up soon. Xxx'

While I'm texting, Astrid goes up to check on Decima. She's back down a few minutes later.

'Her breathing and pulse are very weak, but they're steady. She's trying to speak, but I couldn't catch what she was saying. It sounded like "Rigby". '

'Digby', I say. 'She's saying Digby. Her bear. I have to go back.'

'Don't be foolish. It won't have survived the fire.'

'I know. Maybe. But I have to try. It means everything to her. I'll be back soon.'

Without my phone, I have to use the old, unreliable **Broomstick** spell. It dumps me unceremoniously in the shallow ornamental lake in front of the tower.

The devastation of the Tower pierces the sky like a black skeleton, illuminated by the lights of the firefighters. Ambulance crew are tending to people wrapped in foil survival blankets.

I wander around, unnoticed in the surrounding chaos, catching fragments of conversation from the crowds.

'...only building touched.'

'No tremor in the area...'

'Came down like a pack of cards...'

'Meant to be indestructible...'

'Only way it could have come down was if explosives were used....'

'...defo an insurance scam...'

I remember I still have my wet hair wrapped in a towel; but nobody's going to notice me here in the dark. I get to my feet and walk around scuffing the piles of hot ash and singed papers. My foot bangs into something hard. I pick it up and move to where there is some light, and see the ceramic pot that held the Chinese Money Plant, strangely intact. The plant itself lies a few feet away, a mess of bent and broken stems and leaves. I pick it up anyway. I borrow a torch from somebody standing nearby, and flash it around until the light falls on a small bundle of charred fabric and something glistening. I gingerly pick up the burnt remains of Digby, brushing off the ash. A pair of bright button eyes peer out.

With my arms full, I **Broomstick** back to Brent Flats and drop the things onto the kitchen table. I fold my arms on the table and lay my head on them.

When I wake up, it's daylight and my mother has wrapped a blanket over my shoulders.

She's sitting on the other side of the table, and slides a mug of coffee and a couple of cinnamon rolls to me.

'How is she?' I ask.

'Weak, but holding her own. She's taking broth through a straw. I'm keeping her sedated to cope with the pain. Those burns are bad. I'm going to try making something to help with them. What's that?'

'That's what's left of Digby, and the plant from her office. I'll see if I can do anything and put them near her. Is there any more news on the Tower?'

'Yes. Several people injured and four bodies recovered. The investigators are working to try to find out the cause. Sean phoned. I've told him you are safe and unharmed, and resting. He's contacted Cory, but hasn't been able to get in touch with Josh yet. He asked if there was news of Decima. I don't quite know why, but I didn't tell him she was here. I had a feeling that it would be better if nobody knew where she was for now. I said as far as I knew she was safe.'

'She had been quite strange over the last couple of months, as if she was afraid of something or somebody. Last night she wanted me to help her find a private investigator. She was shouting something about 'them' wanting to kill her. Why would anybody want to harm her? And yet, the Tower collapsing when she's there, that can't be a coincidence. But I think you're right, we shouldn't let anybody know where she is. If somebody is trying to kill her they won't think of looking here. We need to keep quiet until we know more.'

'She'll have to stay here then. In your room. I'd rather you don't go home until we know more. Just in case. But where are you going to sleep? '

'I'll sleep in the room with her for now.' I don't have any choice because the only other room in the house is the 'living room' which is filled with jars and bottles and buckets which Astrid uses to produce the *Salvheal* oil, and it smells vile and the fumes burn your eyes. You can't stay in there without wearing protective clothing and a mask.

I go upstairs and find Decima sleeping, jerking and whimpering like a dreaming puppy. I pull two chairs together to make myself a bed. I grab a couple of cushions for a pillow, close my eyes and curl up. I'm almost asleep when something soft jumps up beside me and nuzzles into my neck. I put my arms around Zylch and hold him close.

56

Number unavailable

Alice

From the depths of sleep I hear a voice calling weakly.

'What's happened? Where am I? I can't see!'

Decima has pulled herself up onto the pillows and is trying to sit up, turning her head from side to side, plucking at her bandaged face with her bandaged hands..

'You're safe, Decima. You're here with me, Alice. At my folks place. Don't touch your face.' I put my hand over hers.

'We're looking after you. You were hurt at the Tower. There was a fire. You are going to be fine, but you need to rest while you heal. Try to relax. I'll get you a drink.'

Astrid has left a jug beside the bed, with one of her calming potions. I place a straw in it and hold it to Decima's mouth.

'Drink this.'

She sucks slowly, and sinks back onto the pillows.

'Why can't I see? Am I blind?'

'You're not blind. My mother has bandaged you to help you heal. You were burnt, but you'll get better.'

'Where's Digby?'

'He's right here beside you. Feel.'

I place poor Digby by her hand.

'There. You see, everything is going to be alright.'

'He doesn't feel right. What's...' The sedative takes effect, and she falls asleep with a sigh.

Zylch follows me down to the kitchen.

There's a note on the table: '*Your lunch is in the microwave. I'm making more Salvheal for Decima.*'

I take my lunch outside, and sit in the quiet of the garden with my eyes closed, listening to the birdsong and rustling of the trees in the warm breeze. It's so peaceful, hard to believe the events of last night actually happened.

My reverie is broken by the sound of a motor vehicle. It's too early for my father to be home, so I'm alarmed and dash into the house, peering out from the kitchen window.

It's Cory's car. Sean jumps out and comes running to the door, banging and shouting.

As I open the door Sean hurls himself at me.

'Oh my days, oh my days Alice, I've been so afraid. Are you alright? Are you sure?' He pushes me away and looks at me, then he starts crying and drags me into his chest.

Cory is standing behind him and puts his arm on Sean's shoulder.

'It's OK man, you can see she's fine.'

'How did you find me?'

'At the barbecue, your mother told me you lived on the Brent Flats. I got Cory to drive over here and we drove around until we found you. Every other property is empty. I had to know you were safe Alice.'

'Well, as you can see, I am. You'd better come in.'

I lead them through the hallway, past the stacked transport cages and into the kitchen, where they stand looking rather bewildered. Astrid is not the tidiest housewife.

While I'm making coffee and looking for cookies, they ask about what happened, and how we escaped. This is going to be hard to explain. I'll have to be 'creative'.

'It all happened very suddenly. The building began moving and we had to get out quickly.'

'How?' asks Cory, looking at Sean.

'It's lucky that we moved fast,' I say ambiguously.

'Extraordinary,' says Cory. 'How you managed to do that from the 17th floor when the lift had collapsed.'

I stare at him. 'What are you trying to say Cory?'

'Simply that it's remarkable how you were both able to escape.'

I see a look pass between him and Sean, and that's when I know that they know about my powers.

'Where is Decima now?' asks Cory.

'I'm sure she's safe somewhere and we'll hear from her soon,' I say. 'It was all very confusing when we got out.'

'But are you certain? They've found bodies.'

'No, she definitely did get out. She was very shaken, but I saw her. She's probably resting somewhere.'

'But she's not answering her phone,' says Cory. 'Which is very unlike her. I'm going to go to her place and see if she's there, because if she isn't somebody is going to need to look after her dogs until she turns up.'

'You go,' says Sean. 'I'm staying here with Alice.'

'You can't, Sean. There's nowhere for you. I'm sorry, we don't have anywhere at all for you to sleep.'

'I'll sleep anywhere, but I am NOT LEAVING.'

My mind is all over the place. What is going on, who is behind it, and is there any news of Josh? I remember all that has happened while I've been working at the Tower. The good times with Lorelei, the roller coaster ride with Decima, and the guys.

'What's going to happen to us all? What about the program? Our jobs?' I ask.

'Let's worry about that once we've found Decima and know that Josh is safe.' Cory stands up. 'His phone keeps saying the number is unavailable.'

Sean says slowly 'Josh mentioned he was working late tonight. And they are reporting they've found four bodies. One was in the basement. They are also saying that it was sabotage. Latest news is that they've found evidence of explosives. Sounds as if somebody deliberately blew the Tower up.'

A shiver runs down my back.

That's when Decima starts screaming.

'WAAAAAH! WAAAAH!'

Dear Reader,

I hope you have enjoyed your time with Alice, Decima and the boys. This is the first novel series I've ever written and it has been quite an experience. No need to try to imagine what everybody will do next – they decide and do it themselves, frequently waking me up during the night and interrupting at sometimes inconvenient moments to nudge me to write down their thoughts and deeds. I've come to love each of them, despite their faults .

This trilogy is complete, details of the other books in the series are on the next page, but I'm looking forward to finding out what the future holds for them all as their stories continue. If you would like to know too, do sign up to my mailing list (*http://eepurl.com/GKLiL*) and I'll let you know just as soon as the next episode in their lives is ready for you.

New authors and books rely so much on positive feedback, so if you have the time and the willingness, please do an Alice and cast a #review spell for me onto Amazon.

May whatever you read always bring you joy,

Kelly

The BEWITCHED Trilogy

****** Such a fun and exciting read.*
****** Utterly blown away, could not put it down.*
****** Got me hooked and then, before I knew it, I had finished it!*
****** Book 2 is even more of a page-turner!*

1: The Tower of Secrets
A love triangle with a twist

Powerful, driven, TV presenter Decima is a wounded soul with all the trappings of wealth and fame. She compensates for her inner unhappiness by using her position to dominate all who work for her. Alice, her naive, kind PA, has always been an outsider because of her strange powers. She will need to use them to stand up for herself if she is to survive in Decima's world. When evil forces threaten, they must unite to survive, as each strives to find love and security in a world of danger.

3: Twists of Fate
A bombshell confession reveals the Tower's final secret

Through the highs and lows of love and loss, hope and fear, it takes a touch of magic to bring Alice and Decima the true happiness they seek. In a shocking final twist, the Tower's biggest secret is unveiled.

blackbird
blackbird-books.com

www.ingramcontent.com/pod-product-compliance
Lightning Source LLC
Chambersburg PA
CBHW031250120726
47906CB00003B/675